RIO FUEGO

Center Point
Large Print

Also by Wayne D. Dundee and available from Center Point Large Print:

Dismal River
Rainrock Reckoning
The Forever Mountain
The Coldest Trail
The Gun Wolves
Massacre Canyon
Wildcat Hills
Devil's Tower

RIO FUEGO

A Lone McGantry Western

WAYNE D. DUNDEE

Center Point Large Print
Thorndike, Maine

This Center Point Large Print edition
is published in the year 2025 by arrangement with
Wolfpack Publishing.

Copyright © 2023 Wayne D. Dundee.

All rights reserved.

This book is a work of fiction. Any references to historical events, real people or real places are used fictitiously. Other names, characters, places and events are products of the author's imagination, and any resemblance to actual events, places or persons, living or dead, is entirely coincidental.

The text of this Large Print edition is unabridged.
In other aspects, this book may vary
from the original edition.
Printed in the United States of America
on permanent paper sourced using
environmentally responsible foresting methods.
Set in 16-point Times New Roman type.

ISBN: 979-8-89164-456-4

The Library of Congress has cataloged this record under Library of Congress Control Number: 2024948298

Chapter One

Lone McGantry had just ridden through a narrow pass bracketed by low, weathered, brush-choked sandstone walls giving way to high, shoulder-like slopes of sun-browned grass. Beyond, the land spread out flat for as far as the eye could see in the fading dusk. A short ways off to the left there was a small stand of cottonwoods next to a thin stream whose dimpled water caught glints of silver-blue early starlight. Lone swung his big gray stallion, Ironsides, toward these trees.

Throughout the afternoon, Lone had been figuring to reach the town of Rio Fuego, Colorado, by nightfall, which was why he'd pushed on past sunset. Now, however, with no sign of the community yet in sight and the cluster of trees and nearby stream presenting a suitable alternative, he decided he'd be making another trail camp tonight after all. It wasn't like spending a night under the stars was an uncommon occurrence to his roaming ways; in fact, in his adult life, he'd probably slept more often out of doors than under a roof. Far less common was miscalculating his bearings to the point of not reaching an aimed-for destination closer to expectations. But, since he'd never traversed this part of southeast Colorado before, he reckoned that was a fair reason to blame for his misjudgment.

As for Ironsides, since the stream and the richer, greener grass bordering its banks were fully evident, making a stop here meant no hardship for him either. And while the big gray could have maintained the pace Lone had been holding him to for hours more, the day had been plenty long enough and hot enough so that bringing it to a close was welcome for both man and beast.

Reining up over on the edge of the flat, Lone dismounted and stripped Ironsides of his saddle and gear. Ordering the gray to stand ground-reined until he was cooled enough to drink, Lone carried the gear to the fringe of the trees and deposited it on the ground. Next, he began gathering up twigs and fallen limbs for a fire.

Lone moved smoothly, gracefully for a big man. He stood well over six feet tall, wide-shouldered and thick through the chest and torso with none of it fat. The rest of his physical make-up consisted of a squarish, weathered face anchored by a prominent nose extending down from between sun-squinted blue eyes. It wasn't a face likely to bring the word handsome to mind yet more than a few women had been known to give it a lingering sidelong look; and men tended to eye it somewhat warily. His simple trail garb of denim pants, buckskin vest worn open over a boiled white shirt, and a faded, flat-crowned Stetson were evidence, along with the squinted eyes, of someone who made his way on the rugged edge of the frontier. The Colt .44 holstered on his right hip and the ten-inch Bowie sheathed on his left completed the air of overall competence and quiet confidence he projected.

By the time Lone had a sufficient pile of fuel collected, Ironsides was ready to be led on to the stream. It was while the gray was slurping thirstily and noisily that Lone first became aware of the distant rumbling sound. His eyes swept upward involuntarily, even though he already knew there was nothing but clear sky above. The moon hadn't begun to rise yet. Only a few wispy clouds, none holding the remotest hint of building into a storm, could be seen breaking up the sprinkle of gradually brightening stars. Lone's eyes dropped to sweep the horizons. He saw nothing that could be associated with the rumbling sound growing slowly but steadily closer and louder.

What he was hearing, Lone decided, was the pounding of several hooves. But from what source? Cattle? He'd seen signs of cattle ranching as he'd ridden along throughout the day, though no herds of any significant size. And the presence of buffalo in any number hereabouts seemed unlikely. Plus, in either case, what would send them into what sounded like a hard run, possibly a stampede? It could also be a horse herd, but the same question would apply . . . unless it was horses being spurred hard by riders.

Lone pricked his ears, listening intently as the rumble continued to grow still closer and louder. Lone adjusted his earlier assessment. Maybe it wasn't as many pounding hooves as he'd first thought. Maybe only a half dozen or so animals and, yes, he was now leaning stronger toward it being horses. What was more, something in him found the notion of that many mounts being pushed so aggressively through the deepening dusk an unsettling thought. He took Ironsides by the reins and led him over into the middle of the trees, glad he hadn't yet lit his campfire.

Standing motionless within the dappled shadows thrown by the cottonwood leaves, Lone looked southward, the direction he'd been headed, and watched a murky dust boil kicked up by hammering hooves reverse melt into sight and then draw nearer. Pretty soon, the heads of horses and the blurred faces of their riders started to become discernible. They were seven in number as best Lone could make out in the swirling dust. They were following the same trail he'd been on and seemed bent on pouring through the same narrow pass he'd recently exited.

But just before reaching the pass entrance, the pack suddenly reined up and came to a milling, stamping halt. The man riding in the lead wheeled his horse about and faced the others. All had their wide-brimmed hats pulled down low, obscuring their faces in murky shadows. Also, somewhat curiously given the mild weather, Lone noted that each man was wearing either a long slicker or serape that turned their bodies into shapeless, indistinguishable forms perched in their saddles. Four of the riders were brandishing repeating rifles with the butts braced against their hips now that they'd drawn to a stop.

Addressing the others in a voice that carried easily through the still air to where Lone remained watching and listening within the trees, the lead rider said, "Okay. This is our spot, men. Bartlett thinks he's being pretty clever skinning his prisoner out of town before an even bigger mob than last night gets worked up. If he's looking for trouble, he'll be watching his back trail. We'll not only catch him by surprise, but once we corner him in that pass, we'll have him trapped like a mouse in a box."

"Maybe so," grunted one of the other men in the pack. "But Tom Bartlett's got considerably more bark on him than any mouse, boxed in or not. He showed that when he backed down last night's mob in front of the jail."

"I ain't saying Marshal Bartlett's a pushover, not by any means," responded the lead rider. "He had no choice but to stand his ground last night. He takes his job serious and he had the whole town watching. But the fact he's attempting to move his prisoner to Ford City shows he's unsure he can hold off another mob. Out here he'll be outnumbered and outgunned all over again, but he won't have so many eyes looking on."

"What are you driving at? What are you trying to say?" somebody asked.

"Let's just say I'm thinking out loud. And what I'm thinking is that Bartlett and Judge Thorndike were pretty good friends for a lot of years. Hell, they tamed Rio Fuego together. Given that, you can't convince me that the marshal, down at his core, don't want to see that murdering greaser bastard swing just as bad and as quick as the rest of us. How could he not—seeing his old friend, already sick and frail and teetering at death's door, knife-gutted like a trout and knowing plain as day it was the work of that ungrateful pup Rodero?"

"So you saying you don't expect Bartlett to put up much resistance against us?"

The leader heaved an exasperated sigh. "I ain't saying it's gonna be that easy. But, at the same time, I don't figure Tom's heart is really in protecting his skunk of a prisoner. Still, as has already been said, he takes his badge mighty serious. So we got to play it tight and not give him any kind of opening. We do that, I don't picture him putting either himself or his young deputy at too much risk to stop us."

"Enough talk," spoke up another voice. "We been all through this before and made up our minds we're gonna do it, so let's quit chewing it more. How do you want us to position ourselves, Trent?"

Trent, the lead rider, leaned back in his saddle. "That's more like it. We know what we're here for and we know it's the right thing, so let's get set to do it. Like I said before, we keep it tight and simple . . . O'Toole, Dooley, and the two Brady brothers, you four go into the pass a ways. Twenty yards or so, far enough so you won't be seen right away by anybody riding in. It'll be still darker by the time Bartlett shows up, so you can use that along with some brush or rocks on the sides to help conceal yourselves . . . me, Brown, and Hollister will conceal ourselves out here until the lawmen and their prisoner enter the pass. Then we'll close quick-like behind 'em and make our presence known with some shots fired in the air. You boys spring out farther down and do the same. We'll have 'em boxed in cold."

"You make it sound awful easy."

"No reason it shouldn't be," Trent declared confidently. "They'll quick see they're blocked on both ends and exposed to a crossfire if they try to fight it. Like I said, I don't think Bartlett wants to save that greaser's neck bad enough to risk his own against odds like that. So we'll disarm the law dogs, hogtie 'em long enough to do what we came for—I expect a limb somewhere over in that yonder stand of cottonwoods will serve plenty good—and the deed will be done."

"Sounds okay to me," somebody said. "Part I hate worst is the thought of pullin' a damn sack over my head."

"We can only expect Bartlett to bend so far," Trent told him. "Remember the old saying about an ounce of prevention? We spend that ounce and mask our identities, I'm betting the marshal won't work too hard trying to figure out who we are. We *don't* hide ourselves, he'll recognize every damn one of us—no matter how dark it is—and be forced to come huntin' afterward. Unless we make certain he don't by killing him and the deputy too . . . you up for that?"

"No. A-course not."

"Then we wear the hoods. Matter of fact, we might as well put 'em on now so's we get 'em adjusted proper and are used to 'em when it counts."

As Lone continued to watch, the men all pulled wadded-up handfuls of cloth from within their wraps. Once shaken out, these were revealed to be sacks converted into head and face coverings by virtue of eye holes cut out of them. Lifting their hats, each of the men pulled on the hoods and adjusted them in order to see out of before replacing their hats. Most of the riders simply tucked the ends of their hood into their shirt collars to hold it in place; two or three of them produced pieces of string that they tied around their necks to hold their hood more securely in place. When all were masked up, a part of Lone found the sight slightly comical—but more than that it was eerie and menacing due to the intent behind it.

"Okay, let's take our places," Trent said, his voice slightly muffled now by the cloth hanging loosely over his mouth. "I don't know how far they are behind us, but they oughta be coming along before too long. When they show, let me do most of the talking. Although neither of the law dogs know me as well as some of you, I'll disguise my voice. No sense giving 'em even a hint of a suspicion who we are if we don't have to . . . any final questions?"

When none of the others responded, Trent made a sweeping motion with one arm. "Alright, spread out. Like I said, it shouldn't be very long. Not soon enough, though, before we got that murderin' greaser bastard doing the hemp dance!"

Chapter Two

Lone hated lynch mobs. He hated the way gutless individuals too cowardly to act on their own could find courage in a violence-bent pack of like-minded fools. Most of all he hated how they could convince one another that what they were doing was somehow righteous and fitting.

Yet now here he was, faced with what was surely a lynching on the verge of taking place. What was worse, instead of the usual drunken rabble whipped up by some saloon loudmouth, this bunch appeared more or less sober and coolly focused. Right down to kicking their necktie party off with what sounded like a pretty well-planned ambush.

Damn.

It wasn't in Lone to call a matter so serious none of his business and just ride off to leave it play out. But what should he do? What *could* he do? Seven-to-one odds hardly stacked up as something a fella ought to be in a hurry to go charging up against. Not knowing for sure how long before the lawmen showed up with their prisoner—the unfortunate "Rodero" or "greaser bastard" the pack wanted so badly to get their hands on—Lone decided his best bet might be to try slipping away and making it up the trail in order to warn of the awaiting ambush.

No sooner had he seized on this notion, however, than the rataplan of approaching hooves once again reached his ears. If it was the marshal, deputy, and their prisoner, as was most likely the case, then there was no time to give warning. They were already too close to the pass, coming at a fairly crisp pace, and Trent and the others were by now in position. Ready and waiting.

Lone held motionless, cursing under his breath. His mind raced. His most sensible option now, the way he saw it, was to wait and see how the ambush went. If he tried to intervene sooner, there was the risk he might trigger added panic resulting in a greater possibility of gunplay that could turn things worse. If he held back there was a chance, albeit what seemed like a slim one, the lawmen and their prisoner might break through and manage to escape. If, on the other hand, the ambush went as planned, then the whole bunch would be coming over to the trees where Lone remained hidden in the deep shadows. The lynch mob should be less keyed up, somewhat more relaxed by that point, maybe even feeling a little cocky in the belief they were close to succeeding at their grim mission . . . but that would also mean they'd be coming closer to a former Army scout and veteran Indian fighter who would be poised to take advantage of the slightest opening their smugness hopefully presented.

• • •

So that's the way it went. The new riders were indeed the Rio Fuego marshal and deputy and their prisoner, and the ambush of them as soon as they entered the pass succeeded exactly as Trent had outlined. The lawmen were boxed in, disarmed, and their hands bound behind their backs. Then they and the intended lynching victim, already handcuffed and secured, were pushed in the direction of the cottonwoods to select a proper limb for the hang noose to be thrown over. The mob members were guffawing and whooping and displaying mighty high spirits as they swarmed close around their captives and herded them along.

During the time it took for the confrontation in the pass to play out, Lone had the chance to move both Ironsides and his saddle gear to the back fringe of the tree stand, where they were less likely to be seen. Then he ghosted back, Yellowboy rifle in hand, to the front and crouched in some thick bushes near a couple of the larger cottonwoods with fat branches jutting out that he calculated the lynchers would find suitable for their purpose.

With darkness settling in thicker, two of the mob members had produced torches that they wasted no time lighting once the ambush had been sprung. They were now holding these high and lighting the way as the group proceeded toward the trees. This worked to Lone's advantage in two ways. First, it illuminated those in the mob much more clearly to him. Second, being in the wash of flickering torchlight would adversely affect the night vision of the same bunch when it came to the darker reaches beyond. As long as he made sure not to look directly into the torch flames, Lone could maintain benefit both ways.

"Right there. That one looks like it'll do the job just fine," announced Trent as the pack reached the cottonwood stand. He was speaking in a low, sandpapery growl and pointing to one of the trees that Lone had reckoned might be selected. "Get our guest of honor up here. That murdering sonofabitch has been left to breathe up good air for way too long. Time to put an end to that and make him pay for what he done to the judge!"

Up closer and in the pulsing glow of torchlight, the men who made up the mob didn't appear any different than Lone had already noted. Heads covered by hoods with cut-out eye holes, bodies draped in shapeless slickers or long serapes. All were openly brandishing weapons now—four still with repeating rifles, the other three, including Trent, opting for long-barreled revolvers.

The three new additions in their midst, however, were better displayed. The individual being pushed forth as "the guest of honor" proved, not surprisingly given the ugly references made regarding him, to be a young man clearly of

Mexican blood. He was hatless, showing a shock of thick black hair above handsome facial features set in a defiant expression. Back in the middle of the pack, held in place and crowded tight together by a pair of rifle-wielding lynchers, were the two lawmen. The one Lone judged to be the marshal was a middle-aged man, wide-shouldered and thick-bodied, with a craggy face and bushy eyebrows currently scrunched together in a fierce scowl. Beside him, his deputy appeared to be not very far past the twenty mark, tall and lean, solid-looking, with a boyishly handsome face that was making it harder for him to look effectively stern and disapproving.

As the intended hanging victim—Jaime Rodero, his full name would turn out to be—was led up next to Trent and his horse positioned under the tree limb designated for his noose to hang from, Marshal Bartlett suddenly spoke out. "You fools are making a grave mistake," he declared. "It's not too late to call this off and keep from doing something you'll regret for the rest of your lives. Part of that regret won't take long because, in spite of those ridiculous spook hoods, I can still figure out who most of you are and you know damn well I'll have to come after you."

"You might *think* you know who we are," responded Trent, "but you can't prove shit. Happens each and every one of us has a solid alibi for being somewhere else this whole evening.

You want to talk being foolish? Keep pushing too hard to try and convince us you're bent on making more trouble out of this, you might cause us to change our minds about letting you and junior there off with just some bruised feelings over allowing your prisoner to be taken away from you."

"Take off these ropes holding my hands behind my back," grated the young deputy, "and I'll show you what 'junior' can do, you yellow cur!"

Trent chuckled tauntingly. "The only thing you can show me, you pup, is how you can keep your stinking mouth shut. Elsewise I'll have you gagged and tied face down across your saddle. Then send you back to Rio Fuego that way where you can impress the townsfolk with how tough you *would* have been if only we'd played fair."

The marshal muttered something to his young partner that Lone couldn't quite hear.

Trent could, though, and he nodded approvingly. "That's good advice. Keep your pup in line, Marshal, and you can both ride away from here with no further harm done to you."

The mob leader paused for a minute to make sure the lawmen were going to hold their tongues. Then, taking the reins of Rodero's horse, he waved his gun at the man who handed them over and said, "Alright let's get on with it. Swing that rope up over the big limb right above his head and then hop down and tie off the other end . . .

you"—motioning to another mounted lyncher a couple feet away—"move up and give him a hand. Get that noose around the greaser's neck."

In only a minute or so the tasks were completed. The noose was around Rodero's neck and the remaining length of the rope was up over the limb, leaving just the slightest bit of slack, with its opposite end tied securely around the tree trunk.

Pointing, the man who'd applied the noose said, "He's handcuffed to his saddle horn. Gonna have to take them off or we'll be tryin' to swing him and his horse too."

"Well do it then," Trent growled impatiently. "Who's got the key? You, Marshal? Cough it up and don't try anything cute."

"Damn it, man, you still got a chance to end this," wailed Bartlett in a final desperate plea. "Can't you see it's not only wrong, but not even necessary? All the evidence is against the kid! There's no doubt he's gonna swing anyhow, but let it run its course and get handled the right way!"

"I warned you once about running your mouth. Don't make me say it again," threatened Trent, waving his pistol recklessly.

The marshal's shoulders sagged in resignation. In a low, hoarse voice, he said, "The key's in my shirt pocket."

The horseman crowded up against Bartlett

reached out, fished the key from his pocket, turned and tossed it to the noose hanger. The latter began applying it to the cuffs. As he was busy with that, Trent extended his six-gun to arm's length, bringing the muzzle to within an inch of Rodero's temple, saying, "Just sit real easy, boy. Don't get no funny ideas."

While all of this was taking place, Lone eased out of the bushes he'd been crouched in and glided as silently as the shadows he was moving through until he dropped into a new crouch directly behind the tree trunk where the end of the hang rope was tied.

When the man working on the cuffs had them freed from the saddle horn though still with Rodero's wrists locked together, he leaned back and told Trent, "He's ready now."

Still keeping his gun muzzle close to the prisoner's head, Trent said, "You hear that, bean eater? You're ready now. Ready to pay for what you done to poor old Judge Thorndike—splittin' him open like a damn taco shell!"

Rodero slowly turned his head, ignoring the gun muzzle, and glared straight into the eye holes of Trent's hood. The Mexican's chin jutted out more defiantly than ever and his own eyes gleamed like two points of fire.

"Oh, you're a bold one, ain't you?" Trent crowed, enjoying the moment. "Not that you deserve it, but I'm gonna grant you a few more seconds of life and give you the chance to say some final words. Got any?"

In the time it took for Rodero to form an answer, Lone laid the ten-inch blade of his Bowie knife flat against the surface of the cottonwood trunk and slipped it up between the bark and the tied-off hang rope.

Still glaring at Trent, Rodero said, "Last words? Si. I wish upon you a very slow, painful death and then for your remains to be fed to a pen of filthy pigs like the sow who gave birth to you!"

Trent emitted a harsh laugh. "Bold to the end, eh? I gotta hand it to you. But I still get the last laugh. My mother wasn't no sow, you see—she was a bitch!"

With that, Trent tilted his gun barrel upward and fired it while simultaneously hollering, "Hee-yah!" At the crash of the gun and accompanying shout, Rodero's horse bolted.

But behind the tree, an instant before Trent's trigger finger tightened, Lone gave a twist of his wrist that rolled the razor-sharp edge of his Bowie blade upward, cleanly severing the hang rope at its base. The result out under the cottonwood limb was that, when Rodero's horse leaped away, its rider rocked back only slightly in his saddle and then—rather than being left behind dangling by the noose around his neck—remained astride as the animal broke into full flight with the length of the hang rope trailing in their wake, alternately slapping the ground and flapping in the air almost like a taunting wave goodbye.

For a long moment, the would-be lynchers as well as the two lawmen were left in stunned silence and frozen with slack-jawed disbelief.

Finally somebody blurted, "What the hell!"

More voices quickly joined in: "How did that happen?" . . . "Who tied the damn knot?"

At last finding his own voice, Trent roared, "Never mind that! Somebody get the hell after—"

But he was cut short by another gunshot, this one the louder, sharper report of Lone's Yellowboy sending a second bullet into the sky. Immediately chambering a fresh round, Lone stepped out from behind the cottonwood and came into full sight with his rifle now leveled straight at Trent. "I don't think anybody ought to go anywhere," he said in a commanding tone. Then: "And I suggest you be quick to second that motion, Mr. Lynch Boss—or my next slug will put a third hole in that stupid sack you got pulled over your face."

Once again, everybody went silent and frozen for a tense beat.

This time it was Trent who broke it up, saying, "I hope you're satisfied, you meddling ass. You just allowed a cold-blooded murderer to escape!"

"Way I see it," Lone countered, "I just *stopped* a murder by you and your pack of yellow dogs.

I figure the law can manage to catch that boy again. And if it turns out he's truly guilty and is judged to deserve a noose, this time it'll be done the fair and legal way."

"Fair and legal," Trent echoed mockingly. "Who are you to know anything about—"

"Shut up," Lone grated, cutting him short again. "I want any more noise out from under your sack, I'll let you know. But what I *do* want is for one of you other masked goons"—he said this without ever taking his eyes off Trent or without the Yellowboy muzzle wavering the slightest—"to cut the marshal and his deputy loose. Be quick about it."

The deputy reacted to this with considerable enthusiasm. "You heard him. Cut these damn ropes and give me back my guns!" So eager was he with these demands that he caused his horse, already unnerved by all the shouting and shooting, to do a sudden crow hop. This jostled the lyncher crowded up beside the deputy, bumping away his horse and sending it to bump in turn against the mount of another close lynch rider. The latter happened to be one of the torch bearers and the jostling disturbance awakened in him an unexpected burst of desperation that some might even call bravery. Spotting what he deemed a momentary yet sufficient distraction due to the disturbance among the horses, the man reached suddenly back with his torch and then swung it forward in an overhand arc before releasing it to hurtle straight at Lone.

Lone had no choice but to react to the flaming missile.

Seeing this, Trent also reacted. "Yeah! That's it!" he bellowed. "Come on, boys—trample this meddling sonofabitch!"

After using the Yellowboy's forestock to swat away the flying torch, Lone immediately swung its sights back to re-aim at Trent just as the lynch boss was spurring his mount forward. Lone pitched to one side in order to keep from being run down. But he got off a shot as he did so and had the satisfaction of seeing Trent jerk violently in his saddle even as he and his horse rushed past.

Lone hit the ground rolling, jacking home a fresh cartridge in midturn. He came up on his belly on the other side of the tree trunk. The tableau before him had now erupted into something barely short of chaos. Horses were spinning and raring up on their hind legs, their riders were cursing and shooting wildly. Bullets sang through the air above and around Lone and wood splinters and bark chips splattered out from his cottonwood and also others behind him. Lone returned fire. He sent one of the riders flipping backward off the rump of his horse.

Slugs hammered closer to Lone. He went into another roll, returning to the side of the trunk where he'd first made his appearance. He looked out on increasing chaos. The wild shooting in his direction seemed to grow more sporadic. The second torch bearer had somehow dropped his firebrand and now the dry grass was starting to burn, issuing thick curls of smoke to mingle with the dust haze being churned up by the horses and the layers of powder smoke already hanging in the air. Lone fired twice more through this murkiness and knocked another rider out of his saddle.

That was enough for one of the remaining lynchers to call out what the rest seemed more than ready to hear.

"Let's get out of here! This thing is busted to hell and gone! Everybody scatter—knock on it!"

In a matter of moments what was left of the lynchers was gone, spurring their horses as hard as the beasts would go, fading from sight into the darkness beyond the flames and the mix of smoke and dust haze.

Chapter Three

As it turned out, Lone and Ironsides ended up spending the night in Rio Fuego after all. Though hardly in the comfortable manner Lone had once envisioned.

In the aftermath of the fracas with the lynch mob, it was discovered that Marshal Bartlett had stopped a bullet. Whether it had been planted in him on purpose or inadvertently as a result of the chaotic wild shooting, there was no way of knowing. But, either way, the wound was serious enough to require professional medical attention as soon as possible.

One of the two lynchers Lone had shot out of their saddles was dead, the other just wounded. The latter's injury was fairly serious too, though not nearly as bad as the marshal. Lone was convinced he had also wounded Trent when the mob leader tried to trample him, but there was no sign of him afterward, so he must have been able to remain mounted and ride clear with the others who'd fled.

As soon as Lone freed the hands of the deputy, the young man promptly, angrily jerked the hoods off the dead and wounded lynchers. Recognizing both, he spat out their names in a disgusted tone. "Clem Brady" for the dead one, "Slick Hollister" for the other. Then he went on to say, "Two no-accounts not worth the sweat off Tom Bartlett's brow. If the marshal don't make it, I swear I'll see you swing, Hollister! And just for good measure, I might dig up Clem's rotting remains and give him a hemp dance too!"

"Now that you got that out of your system," Lone said to him, "how about calmin' down and helpin' me do what needs to be done in order to give your friend a chance of bein' *able* to make it?"

The deputy—who gave his name as Steve Leonard—quickly got hold of himself and from there on proved cool and competent when it came to assisting with the necessary tasks. First, after moving the fallen men safely out of the way, him and Lone stomped out the spreading grass fire. Then they returned to the injured and more closely examined and assessed how best to handle them.

Steve rounded up a sufficient number of the scattered horses to make sure they'd all have mounts. Ironsides, of course, was awaiting Lone in the rear fringe of trees. The dead man, Brady, they tied belly down on one of the reclaimed animals. Another would carry the wounded Hollister who, after some rudimentary patching up, was deemed able to sit a saddle when it was time. Such was not the case for Bartlett, however. Lone managed to stanch most of the bleeding from his chest wound but by then the marshal was weak from blood loss and pain-racked to a point of near unconsciousness. A travoise was the only option for him. This Lone and Steve fashioned by cutting a pair of long saplings from the tree stand and tying bedroll blankets between them to form a hammock-like "pocket" for Bartlett to lie in. The ends of the poles they then tied to Steve's horse so he could pull the wounded man behind him as he rode.

This was the battered assembly that trudged off into the night, headed for Rio Fuego. Their pace was a tenuous balance of wanting to hurry so they could get Bartlett the care he so badly required as soon as possible yet at the same time needing to use caution so as not to jounce or jar him too much in a way that might worsen his condition.

The hour was past eight when they reached their destination, clumping over a plank bridge that spanned the Rio Fuego River from which the town had taken its name. The community appeared largely still awake judging by the lighted windows in the residences sprinkled in no apparent pattern off to either side of the main drag. Except for two easily identifiable saloons diagonally across from one another, the downtown shops were closed for the business day and their windows were contrastingly dark. A few pole lanterns placed sporadically along the street provided some meager lighting down its length.

Brighter splashes of illumination spilled out in front of the saloons.

Steve led the way past these glowing, noisy establishments to a narrow wood-frame structure squeezed in between a boot repair shop and a seed and fertilizer store. A sign nailed to a post beside the short plank walkway leading to the front door read: DR. CARL PRAEGER. Through a window could be seen a faint light from deeper inside the house.

Steve skinned down from his saddle, saying, "Let me run in and tell the doc what the situation is. If I remember right, he's got one of those beds you can maneuver around on wheels. If I'm right, we can bring it out, lift the marshal up onto it, then roll him inside that way."

"Sounds good," allowed Lone. "Go ahead and find out, I'll wait here."

The anxious deputy trotted to the front door of the doctor's house and banged his fist hard. Then, impatiently, he tried turning the knob. Finding it unlocked, he pushed the door open and barged through. In a matter of moments, the front of the house glowed with fresh lamplight. Through the door that Steve left ajar, Lone could hear him talking excitedly and another man's voice responding in more measured tones. At the same time, Lone became aware of the buzz of other voices coming from back down the street. Looking around, he saw that a handful of men had emerged from each of the saloons and were standing on the boardwalks out front, gawking this way. It was clear that a group arriving in town with an obviously dead man lying belly down across his saddle and another person being pulled in a travoise, hadn't gone unnoticed when they came down the street and passed between the two watering holes.

Lone returned his attention to the doctor's house and watched as the front door swung all the way open and Steve came backing out pulling one end of a narrow, white-sheeted cot perched on a dual set of chunky wooden wheels. Pushing on the other end of the cot was a middle-aged man wearing suspendered trousers and a white shirt with the sleeves rolled up and the collar undone. He was of average height and build, possessing a bald dome but a full beard. The latter ran thick and black down in front of his ears and along his jaw but turned pale gray, almost white, where it covered his chin.

As the two men came rolling the cot, Lone dismounted and stood ready to assist. Once they reached the end of the walkway, the doctor quit his end of the conveyance and hurried to the injured marshal, leaning close over him.

Looking on, Lone reported, "He took it in the chest, not more than an inch from his heart. The bullet is still in there. He's lost a lot of blood, his breathing is mighty shallow."

"Yes, yes," Dr. Praeger murmured. "We must get him inside. We haven't a second to spare." He straightened up and pointed. "Get those litter poles unhitched from your horse, Steve. We'll leave them in place through the blankets long enough to use them for lifting him up onto the cot. Then we'll remove them before rolling him on in."

Steve hurried to do as instructed and Lone stepped over to help him. Out in the street, the men from the saloons had grown larger in number and the crowd was moving closer. And getting more vocal. "Oh, damn. That's Marshal Tom on the litter. And he looks in a bad way," somebody said . . . "Who's the belly-down one? Can anybody tell?" came a question . . . "I don't know—but ain't that Slick Hollister on the other horse? He's lookin' kinda worse for wear too" . . . "What in blazes you figure happened?"

"You men stay back and hold the noise down," snapped the doctor. "Can't you see there's a man fighting for his life here?"

"If you want to do something useful, somebody go fetch the undertaker for Hollister's buddy," Steve told the pack.

The grimness of that statement did more to quiet the crowd than anything the doctor had said. But a moment later a new stirring of motion and murmuring passed through the knot of men and out of this emerged a short, stocky man wearing a dour expression and a deputy marshal's badge pinned to his shirt.

"Zack!" exclaimed Steve at the sight of this individual.

That was enough for Lone to conclude the new arrival must be Zack Mercer, Rio Fuego's chief deputy and the man Bartlett had left in charge while he and Steve covertly (or so they'd intended) transported Jaime Rodero to Ford City. Steve had explained this arrangement to Lone as part of the talking they did during the ride back to town.

Mercer moved up near to where Steve and Lone had finished unhooking the travoise pole ends from Steve's horse and were getting ready to lift Marshal Bartlett up onto the medical cot. "What the hell happened?" Mercer wanted to know, his forehead puckering with concern as he looked down at the ghastly pale marshal.

Steve answered, "Lynch mob. They somehow got wind what we were up to and ambushed us just as we reached Coyote Pass. The bastards would've had their way, too, if not for—"

"Save it," Dr. Praeger interrupted sternly. "You can tell him the rest later. If you want Tom to have any chance, then we need to immediately get him inside to my treatment facilities. Now onto the cot with him!"

Chapter Four

Despite his intense application of all the skills he knew, Praeger was unable to save Tom Bartlett. The marshal died less than half an hour after being rolled into the treatment room.

Praeger's wife Ellen, a slender, handsome woman who served when required as her husband's nurse, emerged from their living quarters in the back and joined in assisting him with his efforts to overcome the injury to Bartlett. When the best they could do failed, she sobbed openly. Still struggling to get herself under control, it was she who opened the door of the treatment room and stepped out into the waiting area to make the regrettable report to those present there—Mercer and Steve, along with Lone, and also Hollister who was under their watchful eyes until the doctor was able to get to him. Lone watched the two deputies visibly wince in reaction to the news and then saw traces of wetness immediately glistening in their eyes even as they set their jaws and pulled their mouths into tight, straight lines in order to hold in check their outward shows of emotion. It spoke well of Tom Bartlett the man, Lone thought, that his passing brought forth such displays.

By that point, the crowd in the street out front

had more than doubled in size. In addition to the men from the saloons, word of the ambush and Bartlett being seriously wounded had spread through the residential section of town and many citizens had left their homes to come join the vigil. It seemed evident that Bartlett had been widely respected and liked by more than just those close around him.

When Chief Deputy Mercer took a deep breath and stepped outside long enough to pass the word that the marshal hadn't survived, the mood of the gathering slowly but inexorably began to change. At first, where it had been somber and concerned and quiet, it became stunned silence. Then, the shock and sadness wearing off, it turned surly and, eventually, angrily demanding. Demanding some kind of accounting for yet another prominent leader of their community meeting a violent end—all in a matter of just a few days.

And while the suspected killer of Judge Thorndike had now escaped and most of the anonymously hooded would-be lynchers responsible for the shooting of Bartlett were also in the wind, one from that bunch remained as a representative for what they'd done . . . the wounded man, Slick Hollister. Even as Dr. Praeger—after closing the marshal's eyes and pulling the sheet stained by his own blood up over his face—was signaling (grudgingly, yet bound by his oath) for Hollister to be brought into the treatment room for the sake of addressing his injuries, the man's name was beginning to be heard as part of some harsh intentions voiced loudly by several of the more boisterous members of the crowd.

"Let that lowdown skunk bleed to death!"

"No, send him out here—we'll take care of him!"

"Not before we make him name the other masked varmints he was riding with!"

"We already saw the undertaker haul off Clem Brady. And everybody knows one Brady brother don't do nothing without the other—So that makes Clyde somebody deservin' to be hunted down, with or without Hollister."

"But that still don't let Hollister off the hook—not by a damn sight!"

As he listened to this from where he sat perched on the edge of a secondary cot in the treatment room, Hollister was hardly feeling let off the hook. Certainly not from the probing and plucking the doctor was doing to remove bone and lead fragments out of his bullet-smashed shoulder. The discomfort from this was considerable, but it didn't completely offset the added discomfort brought on by the ugly mood of the crowd outside.

"You two deputies—you hearin' what they're sayin' about me out there?" he called in a strained voice through the door to the waiting area that had been left partially open. "They want my hide.

No matter how you're feelin' about me right now, you know it's your jobs to protect me from them. Ain't that so?"

"But who's gonna protect you from us?" Steve rasped in response. "You ever think about that?"

"Hey now. That ain't no way for a lawman to talk, not even just kiddin' around," Hollister protested.

Steve jeered, "The sound of a lynch mob working up a head of steam ain't near as entertaining when you might be the target for their noose as when you're one of the rabble throwing the necktie party, is it?"

"That ain't funny neither! You hear him, Mercer?" Hollister's voice was strident. "You're the chief deputy. You know it ain't right for him to torment a body like that. You'd better control your junior man proper."

"What you'd better do," said Mercer in a cold, flat tone, "is shut your damn mouth. You'll have a chance to run it plenty when you're ready to tell us the names of the rest of the hooded freaks who were riding with you and Clem Brady earlier tonight."

"You know I can't do that," Hollister whimpered. "My life wouldn't be worth a plug nickel was I to blow the way you want."

"What's the difference?" Steve sneered. "Your life ain't *never* been worth a plug nickel, you wretch."

"You think I don't know that?" Hollister's tone sounded suddenly meek, dejected. "And with just one arm, it's only gonna get worse . . . but it's the only life I got. I still want to hang on to it."

Responding to this, Dr. Praeger said, "If you'll hold still so I can be sure to get out all of those bullet fragments in order to prevent blood poisoning, you may come out of this in better shape than you fear. Yes, the wrecked shoulder joint will certainly limit the use of your arm. But there's a good chance your hand and fingers will still function. I'd say you ought to consider that lucky."

"Yeah, I guess you're right. That's better than what I figured would be the case." Hollister's tone now turned earnest, even a bit hopeful. "I really appreciate all you're doin' for me, Doc."

"Don't read too much into it," Praeger replied brusquely. "Tom Bartlett was a friend of mine. A good friend. On a personal level, I despise you for whatever part you played in him getting killed . . . but, professionally, I am bound to care for you regardless."

Steve chuckled. "You tell him, Doc. Detest away. And while you're at it—"

He was cut short by the front door abruptly opening to allow the entrance of a portly, harried-looking gent in a frock coat and bowler hat. He quickly closed the door behind him, once again partially blunting the noise from the crowd outside that had surged alarmingly louder for the short time the door was open. The man's eyes swept the faces in the waiting area. He had some years on him, as evidenced by bushy white mutton chop sideburns and wispy strands of equally pale hair floating around his ears and out from under the sides of his hat, as if he'd clapped the lid on hastily. His fleshy cheeks were flushed to a rosy hue and his cottony tufts of eyebrows were pinched together by anguish. "Is it true?" he asked, locking his gaze on Mercer. "Is Tom Barrtlett really dead?"

The chief deputy grimaced. "I'm afraid so, Mayor Jepson. He passed just a few minutes ago."

"Oh dear, oh dear," Jepson murmured in a barely audible whisper.

Ellen Praeger came out of the treatment room again. She and the mayor embraced. "It's a sad day for our town, Miles," she said, fighting not to break into sobs once more. "Carl did everything possible to save him."

"Of course he did," Jepson replied, his own voice cracking a bit. "First Reginald Thorndike. Now Tom . . . these are sad and bleak times indeed. Hard as it is, we must be at our strongest."

From the other room, Hollister let out a loud groan of pain.

"Who else is in there?" the mayor wanted to know. Without waiting for an answer, he disengaged himself from Mrs. Praeger and stepped over to the treatment room's open doorway to have a look for himself. The sight of the patient's shredded, bloody shoulder caused him to quickly turn back around. His eyes darting back and forth between the two deputies, he said, "Who is that man? He looks vaguely familiar."

"You've likely seen him around town, Mayor. Goes by the name of Slick Hollister," Steve told him. "Been in the area a while. He's worked for a couple different outlying cattle spreads, don't seem to stick at any one job for too long. Likes to hang around the saloons as much as he can—until he needs to stop and earn money so's he can come back and hang around some more."

"What happened to him? Looked as if he'd been shot too."

"He was. By me," spoke up Lone.

Chapter Five

Jepson seemed to notice Lone for the first time. "And you, sir, are . . ."

"Name's McGantry."

"McGantry's from up Nebraska way," Steve explained. "He came here looking to buy some prime horseflesh from Judge Thorndike's spread."

When the mayor lifted his brows questioningly, Lone said, "Bein' on the trail for the past few days, I hadn't heard about the judge's demise. Not until a lynch mob showed up near where I was fixin' to make night camp and I overheard 'em talkin' about why they meant to string up the Mexican kid they were so all-fired convinced was the judge's killer."

"That's when McGantry thankfully decided to step in," Steve added. "It was him who busted up the lynch mob Hollister was part of—the bunch that ambushed Marshal Tom and me out by Coyote Pass. Caught us by surprise, captured us and had us hogtied, was fixing to string up Jaime Rodero right there on the spot. Would have got away with it, too, if not for McGantry here."

"And what of the prisoner—the murder suspect you and the marshal were attempting to spirit away to Ford City precisely to *avoid* a lynching?" asked the mayor.

Steve averted his eyes. "Sorry to say he escaped in the process of the mob getting their plans interrupted."

"My god." Jepson wagged his head. "I'm certainly not advocating for having allowed the lynchers to succeed . . . but the life of Tom Bartlett for a young rascal who all evidence points toward very likely being a murderer—can we agree that was a horrendous trade?"

"Maybe so," Mercer grated after a brief, strained pause following the mayor's words. "But transporting Rodero, the prisoner, to Ford City's more secure jail to await trial was Marshal Tom's idea after a lynch mob damn near tore him out of our jail here. The risk of trading your life to uphold the law—and, yeah, that means sometimes protecting lowlifes who don't deserve it—goes with pinning on a badge and honoring everything it stands for. Nobody understood that better or took his badge more seriously than Tom Bartlett."

The mayor placed a hand to the side of his head and rubbed at the temple. "It seems I have much to try and accept about this whole dreadful incident. Unfortunately, I doubt nothing will help me understand the why of it any better. And it surely won't bring back Tom . . . or poor Judge Thorndike before him."

"No, sir, I'm afraid there's nothing we can do about that," Mercer said somberly.

Jepson lowered his hand, and his frown deepened. "I heard another man was also shot. Shot and killed. One of the Brady brothers—is that true as well?"

Mercer nodded. "Clem Brady. The undertaker already claimed his body."

"What about his brother? You never see one without the other. Where is Clyde—was he part of the ambush too?"

"We're figuring he probably was, for the reason you just said," Steve answered. "But we can't say for sure on account of the ambushers all wore hoods to mask their identities."

"Come first light, though," added Mercer, "you can bet we'll be looking to have a talk with Clyde as soon as we're able to locate him."

Dr. Praeger appeared in the treatment room doorway wiping his hands on a blood-splotched towel. "I'm about ready to turn your prisoner back over to you," he said to the deputies. "I've got some final bandaging to do and Ellen is fashioning him a sling. After that, he'll be all yours."

"Is he fit enough to be put in a jail cell?" asked Mercer.

The doctor shrugged. "Don't see why not. He's going to be in pain and discomfort wherever he is. Might as well be in a cell as anywhere." He cut a meaningful glance over at the front door and the steady growl coming from those gathered on the other side, out in the street. "But no matter where you intend to take him, you're going to have to first get him past what sounds like another pretty ugly crowd outside."

"Oh, it is. I can vouch for that," the mayor was quick to attest. "The way they were shoving and pawing, I wasn't sure for a minute if they were going to let *me* through." He frowned at Mercer and Steve. "Maybe you should have done something about breaking them up before this."

"The way me and Steve saw it," Mercer countered, an edge to his tone, "was that we wanted to be here for Tom, and one of us had to stay and keep an eye on Hollister anyway. He is a prisoner after all, and he still poses a threat even with a shoulder wound. Don't worry, mister mayor, we know about facing down angry crowds when the time comes. We've had a lot of practice lately."

"And it appears to me like we may be in for plenty more," added Steve. "Even if we break up that bunch out there now, they're likely to form up all over again after we get Hollister to the jail. I'd say there's a chance we'll have a repeat of last night—only with a different target for those looking to throw a necktie party."

The mayor shook his head sadly. "Oh dear, dear. What has become of our peaceful little town?"

"We're experiencing a rough patch, is all. A

damn rough patch," stated Mercer. Then, doing his best to sound firm and confident, he added, "But we'll make it through. The good people of Rio Fuego, and that's most of 'em, just have to buckle down and stick together until we clear out the trash and get squared away again."

"I like the sound of that," said Dr. Praeger. "Zack's right. We've got enough folks who won't let this current rash of trouble define our town. But that means some of them, for starters, may have to step forward right away tonight in order to help hold off that mob."

Lone gave it a beat, then said, "Since I've stepped into the middle of this already, reckon I might as well offer to wade in a little deeper."

Mercer eyed him. "You sure you understand what you could be getting yourself into?"

"Figure I got a pretty good idea out on the trail," Lone told him. "What's more—seein's how a handful of those hooded ambushers got away—until they're run down, it don't seem out of the question for some among 'em to maybe have a grudge against me for bustin' up their party and come lookin' to dish out a little payback. In other words, me helpin' you and Steve clear out the trash, as you put it, could be in my own interest as well."

"He's got a point, Zack," said Steve. "And he's good. I've seen it. He ghosted out of the darkness back there at Coyote Pass and tore into those ambushers like nobody's business. He'd be a mighty good gun to have backin' our play. A sight better than—and don't take me wrong, I mean no offense to anybody—the townies we've got to draw from otherwise."

"We could sure use another good gun," Mercer allowed.

"Oh, come now," said Mayor Jepson, working up another of the disapproving frowns he seemed so quick to display. "Wouldn't further involving a complete stranger at such a crucial time be awfully hasty? Yes, it was very brave and well-intentioned of Mr. . . . er, McCarthy, is it?"

"McGantry."

Jepson bobbed his head. "McGantry then . . . so it was all well and good for Mr. McGantry to break up the attempted lynching at Coyote Pass. But one could argue it was also rather reckless. As an unintended result, don't forget, our beloved Tom—"

Steve didn't let him finish. "Oh no you don't! Mayor or not, I ain't gonna stand for that. It was those lynch-crazy goddamn ambushers who were responsible for Marshal Tom's death. Period. Whether McGantry showed up or not, there was a fifty-fifty chance they'd've gone ahead and killed Tom and me after they got done with the Mexican kid anyway!"

"Steve's right, Mayor," Mercer was quick to add. "Unless you want to pick up a gun and walk out through that crowd with us and then stick around to side us after we get to the jail, I think you'd best leave the law-enforcing work to us. If you don't like the way we're doing our jobs, go ahead and get together with the city council and find somebody else. Until then, I'd appreciate it if—with all due respect—you stay out of our way."

After issuing an indignant "Harrumph!" the mayor stood back and kept quiet.

The two deputies exchanged looks that seemed to silently question the wisdom of what they'd just done. But it was too late now and there were more pressing matters to worry about.

Mercer sighed and said, "Reckon it *is* time we scattered that crowd out front. Even if a handful of the more determined rowdies go somewhere and work themselves up all over again, we can at least cull out some of the less threatening gawkers."

"Sounds reasonable," Steve agreed.

Mercer cut his gaze to Lone. "If you're still willing to hop on board, how about you hold here inside for now and keep an eye on our friend Hollister so he don't try any funny business?"

Lone nodded. "If that's the way you want it. I shot him once, be no trouble to do it again if he gets too frisky."

"Let's hope it doesn't come to that. Within the walls of this establishment," Dr. Praeger remarked dryly, still standing in the treatment room doorway, "we have a rather quaint tradition of taking bullets *out* of people, not putting them in."

Lone grinned. "I'll try to keep that in mind."

From inside the room, Hollister wailed, "There's some more of that talk somebody thinks is cute but ain't funny at all. Keep that crazy bastard away from me. He ain't no kind of official law dog. You know better, mister mayor—I heard you say so. It ain't right to sic him on me!"

Jepson's eyes darted around but he said nothing.

"What I heard," said Praeger, turning back to the patient, "was the deputies telling you to keep quiet. If you don't comply, I might have to slap a chloroform-soaked rag over your face to make sure you do."

Lone took the doctor's place in the treatment room doorway so he could keep Hollister in full view. "Only trouble with that," he remarked, "is he might enjoy it. He's a fella who likes to wear a hood over his head, remember. 'Course anybody as butt ugly as him is doin' the world a favor by coverin' up that mug of his."

Hollister's eyes burned with hate, but like the judge, he held off making any further comment. At least for now.

Once Mercer and Steve began addressing the crowd outside, it didn't take long for it to start dispersing. Men and women who'd flocked from their homes—several of them likely feeling uncomfortable and maybe even a bit ashamed at now finding themselves jammed into a mass that contained such ugly undertones and so many vulgar, violence-inciting voices—were the first to drift away. A sizable segment wanting to steer clear of trouble, mixed with the mildly curious and easily bored, splintered off next. Until what was mostly left were the hardcore rowdies and half-drunks too stubborn to back down easy. Among these were a few sincerely seeking a measure of accountability; the rest were the kind who made the saloon rounds regularly looking for a reason—any reason—to raise hell.

Mercer, as befitting his role of chief deputy, did most of the talking. Based on what he was able to overhear from inside, Lone was impressed with how he handled the task. He was calm yet firm, didn't lose his temper, nor did he take too much guff. When the pack got whittled down to only the surliest and loudest, Mercer hardened the tone of his demands for them to clear out too. They finally did, issuing a few lame, hollow-sounding threats and promises of "you ain't heard the last of us" as their voices faded.

By the time the deputies came back inside, Hollister's bandaging was completed and his arm was in a sling. Lone had gone over to stand directly beside him.

"He's ready whenever you are," Praeger told Mercer. "He's weak from blood loss and I gave him a dose of something for his pain. He shouldn't be up to giving you much trouble any time soon. I'll come by and check on him in the morning."

Mercer nodded. "Sounds good, Doc. Thanks to you and Ellen for everything. I know none of it was very pleasant. Soon as we get Hollister over to the jail and tucked into a cell, I'll send somebody to fetch the undertaker—unless he's already heard—to come for Marshal Tom."

"I can see to that," spoke up a subdued, almost meek Mayor Jepson. "Culbertson's place is right on my way home, it's the least I can do."

"Appreciate it, Mayor." Mercer acknowledged. Then, sweeping his gaze over Lone and Steve, he said, "Well, we'd best get a move on while things are quieted down outside. Hopefully for at least the rest of the night. But keep your eyes peeled for any flare-ups once we're out on the street."

"How about I go first to see if I draw any attention," suggested Steve. "Then you and McGantry follow along if it looks clear."

"Go ahead," Mercer replied. "But stay sharp."

"Be careful. All of you," Ellen Praeger murmured.

They proceeded in this manner. Steve went out first, down the plank walkway and slowly out into the street. He was carrying a lantern he'd commandeered from out of the mob. He continued at an angle off toward his left—the direction of the jail, Lone reckoned, but also the direction of the two saloons. Splashes of light and a renewed level of noise once again poured from each.

"Your way is the opposite, Mayor," Mercer said to Jepson. "You might want to go ahead while everything seems tame."

The mayor promptly took his advice. He reached the edge of the street, glanced furtively in either direction, then veered to his right and hurried off.

Mercer cut his eyes to Lone. "Guess that makes it our turn now. You ready?"

"Lead the way. Me and Slick here will be right on your heels," Lone said, getting a grip on Hollister's good arm and tugging him off his cot. The wounded man stood, seeming a little unsteady for a moment. As Lone steered him out of the room, he moved sluggishly, no longer displaying his former belligerence.

When they reached the end of the walkway and started out onto the street, Mercer said over his shoulder, "The jail's not far. It's on the other side, a few yards down a side street that juts off just this side of the Morocco Saloon. There's a red brick hardware store on the corner."

"Okay, I see the hardware store," responded Lone, looking past Steve who had slowed his pace out in the middle of the street, waiting for them to close the gap on him and benefit from the illumination thrown by the lantern he was carrying. A cool breeze abruptly sighed down between the rows of buildings, stirring up some dust and one lone tumbleweed that dislodged from somewhere and came skittering along. Lone was struck by how the soft breeze seemed to take the dim, peaceful quiet that lay so near in the outskirts beyond either end of the street and drag it through the saloon splatter of gaudy lighting and noise that was like a stain in the center of the main drag.

Almost like he was thinking something similar, Mercer said, "If we get any fresh trouble, I expect it will boil out of one of the saloons again. We make it past them without another incident, I'm thinking the smartest thing might be for all of us to just bunk in the jail for the rest of the night. That oughta dissuade any whiskey-brave idiots from trying anything too crazy and give 'em a chance to sober up and cool down by morning."

"Much as I dislike the thought of being cooped up and breathing the same air as that skunk Hollister," Steve muttered. "I gotta go along with your idea sounding like a good one."

Tossing a quick glance back at Lone, Mercer said, "How about you, McGantry? With the mood the way it is on these streets tonight and you having thrown in with us the way you're doing—you must see how it's smart for you to continue sticking close too. At least for the short term. Right?"

"I got no problem bunkin' at the jail tonight. I can see where it's a sensible precaution," Lone answered. "But that big gray stud of mine back there hitched in front of the doc's place—Ironsides I call him—I *do* have a problem with leavin' him on the street all night."

"Well hell, that ain't no problem at all," said Steve. "We got a small barn out back of the jailhouse where we put up our own mounts now and then and sometimes the animals of short-stay prisoners. We keep some straw, hay, even a little grain in there. Soon as we get Hollister behind bars, I'll come back to fetch Ironsides and bring him to our barn. That solve your worry?"

"Sounds like it'd be fine."

A sudden boisterous whoop came out of the Morocco Saloon, followed by waves of shrill laughter.

Mercer grimaced. "I probably should have known better, but I was hoping more of the fools might have tamed down after we broke up the pack in front of the doc's house. Due to respect for Marshal Tom, if for no other reason. From the sound of it, though, there's still plenty of liquored-up jackasses braying as loud as ever in both the Morocco and the Grizzly Den across the way."

"Jackasses, the human kind and the four-legged ones alike, have a way of not showin' a whole lot of sense *or* respect," Lone remarked sourly. "And no offense, Deputy, but you were right to say you should know better than to expect otherwise. If you don't and you intend to take over as top law dog around here—which you show the savvy to do, based on what I've seen—then that's a lesson you'd better learn in a hurry."

Mercer slowed to nearly a stop and twisted at the waist to look around at Lone. "I'm not sure," he said with a thin smile, "whether you just scolded me or complimented me . . . or a little of both."

Lone shrugged. "Said you showed savvy, didn't I? Ain't a brand I slap on somebody without—"

The crack of a gunshot cut short Lone's words, rolling out sharp enough and loud enough to also shatter the stillness at both far ends of the street as well as the clamor coming from the saloons.

"Hit the dirt!" Mercer hollered, even as he, Steve, and Lone—caught wide open in the middle of the street and startlingly close to the hardware store window where the shot had come from—were already pitching themselves to the ground. As each did so, he clawed for the gun holstered on his hip.

With his free hand, Lone was also clawing to regain the grip he'd been maintaining on the prisoner Hollister ever since they left Doc

Praeger's. The man had jerked loose simultaneously with the sound of the shot.

Lone cursed, thinking Hollister must have used the disruption of gunfire to try and bolt free. However, swinging up his Colt and squirming on his stomach to look frantically around, Lone quickly saw that wasn't the case at all. Slick Hollister wasn't making a bolt for anywhere—except maybe to Hell. He was sprawled flat and lifeless just a couple feet from Lone. It was plain why he'd jerked away so tightly timed to the sound of the shot . . . the slug had ripped into his throat just below the chin, instantly killing him and dropping him in his tracks!

Chapter Six

A second shot crashed from the hardware store window, resulting in a long furrow being gouged into the ground between Lone and the fallen Hollister. Lone immediately pushed into a side roll, distancing himself from where the bullet had struck. A third report sounded, this time sending a slug sizzling mere inches above Lone while he was still in motion, clipping the heel of his left boot before burrowing into the dirt somewhere beyond.

Lone came to rest once more on his stomach, this time with his eyes locked on the front of the hardware store and his gun hand extending out, aiming his Colt in kind. Before he could trigger a shot, though, Steve and Mercer opened up with their own drawn Colts—pouring lead at where they'd seen the muzzle flashes. The store's window disintegrated under this barrage, sheets and shards of glass making shattering, tinkling sounds amid the gunfire. As the bullets streaked deeper into the store, the thump and clatter of them striking inanimate products could also be heard.

Lone got off a couple rounds of return fire before shoving to his feet and shouting, "Out of the street! Take to cover!"

The two deputies were instantly in motion, same as him. Steve wisely discarded the lantern he'd been carrying, tossing it away to remove the wash of illumination it was bathing him in. He'd been farther across the street and part way past the hardware building when the shooting started. In a burst of speed while bent forward at the waist, blindly snapping rounds in the direction of the shattered window as he ran, he raced on past the corner of the building and then disappeared into the shadows of the side street that led back toward the jail.

Lone reached the edge of the street and ducked in low behind a watering trough about a dozen yards diagonally down from the hardware store window. Seconds later, Mercer came skidding in next to him.

"Damn kid runs like an antelope," he panted, marveling proudly at his partner's prowess.

"That he does," Lone agreed.

Both of them began nimbly, automatically replacing spent shells in their cutters. Starting to catch his breath, Mercer said, "Didn't hurt that the shooting seems to have stopped . . . but still." Then, as if an afterthought, he asked, "You didn't get hit, did you?"

"Heel of my boot got stung a little. Nothing worse," Lone told him.

"Too bad for our boy Hollister, he got stung considerably harder."

Lone made no response to that. He lifted himself just enough to peer cautiously over the weathered wood rim of the water trough.

Mercer said, "What do you figure the shooter's doing in there? Calling it quits? Or just re-positioning himself and lying in wait for one of us to give him a fresh target?"

"I'd be inclined toward him callin' it quits." Lone cut a glance down the street to where saloon patrons—drawn by the sound of gunfire and their curiosity outweighing their caution—were starting to dribble out through the batwings again. "Gonna get a mite crowded out here in a few minutes."

"Then we wouldn't want the shooter to feel lonely trying to squirt out the back all by himself, would we?" Mercer said through clenched teeth.

When Steve picked that moment to lean out and look their way from the corner of the hardware building, Mercer was quick to wave one arm and then point its hand in frantic jabbing motions toward the rear of the structure. Steve looked blank for a couple beats, but then suddenly got it. He gave a choppy wave of his own before spinning away and disappearing into the side street shadows again.

Mercer expelled a satisfied grunt. "Okay. Good. That street will take him to the rear in no time. Me, I'm gonna make my way down this alley on the other side in case the building has any side doors or windows along the way our rabbit might try to hop out of. You wait here, McGantry, and keep covering the front on the off chance—"

"Not this time," Lone grated.

"What do you mean?"

"I mean, I had my fill of waitin' back at the doc's office. I ain't playin' it that way again." Lone jerked his chin, indicating the bullet-blasted store front. "I'm goin' straight at the sonofabitch. Right down his gullet. If he ain't on the run already, he quick will be. You go ahead and work around, get yourself set. I'll either nail him on the inside or flush him into the laps of you and Steve."

Before Mercer could protest, Lone surged to his feet and broke into a bent-over run. He blindly fired a pair of rounds ahead of himself, then followed them in—leaping over the low sill of the busted-out window that swallowed him like the giant maw of some menacing beast with shards of broken glass thrusting in fanglike from all sides. Once inside, he dropped into a low crouch and froze with his Colt extended out at arm's length. He held motionless for several beats, willing his breathing to level off and letting his sight adjust to the denser darkness.

Somewhere up ahead there was a small, curious glow. Otherwise the high-ceilinged interior of the store was a mass of inky blackness. And totally silent. When Lone shifted his weight slightly, the bits of broken glass and splintered wood under his boots crunched in amplified contrast. The only other sound came from out in the street—the muted though steadily increasing murmur-buzz of more and more saloon patrons filtering out in the wake of the shooting.

The thought of how some of them might react upon closer examination of Hollister's body pulled Lone's mouth into a bitter grimace. He was willing to bet it wouldn't take long before there'd be at least a few in the crowd who—even though they'd been clamoring for Slick's hide just a short time earlier—would start lamenting about how he'd been mercilessly gunned down. The way a pack mentality could too often take hold of some folks never ceased to make Lone wonder. And it ranked high among the reasons for him having spent such a big chunk of his life living up to his name and generally steering clear of others.

But at the moment he wasn't looking to steer clear—certainly not of the ambushing bastard who'd made the mistake of opening fire on a street that Lone was in the middle of.

The former scout straightened up and began to move slowly forward. With the Colt up and ready in his right hand and his left reaching ahead in slow sweeps to help feel his way, he took careful steps to minimize the scrape of his boots on the littered floor. Outside, the buzz of those emerging more boldly from the saloons grew louder.

Lone felt his way along the edge of what he took to be a service counter. When that ended, he found himself in a fairly wide aisle that ran between displays of available merchandise—shovels, axes, kegs of nails—and seemed to reach straight back for as far as he could tell. His vision had adjusted as much as possible to the darkness within the spacious room. He proceeded more by feel than sight, though as he grew nearer to the curious glow up ahead, he began to rely on it as a sort of beacon. And then, when he got closer still, he saw that's exactly what it was. It was a modest-sized candle placed atop a chest-high stack of wooden crates. Not there for the meager illumination its small flame provided, Lone concluded—but rather as a signal marker the rifleman had had the foresight to leave behind in order to aid what he anticipated might be his hurried departure out of the darkened building.

Lone swore under his breath. If that was the case and the ambusher had begun his withdrawal right after taking his third and final shot, then the maneuvering Lone and the deputies were doing to try and head him off might already be too late. Lone started past the guttering candle, meaning to quicken his pace as he continued down the long aisle. In midstep, however, he paused. When his groping hand touched the crate where the candle rested, it grazed a sticky wetness that warranted closer examination. Lifting the hand directly into the candlelight, he saw his fingers were smeared scarlet . . . by fresh blood.

Lone gave a satisfied grunt. The fact the shooter appeared to be wounded was a promising turn. If he was hurt badly enough, then it might slow him sufficiently to aid in his interception after all. Or, at least, provide a blood trail to follow.

Up ahead, Lone could now see another even dimmer glow standing out against the gloom. The faint touch of cooler night air, coming from outside, told him what it was—a rear exit door left standing ajar. He started in motion again, urged on and guided by this new beacon.

And then came a loud curse issued by somebody from out beyond the patch of murky gray that marked the open door beacon. Immediately on the heels of that, guns began blasting. Two shots rapped in quick succession, followed by a third only a half second later.

Lone broke into a run, hoping he didn't crash into any unseen object in his path. More gunshots and curses barked from outside, suddenly joined by the clatter of hoofbeats from a galloping horse.

"Stop, damn you!" shouted a voice recognizable as Zack Mercer's.

But it did no good. The pounding of the hooves grew momentarily louder and faster before beginning to fade. Two more shots chased them.

By the time Lone reached the open door, it was over. The shooting had stopped, the rataplan of the fleeing horse (presumably with a rider) was diminishing into the darkness to the point of being barely audible.

Before stepping through the doorway, Lone called, "Zack! Steve! It's McGantry, I'm comin' out."

"Come on ahead," Mercer responded. "It's all clear, but I think Steve's been hit."

"I'm over here," Steve spoke up. "I'm okay. It's just a scratch."

The rear of the building was throwing a long shadow over everything, but even at that there was enough light filtering down from the moon and stars to make visibility markedly better for Lone than it had been inside the store. Mercer moved up on his right, motioning past him. Lone turned and the two of them stepped over to where Steve was sagging against the corner of the building, his left hand clamped tight to his thigh.

"The slippery rat was already out here when I showed up," he rasped as Lone and Mercer edged up closer. "Must've just came out. He was reaching to untie the horse he had waiting. When he saw me, he cussed and right away swung his gun my way. We fired at the same time. I hurried my doggone shot and missed him. His slug tore this burner on the side of my leg, causing me to stagger and miss a second time—damn the luck!"

"Guess that's when I came out of the alley," Mercer picked up. "I saw Steve stagger, and I pulled my first shot on account of the darkness and knowing he was in my line of fire. Then me and the ambusher traded leads without either of us scoring a hit. The lucky bastard kept me pinned back enough for him to gain his saddle, though, and then he was off. Me and Steve both sent some rounds chasing him, but I don't think we did any good . . . like Steve said—damn the luck!"

Up at the mouth of the side street, where it fed off the main drag, several of the men from the saloons were milling. A couple of them had lanterns.

"You up there!" Mercer hollered. "Somebody bring one of those lanterns down here. We've got a wounded man."

As one of the lantern carriers and a couple followers started down the side street in response, a voice from among those hanging back called, "Want we should fetch the doctor?"

"Yeah, good idea," Mercer answered. Then, after a slight pause, he added, "While you're at it, somebody also let the undertaker know he's got another customer up there in the middle of the street."

Chapter Seven

Steve Leonard's handsome face was scrunched into a troubled expression as he said, "I'm trying, McGantry, but I gotta tell you, I'm havin' a hard time wrappin' my head around this notion of yours . . . you really think there's a chance the shooter who opened up on us and killed Hollister wasn't no part of the bunch who'd been howling for his hide just a little while earlier?"

"Yeah, I think there's a good chance of that bein' the case," Lone replied. "Matter of fact, the more I ponder it the more I'm convinced."

"Feeling so strongly the shooter wasn't a carryover from that earlier mob, does that mean you also think his motive for gunning Hollister was something other than seeking revenge on Hollister for his part in Marshal Tom's killing?" This question came from Zack Mercer who was rocked back in a chair behind the marshal's desk in the front office of the Rio Fuego jail.

It was well past midnight. The three men were having this discussion as part of their first opportunity for a private review of events since the gunman had opened up on them out in the street. Elsewhere—except perhaps for Cormac Culbertson, the inordinately busy undertaker—the rest of the town had settled into the kind of peaceful quietness to be expected for the late hour. The ruined hardware store window was temporarily boarded up, citizens who'd been stirred from their homes were now bedded down back in same, even the saloons were mostly emptied out and tame.

Lone sat in front of the marshal's desk on a turned-around wooden chair with his arms folded atop the backrest. Steve was perched on a corner of the desk with his wounded leg thrust out in a stiff, rather awkward manner. The wound, a deep bullet burn, had been treated by Dr. Praeger and left heavily bandaged under a split open trouser leg. Each man had a cup of fresh-brewed coffee in front of him, the steaming black contents spiked with a generous splash of whiskey from the late Marshal Tom's desk drawer bottle.

Lone took an unhurried sip from his cup before responding to Mercer's query. "That's right," he said. "What I'm thinkin' is that the hombre who shot Hollister was likely a carryover with motives goin' back to an even earlier mob—the would-be lynchers who ambushed Steve and Bartlett out at Coyote Pass."

This got an eyebrow-raising reaction from both deputies.

"Whoa," exclaimed Steve. "Now you turned down an even twistier canyon. How much tanglefoot did you pour in that coffee of his, Zack?"

"Not *that* much."

Lone grinned crookedly. "If you two will concentrate on nursin' your own coffee for a couple of minutes in order to allow for hearin' me out, you might surprise yourselves by decidin' I ain't as loco as you're so quick to think."

Mercer made a gesture with one hand. "Go ahead then. Surprise us."

"Okay. It starts with the amount of preparation the shooter—if we reckon it was just one man, like all signs indicate—put into settin' up his ambush," Lone said. "What that amounted to was this: He had to get a horse around back and leave it ready for his getaway; then he had to break into the store and make his way to the front, leavin' off his beacon candle along the way, again to help for a quick getaway; then he had to position himself at the front window, which, since we didn't hear no breakin' glass until we started blastin' return fire, must've included takin' out one of the panes for him to initially shoot through . . . that all sound about right?"

The two deputies nodded. "Like you said, it's what all the signs indicated," Steve agreed.

"So how much time," Lone continued, "do you reckon passed between when you got the crowd broke up in front of the doc's house and we headed out to bring Hollister here to the jail? Couldn't have been more than ten, fifteen minutes at the most. That also sound right?"

"Yeah. Keep going," said Mercer, his brows starting to pinch into a scowl.

Lone took a drink of his coffee. "So add it up. You see the problem?"

"Shit," Steve muttered. "No chance anybody leaving the crowd at Doc Praeger's would have had time to go through that much preparation."

"Not hardly. That's the first thing that made me figure the shooter didn't come out of that crowd," Lone stated.

"Alright, I'll go along with that much," said Mercer, scowling fully now. "But he still could have been out to get Hollister as revenge for Marshal Tom—acting on his own, having never been part of those who gathered in front of the doc's. What makes you think the shooter connects back to that Coyote Pass bunch instead?"

"Couple things," Lone told him. "He got Hollister with his first shot. Why did he keep shooting after that when he could have called it quits right then and there and been started on his getaway before any of us ever began throwing return fire? And where did he aim those additional shots? At me, that's who . . . not you, Zack, even though you were walking ahead of me and Slick and therefore were a closer target. And not you either, Steve, even though you were closer still and carrying a doggone lantern to boot."

"So what does that mean—why would the shooter be after you in addition to Hollister?" Steve wanted to know.

Mercer sat forward in his chair. "Because of

what McGantry said before when he first offered to throw in with us and help clear out the trash. It was in his own best interest, he pointed out, because some of that trash could very likely hold a grudge against him for busting up the Coyote Pass necktie party. Remember?"

"Yeah. Of course." Steve frowned. "So okay, maybe the hardware store shooter saw a chance to get even with Lone because of that business. But how does killing Hollister fit with . . ." The young deputy stopped short and his eyebrows lifted sharply once again. Then, providing his own answer to the question he'd started to ask, he blurted, "Because Hollister needed shutting up before he could identify the rest of those hooded, lynch-happy bastards who ambushed us and caused the death of Marshal Tom!"

Mercer's gaze locked on Lone. "By God, McGantry, it looks like maybe you ain't so loco after all."

Lone's mouth twisted wryly. "Not in this instance maybe. But there's plenty of folks who'd argue against that as an overall blanket statement."

"Damn it, I should have leaned on Hollister harder right away to get some of those names out of him," Mercer rasped, tightly clenching the fist not wrapped around his coffee cup. "I figured we'd be able to sweat 'em out easier once we had him behind bars!"

"And there wasn't nothing wrong with figurin' that way," Lone told him. "No use back-trackin' and second-guessin' now. What's done is done. None of us had any reason to expect a street ambush like that."

"Besides," added Steve, "we kinda had our hands full worryin' about a newer—albeit more half-assed—lynch mob."

"I guess so," Mercer allowed reluctantly. "But that don't change the fact that losing Hollister lost us an important link to the other curs responsible for Tom Bartlett being dead. On top of that, the suspected killer of Judge Thorndike is in the wind without the slightest clue where he might be headed . . . if that don't add up to a shit storm, I don't know what does. And you can bet Mayor Jepson is gonna be wailing that tune first chance he gets to anybody and everybody willing to listen."

"To hell with that pipsqueak," Steve chuffed. "We put him in his place once tonight, we can do it again."

Lone drained his cup. Lowering it, he said, "I think Steve's got the right idea. Jepson is a prime example of somebody who talks too much and says too little. And I'd put anybody who seriously listens to him in the same category. So you fellas can worry about the gut wind that comes out of him, or you can ignore it and go ahead with what you have to do."

"I'd love to go ahead with something," replied a sour-faced Mercer. "Trouble is, I don't see a hell of a lot to go ahead *with*."

"You're wrong," Lone said bluntly. "Things ain't as dead-ended as you're makin' 'em out to be."

Mercer eyed him. "How so?"

"What about the other Brady brother? Ever since we got to town with the one I killed," Lone said, "all I've heard is how the two brothers always stuck tight together. Even the mayor mentioned it. So if the dead one was part of the Coyote Pass necktie party, don't it reason out as bein' likely his brother was in on it too?"

"Yeah, it's almost a certain bet," confirmed Steve. "Like Zack told the mayor, we been figuring all along to look him up soon as—"

The sound of Mercer's palms slapping down hard on the desktop cut him short. "But 'soon as' is no longer good enough!" the stocky chief deputy declared with sudden intensity. "Lone's right—we need to make Clyde Brady a priority and do it pronto. If we can run him down and get him to confess being part of the same bunch as his brother, then he becomes the replacement for Hollister as somebody who can identify the rest of them."

"See? There's always tracks to be found if you scan the ground tight enough," Lone said. Then he added, "And I got something more."

"Spit it out," Mercer encouraged him. "You've been damned helpful so far, don't hold back now."

Lone grimaced. "This is something I should've coughed up a lot sooner. My only excuse is that the way things have been poppin' at such a breakneck pace ever since those would-be lynchers showed up to disrupt my camp, damned if some stuff didn't get fogged over in the dust. So, before the dust has any chance to settle again, grab a pencil and piece of paper, Zack, and get ready to write."

Without question Mercer produced the requested items and laid them out on the desktop. "Okay, we all know about Hollister and the Bradys," Lone said. "Now write down these . . . Trent . . . O'Toole . . . Dooley . . . and Brown."

When Mercer was done writing, he looked up questioningly.

"I was over in that grove of cottonwoods—like I said, gettin' ready to make night camp—when the riders first showed up and checked down their mounts at the mouth of the pass," Lone explained. "It was dusk, I couldn't make out their faces even before they put on their hoods. But I could hear 'em talkin' plain enough. The one the others called Trent, he seemed to be the he-bull of the herd, started tellin' the others where to take up positions for the ambush . . . what I just gave you was the names he used to direct 'em."

"Hot damn! This is great, McGantry," said

Mercer, slapping the sheet of paper he'd just made the list on. "This identifies the whole stinkin' bunch!"

Lone's grimace stretched wider. "Rotten shame I didn't think of it sooner. Like I said, that happened right at the start, before I had any idea what all was shapin' up. What they were callin' one another didn't really register as bein'—"

"That don't matter," Mercer cut him off. "It finally did register, and that's what counts now!" He shook the paper excitedly. "We went from being dead-ended to now having five leads to follow."

"So you think you'll be able to match those partial names to some hombres in the area?"

"We damn well oughta be able to," said Steve, moving around the end of the desk and leaning over to peer down at the paper Mercer had smoothed out flat once more. In a matter of moments, the lawmen confidently identified two men suggested by the list—Reece Dooley and Gus O'Toole. Since there were a number of Browns around town, they were a little less sure about locking on a single individual to fit with that handle; but they narrowed it down to either a Merl or a Frank, both of whom were well-known rowdies and each having been seen as part of the mob that had stormed the jail the prior night. That left the one called Trent . . . and he presented a stone wall.

"Could be a first name, could be a last. Either way," Mercer said grudgingly, "I'm coming up empty as far as anybody to fit it."

"Same here," allowed Steve. "But we still got those others to make a run at. One of them is bound to spill on this Trent character."

"Before that," interjected Lone, "I got something else to add about him . . . I believe he's wounded, maybe still packin' around the bullet."

"What makes you think that?"

Lone answered, "For one, when things busted open after I cut loose the Mex kid they were fixin' to string up, Trent tried to trample me with his horse. I got a shot off at close range and was pretty sure I hit him, even though he stayed in the saddle and rode off . . . then, just a while ago back in the hardware store when I came upon that beacon candle, I found a small puddle of blood beside it. I'm thinkin' now that might've been left by Trent, makin' him the shooter who got rid of Hollister."

Mercer looked thoughtful. "If he's on the prowl with a bullet in him, you gotta think he'll need to seek out a doctor before much longer."

"He ain't likely to try local, figuring Doc Praeger would no doubt raise an alarm," pointed out Steve. "So, now that he's eliminated Hollister, the closest place for him to find a sawbones to patch him up would be ol' Doc Greeves over at Singletree Junction."

Mercer's mouth pulled into a tight line and he gave a slow shake of his head. "Thing is, the shooter ain't done eliminating yet."

Steve looked puzzled. "What do you mean?"

"I mean," Mercer replied, "while the shooter has no way of knowing about these names McGantry has provided, it's a pretty sure bet he *is* aware how us and half the people in town would reckon Clyde Brady to almost certain be part of the ruckus that got his brother killed. That would make Clyde—as is exactly the case—somebody you and me'd be bound to want to talk to. Which, in turn, would make him the same risk as Hollister for spilling the beans on the others."

"Holy shit," exclaimed Steve. "All the more urgent for us to run down Clyde then, ain't it? For our sake, to get what information we can out of him . . . and for his sake, to get him out of the way before the shooter makes it to him first!"

Lone smiled slyly. "Now you're catchin' on."

Chapter Eight

Clem and Clyde Brady, Lone was informed, were barely literate brothers who eked out a meager living doing irregular hauling jobs with a big old Studebaker freight wagon and a team of prime, sturdy mules they had somehow gained possession of. They were raised by a bitter, coarse-featured, foul-mouthed widow (a status achieved by her own hand, many believed) and turned out to be mostly just brawnier, hard-drinking, brawling versions of her. Both were judged to be somewhat simple-minded, with eldest brother Clyde a bit less so than Clem. Though they often camped on the trail during long, arduous hauls of the type other freighters were reluctant to take on, and almost as frequently slept in the livery barn where they boarded their mules when in town, they nevertheless owned a hardscrabble piece of property and a rundown old shack some miles outside of Rio Fuego; this being left to them by their deceased mother.

Zack Mercer told these things to Lone during the course of their ride out to the Brady property. It was coming up on dawn. The moon and stars had faded from the sky and, in advance of the first stabs of sunlight, a smear of pinkish-gold was staining the pale gray along the eastern horizon.

"I've never had occasion to ride out to the Brady place before," Zack was saying. "Not that confrontations with the Bradys haven't been called for plenty of times due to some of their saloon ruckuses. But that was always in town and, like I mentioned, when it was time to roust 'em they could usually be found sleeping off the effects of what got 'em in trouble either under their wagon or in the livery barn with their mules. Just speculation on my part, mind you, but I've always sorta figured their reluctance to head home more often probably speaks to the sorry condition of the place."

Lone's brow puckered. "If you're sayin' it might be even less invitin' than sharin' a livery stall with a couple of mules, then it must be in sorry shape indeed."

"Steve pretty much confirmed such when he got called out here a year or so back," Zack said with a chuckle. "That wasn't too long after the ma had passed away, and anybody who ever met her could vouch how she didn't hold very tight to the old 'cleanliness is next to Godliness' belief herself. Nor did any difference show in her sons. And now, since it's been a year of just the boys looking after the place . . . Lord knows what to expect. Steve said the stink from taking one peek inside the shack that time he was there made his eyes water so bad he couldn't really describe it any farther."

"That must explain why he didn't put up more of a fuss about stayin' back to keep an eye on the town while I'm the one comin' on this little ride-out with you," Lone surmised.

"If that wasn't much of a fuss, I'd hate to see him throw a full-fledged fit," replied Mercer. Then, scowling, he added, "I didn't like having to pull rank on him like I did but, doggone it, I *am* the chief deputy and we both might as well get used to it—leastways until the city council puts a new marshal in charge over the both of us, if that's what it comes to."

"Apart from any more hot air outta your friend the mayor," Lone said, "the town would be plumb loco not to give you a crack at the job. If you want it, that is. And as far as Steve, it's plain to see he respects the heck out of you. So there'd be no trouble there. His fussin' was just his young, hot-headed way of showin' he wants in on the action and ain't no shirker at holdin' up his end. He knows full well somebody needed to stay behind and watch over things, just like he knows that fresh bullet burn on his leg only makes it smart for him to keep out of the saddle for a while."

Zack sighed. "It was what was best. Period. I gotta add, though, that having you on hand willing to pitch in yet again was mighty handy and something both me and Steve are obliged for."

"I took on a piece of this as soon as I crashed

that necktie party," Lone reminded him. "But if this shack turns out to be as repulsive as has been advertised, my willingness to pitch in so quick-like goin' forward might get cured once and for good."

The farther west they rode from Rio Fuego, crossing and re-crossing the twisty tributary the town was named after, the choppier and rockier the terrain became. Until, about six miles out, they ascended a long, low hogback that looked down on a shallow, grass-bottomed bowl that contained the Brady property.

Reining up just back from the crest of the rise, they gazed down on the simple layout with the sky overhead growing steadily brighter. Below stood a dilapidated shack of a house. A rusty, tilted windmill rose up out in front and parked between the windmill and the shack was the Studebaker freight wagon appearing well maintained in sharp contrast to everything else in its vicinity. Behind the house was a cramped, rickety-looking corral and an equally rickety lean-to meant to serve as an animal shelter.

"I make those lumpy shapes back in the shadows of that lean-to to be the mules," said Zack. "Them and the wagon out front means it's pretty certain Clyde is down there too."

"Only there's no sign of a saddle horse," Lone noted. "The Bradys don't travel strictly by means of their wagon and mules, do they? If they were part of that shindig back at Coyote Pass, wasn't nobody rollin' around on a wagon."

"They must have borrowed mounts for that," Zack replied. "Otherwise, yeah, their wagon and mules is how they get around. And even if Clyde did have a riding horse at his disposal, he wouldn't go off and leave his mules here unattended. Whatever else anybody can say about the Brady brothers, they've always taken top-notch care of their mules."

"Okay. You got me convinced—Clyde is down there."

"It would fit, too, with how ol' Gus back at the livery barn said he hitched up his mules and tore off so sudden-like," pointed out the lawman. "Clyde must have heard by then that his brother was dead."

Lone frowned. "So he came out here to . . . do what? Lay low? Hide? Wouldn't he figure anybody lookin' for him would try here first, just like we're doin'?"

"Didn't I tell you neither of the Bradys were very bright? And hearing Clem was gone would be enough to send Clyde into a panic, no matter what." Zack glanced skyward and formed a scowl. "Damn, I'm wishing now we'd have gotten here when it was a little darker. Because you're right . . . Clyde ain't so dense as to go very long without figuring somebody is bound to come looking for him."

"Meanin', if he's thinkin' that way, he could be waitin' down there like a cornered animal."

"A very *dangerous* cornered animal," Zack was quick to amend.

Both men went quiet for several beats, their eyes scanning, their minds churning. Until Zack spoke again, saying, "Ain't shit in the way of cover for anybody to try and approach that shack unseen, is there? No trees, no brush for dozens of yards in any direction."

"About the size of it," Lone agreed. "But we need to make a move in what pre-dawn dimness we got left. Only a couple ways to go at it, far as I can see."

"And they are?"

Lone said, "We go straight on in, slow and easy, tryin' to look as non-threatening as we can. We might even catch him asleep, possibly drunk into a stupor out of grief . . . or we fan out wide to the north and south and work our way in separate, still slow and easy, splittin' his attention and one of us possibly even goin' unnoticed."

"Not that I don't appreciate your company," replied Zack, "but I kinda favor the spreading out notion."

Lone pointed. "Whoever comes out of the north will have the advantage of gainin' some cover, slim though it is, when he reaches the corral. You want to flip for it?"

"You're my guest, reckon I owe you the

courtesy," Zack said with a wry twist to his mouth. "Besides, I don't get along good with mules. I'd be too distracted looking out that one of those jugheads didn't slide over and try to bite a chunk out of my behind instead of focusing on Clyde not trying to take a potshot at me from the shack."

"If that's the way you want it." Lone grinned. "Mules love me."

They dropped away from the crest, ground-reined their horses on the backslope, then split in opposite directions on foot. The sun broke above the eastern horizon and Lone found himself mentally echoing Mercer's earlier wish that they'd arrived for this undertaking when it was a little darker. But, as the old saying went, if wishes were fishes then everybody would have something to fry. The thing now was to make the best out of what they had to work with.

Lone double-timed it to a point where he figured he was out wide enough. Pausing, he looked across to Zack who had also come to a halt. The two men exchanged signals then turned to proceed on over the crest of the hogback before curling inward on the Brady shack from their separate points.

Holding his Yellowboy at a ready angle out front, leaning slightly forward at the waist, Lone angled down through the knee-high grass in long, steady strides. His narrowed eyes were locked on the shack, making occasional quick sweeps over to the corral and lean-to. The mules remained still and silent inside the latter, one of them standing, the other lying down. As he reached the end of his descent off the hogback, the high grass gave way to dusty, hard-packed earth under Lone's feet. He moved up to the peeled pole corral and began slowly skirting along one side. He could see Zack approaching cautiously from the opposite direction. Nothing else moved, everything was silent.

Their initial surveillance of the shack from atop the hogback had revealed a front door and two side windows. They couldn't see the back side of the structure to be able to tell whether or not there was a rear door. From his vantage point now, Lone could see that there was. It was old and weathered, hanging crookedly on its hinges and standing slightly ajar. Still, there was no sound or sign of movement from inside.

Lone caught Zack's eye and made a motion to indicate he was moving around to the back. Zack nodded okay.

Lone edged around the corner of the corral. He angled the muzzle of the Yellowboy higher and out ahead a bit more. His gaze swept back and forth between the side window and the back door. As he drew closer, he became gradually aware of mixed sour smells emanating from the shack. Still no movement or sound, though. But wait . . .

along with the increasingly stronger smell, a low, constant noise, a dull buzzing, was beginning to be audible.

There was a vague familiarity to it that Lone couldn't quite place. Only then, after a couple more steps closer to the crookedly hanging door, he abruptly did. His gut tightened and filled with its own sourness.

Out front, from where he had taken cover behind one end of the heavy freight wagon, Zack picked that moment to call out: "Brady! Clyde Brady! This is Chief Deputy Marshal Zack Mercer! No harm will come to you if you step out with your hands empty so we can talk!"

When there was no response for several beats, Zack called again. "Don't make this harder than it has to be, Clyde. And don't be fool enough to try making a run for it—we've got the place surrounded!"

But by then Lone was confident Clyde wouldn't be making any attempt to run. So certain was he that he stepped boldly up to the side window and leaned close enough so that his nose was almost touching the sheet of paper covering it, said paper smeared with a thin layer of grease to create a certain amount of transparency as long as you didn't mind what you saw through it being blurred and somewhat distorted. Even though this was the case, Lone had no trouble being able to make out what he'd more or less expected to see on the inside. Even clearer and louder through the filmy paper came the low, steady buzzing sound. A man Lone had every reason to believe was Clyde Brady sat perfectly motionless at a rough-hewn wooden table. His shoulders were hunched forward in an awkward way and one side of his head lay flat on the tabletop, encircled by an uneven stain turned blackish maroon in color. The man's right forearm also rested on the tabletop, bent so that the hand was pointing in toward his face. The hand was gripping a long-barreled Remington pistol, the tip of its barrel shoved approximately into the man's mouth. It was hard to tell for certain because of the buzzing, swarming mass of flies that covered the ruptured head and face like a living, squirming blanket.

> I AM SORY THE MARSHEL GOT KILT. IT SHOOD HAVE BEN THAT DAM SPIK. I AM EVEN SORYER MY BROTHER CAME TO SUCH A BAD END. I SHOOD HAVE PROTEKTED HIM BETTER. I WILL TAKE MY GILT AND SOROW TO HELL . . . CLYDE BRADY . . . PS I DO NOT CARE ABOUT THE WAGIN BUT PLEASE GIVE OUR MEWLS TO SOMBUDY WHO WILL TREET THEM GOOD.

So read the suicide note left on the table where Clyde sat down to blow his brains out. The paper was flecked with spatters of blood and a few chunks of skull bone, but still legible . . . at least to the extent the rudimentary spelling would allow.

"Jesus Christ!" gasped Zack Mercer as he straightened up and took a step back from completing the task of helping to hoist Brady's tarp-wrapped body up onto the bed of the freight wagon. The exclamation was faintly muffled by the bandanna tied over Mercer's mouth in deference to the stink and swarming flies that filled the inside of the shack from which he and Lone had just carried the carcass. Yanking off the bandanna now, the deputy first used it to swat away some of the flies that followed along with the decomposing corpse, then he pulled the hanky to his face and mopped fat beads of sweat from his forehead. The sun was nearly two hours high now and the morning heat was beginning to build quickly. Continuing his lament while mopping sweat, Zack said, "If that marshal's job—or wearing a badge, no matter what the position—was to involve very many episodes like this one, then there wouldn't be enough money in the whole town of Rio Fuego to keep me hired on!"

Lone turned from where he'd completed closing and fastening the wagon's tailgate. He pulled off the bandanna he also had been wearing over his mouth, revealing a crooked grin. "I thought you was on your way to bein' one of those nail tough, seen-it-all-before veteran lawmen," he drawled. "We left dead men back in Rio Fuego only a few hours ago, and you seemed to handle that okay. What's so different about ol' Clyde here takin' a bite of a pill he couldn't swallow?"

"Yeah, I've seen dead men before. Plenty of 'em. Hell, I even caused a few to end up that way. But none of 'em was ever left in a condition with their heads busted apart like a stomped-on pumpkin and a bucketful of flies and maggots crawling all over it. Not to mention the stink surrounding the whole works." Zack swept a baleful look from the wagon and its grisly cargo to the shack and then back to Lone. His forehead puckered in the process and the "green around the gills" look he'd been fighting to hold at bay threatened once again to take hold. "You sure as blazes seem to be taking it all in stride. How is that?"

Lone's grin faded. "Spent a big chunk of my younger years ridin' scout for the Army. Much of it was while the Indian campaigns were still goin' on. It's a job where it don't take long to see all kinds of death and butchery—laid down by both sides—that make this business with Clyde seem pretty tame by comparison. You either learn to harden yourself to it, or you get the hell out before it makes you go mad."

"I like to think I'm a fairly tough hombre, but I reckon I'd have to do the latter. I don't think I could ever get used to regular doses of butchery worse than this."

"There's plenty who feel that way, and it's got nothing to do with toughness. There's lots of ways for a body to be tough, don't mean it fits every situation," Lone said. "By the look of it, not even our friend who likes to go around eliminatin' folks had the stomach to handle what he came across here."

Zack looked puzzled. "What do you mean?"

"Something I didn't notice myself right away on account of how we worked in wide from off to the sides. But when I brought the mules around to hitch 'em to the wagon, I saw these fresh tracks right here in front. See 'em?" Lone pointed as he issued the rhetorical question. Then he continued, "I make it that a lone horseman rode up only an hour or so ahead of us. Somebody who didn't figure he had to be careful about approachin' Clyde. When he called out and got no answer, he must've dismounted and walked to the front door. You can see his boot prints leadin' up to it. When he looked inside . . . well, he saw same as we found."

As his eyes scanned the ground, following the markings Lone had indicated, Zack said, "And you're thinking this horseman was the shooter who eliminated Hollister and then, like we anticipated, came here to do the same to Clyde?"

"Way it sizes up."

Zack lifted his gaze. "You think he *did* get to Clyde?"

"No. Clyde did himself. Did the shooter's work for him," Lone said firmly. "If you want more proof, take a look at something else I didn't notice right away—outside, next to the doorway, there's a fresh splash of vomit where somebody lost his grub over what was inside. Don't seem likely the shooter would throw up at his own handiwork, does it? What's more, higher up on that outside wall, there's another smear of fresh blood like I found inside the hardware store by the beacon candle."

"For somebody carrying around a bullet in him," Zack muttered bitterly, "that stubborn sonofabitch sure seems to be covering a lot of ground."

"It'll catch up to him sooner or later," Lone predicted. "But speakin' of coverin' ground, seems to me it's time for us to cover some of our own and get back to town. I'll drive the wagon, you lead Ironsides along behind you, okay?"

Zack nodded. "Fair enough. I'm glad you're a muleskinner in addition to your other skills. I admitted before how lousy I am with jugheads."

Lone moved around to the front of the wagon and got ready to climb up into the driver's box. Over his shoulder, he said, "Don't worry. Like I told you . . . mules love me."

Chapter Nine

"Ow! Damn, I thought nurses were always supposed to be so gentle." After voicing this complaint, Eli Trent lifted the half-full bottle of redeye he was clutching in one paw and tipped it up for a long pull.

"Keep in mind," replied the woman who was leaning close and probing at his wounds, "that I never claimed to be a nurse. Leastways not no official one. They got to calling me that while I was helping care for the sick old judge. But all I really did was see to it he took his pills according to the doctor's instructions, made the old gent as comfortable as I could, and cleaned up the disgusting messes he made that his pampered wife was too delicate to manage. That was the extent of my 'nurse' duties."

Lowering the bottle, Trent glared at the third person in the room, a husky, ruddy-faced, middle-aged man clad in standard ranch attire but of a notably better quality and fit than that of a common wrangler. "Hell. While you were at it, Hank," Trent quipped sarcastically, "why didn't you just fetch me some old horse doctor?"

"Findin' a horse doctor would've been easy," Hank Birchfield said, stone-faced. "But one willin' to treat an ungrateful jackass—those are harder to come by."

Trent's eyebrows pinched together. "You're calling *me* ungrateful? After I spent the whole goddamn night running around doing your dirty work, and over half of it with a bullet hole in me?"

"I'm not discountin' that, Eli. Not a bit. And neither am I ungrateful for it," Birchfield assured him. "But I'll point out that most of the reason you kept going with that hole in you was because you had to clean up the mess that got made of the job you originally set out to do."

When Trent stiffened and looked ready to make a heated reply, the woman tending his injury quickly placed a restraining hand on his bared chest and said, "You'd better calm down, mister, or you're going to make that wound worse and what limited skills I do have will be strained even more. And, while we're on the subject, let's get clear on whether or not you *want* me to continue. If you don't think I'm good enough, just spit it out and I'll gladly wash my hands and be on my way. It's not like I asked to be hauled clear the hell out here at the crack of dawn to go digging around in your bloody, smelly old armpit!"

"Clear the hell out here" was a cramped, little-used line shack on the northern fringes of the JT Connected spread, the modest-sized cattle ranching operation owned (until his recent demise) by Judge Reginald Thorndike. The meager furnishings of the place consisted primarily of a rough-cut wooden table and two straight-backed chairs. There was also a small iron cookstove complete with a stack of firewood and a storage bin—lined with tin-plated sheets to keep rodents out—built against one wall. The bin contained blankets, a couple mess kits, some canned goods, and a sack of coffee beans. A thin layer of dust due to lack of use had settled over everything, but otherwise the interior was in good repair.

Hank Birchfield, foreman of the JT Connected, sat on the storage bin. Trent, an old friend and recent hire to the brand, was seated on one of the chairs at the table. Occupying the other chair, hitched up close on Trent's left side, was Rose Ellison, formerly acting as nurse and aid to the ailing, cancer-riddled Thorndike. Though not widely known, in her time thus employed she and Birchfield had become romantically involved.

In response now to Rose's challenging statement, Trent lifted his brows and rocked back his head. Then, cutting his gaze over to Birchfield, he said, "Whooee, Hank-boy. Looks like you got yourself a real spitfire here."

Trent was a big man. Tall, thick-bodied, with large, blunt-fingered hands. His face was a map of rugged features, borderline homely, but with sharp, intelligent eyes that conveyed an overriding sense of confidence and strength.

"No. This spitfire," Rose spoke again, even though Trent's remark was aimed past her, "is what *you* got if you want that wound treated before you risk a dangerous amount of blood loss and possible infection. Now I asked you a question—do you want to risk that, or do you want me to go ahead and do what I can to take care of it?"

Trent's expression hardened as his eyes dropped to her. "Are you capable?"

Rose met his gaze evenly. "I think so. If you'll hold still and quit interfering, that is. Other than the pain and the blood you've lost, you're actually pretty lucky. The bullet went in at an upward angle, grazing just above your ribs before punching up through your armpit and exiting your shoulder a whisker away from the socket. No broken bones, nothing more serious than some meat and muscle torn on the inside. I repeat—lucky."

Birchfield grinned. "Sure sounds to me like she knows what she's talking about, Eli."

"Yeah, I gotta go along with that," Trent said, the harsh edge suddenly lifted from his tone. Then, regarding Rose with a softened gaze, he added, "Reckon I owe you an apology, ma'am. You were put to a lot of trouble to come out here and try to help me. And the thanks you got was me acting like a . . . well, an ornery jackass."

"Forget it," came a rather terse reply. "We're all in this together. We've got to look out for one another or the whole works will collapse in on us like a house of cards."

A couple years past the thirty mark, Rose was still quite an attractive woman. Dressed in a simple white blouse and split riding skirt, she displayed a trim, almost girlishly slender figure. Pale gold hair framed somewhat angular facial features set with smoky brown eyes that conveyed a hint of sad wariness suggesting perhaps some past hard breaks.

Ready now to proceed with the task of ministering to Trent's wounds, she gestured to a large carpet bag perched on the table, the dusty top of the latter covered by a blanket from the storage bin. "I gathered an armful of medical supplies left behind by Doc Praeger at the judge's place. I figured there was bound to be some stuff we could use."

Birchfield nodded in approval. "Good thinkin'."

"There are plenty of bandages, some strong disinfectant, even a bottle of pain medicine."

"I got my bottle of pain medicine right here," Trent declared, brandishing the whiskey he still held in one hand.

"Suit yourself," Rose said with a shrug. "After I've finished cleaning and treating those entrance and exit holes with disinfectant, I can *probably* keep the bleeding stanched with bandages. The surest way, though, would be to cauterize them. You know what that means."

Trent's mouth pulled into a tight, grim line. "Yeah, I've had some miseries cauterized before. If that's what you figure would be best, then go ahead and do it."

Rose glanced over at Hank. "You heard him. Get a fire going in that stove, will you? Doesn't have to be too big, just enough to make some good hot coals we can heat a knife blade cherry red in."

Everybody went quiet for a few minutes. Until, speaking over his shoulder as he got some wood crackling in the belly of the stove, Birchfield said, "So Clyde Brady up and killed hisself, eh? I'll be damned."

"He sure did," Trent confirmed. "Made a hell of a mess doing it, but he got the job done."

"Well, since you'd already taken care of Hollister in town, I guess we can look at it as Clyde tyin' off the final loose end that he himself represented from that Coyote Pass fiasco." Birchfield straightened up and turned away from the stove. "Now, if we can count on that stinkin' Mex kid to keep ridin' into the wind and that big damned McGantry finishin' his business and movin' on . . . then maybe we can still manage to pull this thing off."

Trent grunted. "I don't think you have to worry about that Mex kid. He came so close to getting his neck stretched that I don't figure he'll stop running until he's back eating beans somewhere south of the border." He took another swig of his whiskey then lowered the bottle with a scowl. "As far as that meddling damn McGantry, I don't know that I personally am in such a hurry for him to ride off. I owe that bastard for these holes in me and it would do my healing a powerful lot of good was I to send him on his way permanent-like."

"You had your chance at him last night, didn't you?"

"Yeah, but it was more important to take out Hollister first," Trent snapped defensively. "Once I'd put him down, it was hard to get a bead on McGantry. He moves fast for a big man. And I only had a matter of seconds before him and those two deputies were pouring enough return fire my way to make it slightly unhealthy for me to stick around."

Birchfield made a face. "I guess I can understand you wantin' another crack at him. But me, I'd just as soon see him move on with no more trouble. We've already got a God's plenty of that both behind and ahead of us. Since we know McGantry came here lookin' to do some horse dealin' with the judge, my hope—upon findin' out the old man's dead—is that he'll call it a wasted trip and go back to Nebraska, where he came from."

"Having come all this way, you don't think he might try still dealing with Thorndike's widow?" asked Trent.

Birchfield's face scrunched up even more, taking on a look of distaste. "Jesus. Wouldn't that be awful cold, tryin' to strike up business talk with a widow whose husband ain't even in the ground yet? Besides, half a minute with Amanda Thorndike and anybody would see she's too distraught for anything of the kind."

"I wouldn't be so sure about that," spoke up Rose as she gently applied disinfectant to the exit wound on Trent's shoulder. "Mrs. Thorndike has a close friend at her side now, remember. That lady lawyer from Denver who showed up to console and support her in this tragic time. I don't know about cold, but that gal is mighty cool—and *sharp*. Though Mrs. Thorndike might be too upset to handle much of anything right now, if there was some Thorndike business needing taken care of then I'm betting this lawyer gal wouldn't be at all shy about stepping in and seeing it got paid proper attention."

"That might be true in some cases," Birchfield allowed. Then he was quick to add in a smug tone, "But what is a Denver lawyer—a lady lawyer, no less—likely to know about horse dealin'?"

"Maybe not very much," granted Rose. "But there's something more about this gal—Harriet

Munro, is her name—that I haven't gotten to."

"And what's that?"

"From part of a conversation I overheard between her and Mrs. Thorndike," Rose explained, "it turns out Miss Munro is pretty well acquainted from some past dealings with this McGantry fella. She spoke very highly of him. In fact, at one point I heard her assuring Mrs. Thorndike that if anybody could be counted on to get to the truth—her word—then it would be McGantry."

Birchfield's smugness evaporated. "What the hell? What truth? Is he a horse buyer or some kind of range detective or something? What did she mean?"

Rose shook her head. "I don't know. I'm just telling you what I heard. But I'd bet on this much—if Harriet Munro has her way, then McGantry isn't likely to be heading back to Nebraska any time soon."

"That can leave you two feeling however you want," said Trent with a mean glint forming in his eyes. "But for reasons I already stated, that don't come as worrisome news to me. In fact, it gives me something to look forward to."

"In that case, there's a thought you'd better hang on to," Rose told him. "Because as soon as we can get a knife blade hot enough, what's coming next is something you damn sure ought *not* be looking forward to!"

Chapter Ten

By the time he and Zack got back to Rio Fuego Lone had been more than twenty-four hours without sleep. Exhaustion was starting to grind down on him like the weight of a giant boulder across his broad shoulders. After leaving Clyde Brady's remains at the undertaker's, he returned to the jail with Zack but tarried there only long enough for directions to the nearest hotel and to get Steve Leonard's promise that he would see to it Ironsides was put up in a livery where he'd receive proper care.

Ideally, Lone should have taken time for a hot bath or at least a good washing up. But he was too damn tired for any of that. With leaden feet he climbed the stairs to a second-floor room after checking in at the recommended hotel, the Traveler's Rest. Once inside, he deposited his saddlebags, possibles pack, gun belt, and Winchester Yellowboy in a corner, hooked a straight-backed wooden chair under the doorknob, and then stripped down to nothing but his long handles before flopping onto the bed with his Colt shoved under the pillow. Sleep came in a matter of seconds.

Until, after what felt like the passage of only a few seconds more, the blessed slumber was interrupted by an insistent pounding on the hotel room door. Trained by his years scouting in Indian country to sleep light and awaken fast, Lone immediately pushed up on one elbow with his fist closed around the Colt under the pillow. A quick scan of his surroundings, however, brought a wash of recollection and realization that put him guardedly at ease. Guardedly. After all, Rio Fuego might not be Indian territory, but the chain of events he'd gotten caught up in since arriving in its vicinity didn't exactly paint everything as being calm and peaceful either.

The door rattled under renewed knocking. And now a voice joined in, calling his name.

"Lone! Lone McGantry! Time to wake up, sleepyhead!"

The voice, not surprisingly, was somewhat muffled. What *was* surprising, though, was that it unmistakably belonged to a woman. Furthermore, something about it seemed vaguely familiar.

Frowning, Lone swung his feet over the side of the bed and stood up. "Hold your horses—I'm comin'!" he called. He put the Colt back down on the mattress long enough to climb into his britches. Then, tucking the shooting iron in the waistband at the small of his back, he padded barefoot over to the door. After swinging away the wedged chair, he shifted off-center from the doorway and said, "Come on in."

There was a slight pause before the door swung open and his visitor entered. It took a moment for Lone to match the familiar-sounding voice with the attractive woman now standing before him. When full recognition clicked, he let out a whoop of delight. "Harriet! Harriet Munro! I don't know what you're doin' here, but you sure are a sight for sore eyes!"

Harriet smiled warmly but then, as her gaze traveled the length of him, from his bare feet to his rumpled, sweat-stained undershirt to his unshaven mug and tousled hair, one finely penciled brow lifted in a mix of amusement and feigned skepticism. "Fortunately, I *do* know what I'm doing here," she said. "And you in turn are, well, let's just say . . . a sight."

Lone's ears burned a little, well aware of his partially dressed condition and his failure to get cleaned up earlier. But his relationship with Harriet was such that, even though they hadn't seen each other in quite a spell, he knew she wasn't truly that put off by his appearance. "If I'd expected a visit from you, I would have got myself polished up like a show horse's saddle," he assured her. "And you *could* have given a fella a little bit of a heads-up, you know."

"Relax, you big lug," Harriet said, her brow smoothing out and her smile widening. She came the rest of the way into the room and closed the door behind her. "Your deputy friends explained to me how badly in need of some rest you were, that's why I held off coming by until this afternoon. By the way, there was no need for them to explain how you'd been keeping yourself so busy in lieu of getting a proper night's sleep—I'd already heard plenty of reports elsewhere about that, about your various escapades since arriving in the area."

"Escapades," Lone echoed. "Is that what I've been doing?"

"It's a nice catch-all phrase to, in this case, cover all of the shooting and charging about and piling up of dead bodies you've been occupying yourself with."

"It's not like I came here lookin' for any of that," Lone countered.

"No, of course you didn't. You came in hopes of purchasing some top quality horses. From a man who ended up getting murdered shortly before you arrived—an unfortunate event that led, in a roundabout way, to what you got caught up in instead."

Now it was Lone who cocked an eyebrow. "You seem to know an awful lot about these 'escapades' I got mixed up in."

Harriet smiled fleetingly and said, "As a matter of fact, I do." She gestured to the chair he'd moved aside a minute earlier and said dryly, "Is this suitable for sitting in—or does it function strictly as a door block?"

"Reckon it'll work as a seat too. Help yourself," Lone told her.

As she re-positioned the chair and settled herself upon it, he took a moment to fully drink in the sight of her. God, how long had it been? Nearly four years. On one hand, that didn't seem possible; on the other, speaking for himself, a hell of a lot had taken place during that time. And not all of it had been over smooth trails. Apart from his currently rumpled outer appearance, he wondered what more lasting marks had those rougher stretches left on him that might be evident to someone as perceptive as Harriet.

She, on the other hand, appeared essentially unchanged. For the better, if anything. More poised, more confident seeming (as if that had ever been in short supply). She had to be close to thirty now, Lone figured, still trim and elegantly graceful in her movements, with the same loosely piled wheat-colored hair and penetrating blue eyes. Her face remained smooth and unlined, its features a bit too boldly cut to fit the classic notion of delicate feminine beauty yet thoroughly fetching and handsome in a strong, womanly way. Her attire was simple yet flawless—a pleated pale orange skirt reaching to mid-calf, cream-colored blouse of some silk-like material, short-waisted open jacket of brushed leather nearly matching in color and texture to a pair of (if Lone was any judge) custom-made boots. A touch of Western flair that wouldn't have been out of place in practically any setting.

Realizing he was on the verge of staring, Lone turned and stepped over to take a seat for himself on the edge of the bed. "As I recall, you were never one who cared to have a lot of flattery heaped on you. Nor have I ever been the silver-tongued type when it came to that sort of thing. But I gotta tell you," he said earnestly, "you make one fine-looking lady, Harriet. Even better than I remembered. So I'd appreciate it if you struck that clunky 'sight for sore eyes' remark I blurted out at the start and accept what I just said as more deservin' instead."

"Duly noted. And thank you, that was nice to hear." Harriet smiled. "So now that it's out of the way, no need to lay it on any thicker."

"If you say so. But there's one more thing I'd appreciate . . . that is, unless you're pinched on time for some reason?"

Harriet shook her head. "I didn't seek you out merely to say a quick hi and goodbye."

"Good. I hope that means an unhurried chin-wag is in order to catch up on everything," Lone said. "If so, I'd really appreciate the chance to get out from under this layer of trail dust I'm packin' around, scrape off these whiskers, and crawl into some clean duds before then. I can't promise I'll come out a whole lot more pleasin' to the eye—there's only so much you can do with an old chunk of leather. But I'd sure feel a heap better spendin' time in your company if I didn't look *quite* like somebody just rope-dragged in behind a horse."

"False modesty doesn't suit you any better than silver-tongued flattery, old friend," Harriet replied with a bit of a smirk. "And after what you did four years ago to aid me—not to mention the Bigbee sisters—on that Rainrock case, there isn't a layer of trail dust thick enough to tarnish the way you look to me. However, the same may not be true for another friend of mine who has invited the two of us to dinner this evening. We'll make time for the private 'chin wagging' either before or after. Perhaps both. But I believe this invitation will be of interest and possibly some benefit to you. What do you say? Can I convey that you'll accept?"

Lone shrugged. "Considerin' the company I'll be in and the prospect of a free meal . . . sure, why not? Long as I get my chance for some scrubbin' and scrapin' ahead of time."

"Certainly."

"By the way, who is it we're gonna be the dinner guests of?"

Harriet regarded him very directly before answering, "Amanda Thorndike. The widow of the late Judge Reginald Thorndike . . . the man you came here hoping to buy horses from."

Chapter Eleven

"Ho-lee mackerel," declared Steve Leonard. "You ain't hardly landed here long enough to cast a shadow, yet look at the swath you've cut everywhere you been and where you say you're headed next. First it was wading in to help handle troublesome lowlifes—for which me and Zack remain grateful, by the way—and now, the minute we let you out of our sight, you go and get yourself invited to take dinner tonight with the Widow Thorndike and that high-class lady lawyer out of Denver. Do all horse wranglers from Nebraska operate as fast as you?"

"Can't say about the rest. Hell, I have a hard enough time keepin' up with myself," Lone responded.

"I bet you do," Steve chuffed. "I didn't even remark on the part about you finding time to get all steam cleaned and curry-combed and decked out in new duds and all. I don't know about Zack, but I hardly recognized you when you walked through the door a minute ago. Been much closer to sundown, I doubt I would have at all."

Indeed the shadows of late afternoon were stretching long in the streets of Rio Fuego outside the jail building. And in the time since Lone had been here last, he'd caught up on some much-needed sleep, been visited by Harriet Munro, and then had seen to the bathing and getting generally cleaned up in the manner Steve was now calling attention to.

Striking a more serious tone, from where he was once again seated behind the marshal's desk, Zack Mercer said, "You mentioned your lady lawyer friend told you that having dinner with Mrs. Thorndike might be of some benefit to you—any idea what she meant by that?"

Lone wagged his head. "No. She wasn't ready to go into it any more right then. The only thing I can guess is that, even though her husband has passed, the widow must be willin' to still discuss some horse dealin' with me on account of how I came all this way and everything."

"I guess that could be it," Zack allowed. Then, frowning thoughtfully, he added, "If that was the case, though, I'd be surprised if Mrs. Thorndike was handling it herself. I mean, she might be willing to consider whatever preliminary arrangement you had with her husband and the long trip you made and all, but having the savvy to reach any final sales deal . . . I don't see her being up for that."

Lone said, "Because she's grievin' and upset over the loss of her husband, you mean?"

"Well, that too. But I was thinking more along the lines of her simply not knowing enough about the business end of making a horse sale,"

Zack explained. "You see, Judge Thorndike had begun building up his cattle ranching operation, the JT Connected brand, about seven or eight years ago. Not too long before his first wife passed away. It was sort of a dream of theirs—nothing real big, just a place for them to finish out their years once the judge retired from the bench. After Katherine, that was his first wife, took ill suddenly and died, the judge kept on with the goal of retiring to the ranch for his own final years.

"Then, three or so years ago, he met Miss Amanda, now his widow, on a business trip to Denver and they soon married. It was pretty clear to most everybody right from the get-go that the new Mrs. Thorndike wasn't cut from the same cloth as Katherine, not when it came to being a ranch wife. But the judge was that much closer to retiring and went ahead with his plans for the JT Connected all the same. For a compromise, he started building a grand new house out at the ranch, something that would have all the luxuries and comforts Amanda was used to. She seemed satisfied with this, even took up learning how to ride and such so she could better fit in. Everything seemed on track for it all to work out."

"Until," Steve cut in bitterly, "the judge got walloped by the lousy break of being diagnosed as having cancer and not expected to live out the year. That knocked all of his careful plans to hell and gone."

"Which is what forced him," said Zack, picking up the narrative again, "to abandon his ranch dreams. Knowing that Amanda would have no interest in continuing the JT Connected without him, he made the decision to start taking bids for the livestock, property, and whatever other holdings he had in order to get top dollar so as to ensure Amanda would be left well off after he was gone."

"Makin' it where I came in," concluded Lone, "when I got word through a mutual friend, Frank North, that the judge was aimin' to sell off some prime stock that would be well suited to the horse ranch I'm plannin' to start back up again in my neck of the woods. A sale that sounds like it might still be doable except for the part about the widow bein' sorta ill-equipped to hold up her end. I sure ain't out to take advantage of somebody in her position."

"No, of course not. Nobody's thinking that," said Zack. "If horse dealing *is* what's behind Mrs. Thorndike's invitation, then I gotta expect she'll have somebody more knowledgeable—probably Hank Birchfield—also present on her behalf."

"Who's Birchfield?" Lone asked.

"He's the ramrod of the JT Connected, the fella who actually runs the operation. Been the judge's right hand clear back to the start." Zack's brows pinched together as he gave this description. "Ain't been nobody tore up worse than Hank over the judge's bad turns of luck. First losing Katherine, then the cancer . . . then, the hardest punch of all, his savage murder. Hank was on his way to see the judge that last morning, going to visit him like he did most every day. Arrived right after the murder was discovered. Folks who was there say he wept like a baby."

"I been wonderin' about that, the murder business," Lone said, forming a frown of his own. "It's one of the reasons I stopped by before headin' over to that dinner thing. I wanted to get a clearer understandin' of some of the details so's I don't say something that'll amount to stickin' my foot in my mouth or hurtin' somebody's already tender feelin's."

Zack interlaced his fingers on the desktop in front of him. "The details are pretty simple. Gruesome, but nothing too complicated. The most ironic part was that it happened at a time when the judge was already so bad off from that damn disease. He was weak, either bedridden or at best getting around in a wheelchair. Hardly ate, didn't always have control of his functions, basically being kept alive on the pills and medicines prescribed by Doc Praeger."

"It was a pitiful thing to see," said Steve in a somber tone. "Fella who was a big, strapping man all his life—physically powerful as well as having a powerful influence all through the territory—reduced in only a short amount of time to such a sorry state."

"Anyway," Zack continued, "on the morning of his murder, the judge was alone in his den. It had been turned more or less into a hospital room by then and he hardly ever left it. His wife had hired a live-in nurse, gal by the name of Rose Ellison, to see he got constant care. The night before, the judge had gone through an especially miserable stretch that kept both him and the nurse awake past daybreak. When she at last got him settled down, Rose went to her room right across the hall to get a little rest. The Thorndikes' cook, a Mrs. Gladstone, was leaving at about that same time to walk downtown and pick up some grocery supplies. Mrs. Thorndike was following her usual morning routine of exercising and grooming her horse in the stable and corral area the judge had built for her out behind the house."

"And all of this was—when exactly?" Lone asked. "Just a couple of days ago?"

"That's right. Tuesday morning," Zack conformed. Then, wagging his head in dismay, he added, "This being only Thursday, it's hard to believe so much tragedy and bloodshed—and I'm talking what happened to Marshal Tom, too, on top of the judge—could take place in such a short amount of time."

"And it ain't over yet. Not considering how we

still got guilty varmints for both killings to run down," muttered a grim-faced Steve.

"Gettin' back to the judge, how long after the nurse left him was he found murdered?" Lone prodded.

"By all reports, only about half an hour," said Zack. "That's when Rose heard voices coming from the study and waking her from her nap. She saw that the door to her room, which she'd purposely left ajar so she could hear if the judge started stirring, had been closed. When she opened it and went across the hall, she found the judge dead, knifed, his stomach laid open from belly button to sternum. Both Mrs. Thorndike out in the corral and the cook returning from her shopping trip heard her screams. And it was both the cook and Rose who spotted Jaime Rodero lighting a shuck off to the south on his easily recognizable Palomino stallion."

"So that's what pegged him as the killer, eh?"

"Sure as hell made him the prime suspect. Nor did it help that he was known to carry a big-bladed Bowie knife, like the weapon used on the judge, and had demonstrated on more than one occasion how he was mighty handy at using it," Zack replied. "He denied everything, naturally, when he was hauled in. But he had nothing else to back him up. And something more—he and the judge were known to have had at least two very recent heated arguments."

"About what?"

Zack explained, "Up until just a little while ago, you see, Rodero worked for the JT Connected. Horse breaker and gentler. Kid had a damn near magical way with horses, they say. Among other things, he was the one who taught Mrs. Thorndike how to ride and gentled and trained her buckskin mare, Honeydew. But when the judge made up his mind to sell off the ranch and started cutting back on some of the hired help, Rodero was among those who got their walking papers. Kid took real hard exception to that—claimed he was being singled out, treated unfairly, bunch of crap like that. Hank Birchfield ran him off the spread and Marshal Tom himself got called to the Thorndike house less than a week ago to chase him away from there . . . unfortunately, he didn't chase him far enough. Little bastard went back one too many times."

Steve grunted. "Yet for all that, the lamebrain staged the worst getaway in the history of getaways. We caught him before the morning was out at his sister's place right on the south side of town. And no sooner did we get him back here to the jail than holy hell started breaking loose. Matter of fact, it ain't hardly let up since."

"That first night," Lone said, recapping the events he'd already heard about previously, "was when the first lynch mob stormed you here and nearly succeeded in rippin' Rodero out of your hands. Causin' you to attempt sneakin' him off to Ford City the followin' dusk in order to avoid a repeat."

Steve made a sour face. "Which they damn near succeeded in doing anyway, if not for your intervention. Unfortunately, much as I hate to sound like our pompous mayor, stopping that Coyote Pass necktie party came at a painfully high price."

"So now," summed up Zack with a heavy sigh, "we've got Rodero on the run and this time making a far better job of it—at least as far as we can tell from what little time we've been able to put into looking for him—plus the matter of pinning down those surviving mask-wearers responsible for the death of Marshal Tom. Leaving an ugly, unsettled mood still simmering too hot for comfort while, just incidentally, a whole flock of state-wide politicians and other dignitaries are due in day after tomorrow for Judge Thorndike's funeral. Then of course Tom's to follow a day or two after that."

Lone rose from the chair he'd been occupying in front of the marshal's desk. "With that pile of work restin' on your shoulders, I reckon I ought not be takin' up this much time rehashin' things just for the sake of my piddly worry over keepin' my foot out of my mouth."

Zack stood up also. He and Steve exchanged glances. Then, cutting his eyes back to Lone, he said, "Expect you've earned as much right as anybody to take up our time. In fact, me and Steve talked it over and decided we wanted to try and convince you to spend a little *more* time with us."

Lone cocked an eyebrow. "Care to chew that a little finer?"

"What we didn't get around to telling you yet," responded Steve, "is that, while you were catching your beauty sleep, we got a visit from the town council. They made an offer—a unanimous one, the mayor included—for Zack to take the marshal's job. He accepted."

Lone eyeballed Zack and made a *tsking* sound in his throat. "I took you for bein' smarter than that."

"So did I," said Zack, his mouth twisting wryly. "But when they put it to me, I heard somebody saying 'I'll give it a try' and danged if it wasn't me."

"Aw, he'll do fine. *We'll* do fine," stated Steve confidently. "But, for all the reasons we just went over, in order to keep a lid on this simmering pot and stop it from coming to a boil until we can get some things sorted out so's to start cooling it down . . . well, we could sure use some reliable help."

"What we were hoping," said Zack, "is that we could talk you into pinning on a deputy's badge for a while."

Chapter Twelve

Having received directions initially from Harriet Munro and then again from Steve and Zack, Lone had no trouble finding the Thorndike house. Located on the east edge of town, it was a relatively short walk from the jail. An imposing, two-story wood-frame structure, easily the community's largest residential building, it would have been hard to miss even with less thorough directions.

The evening was clear and warm, barely any breeze. A few stringy clouds hung in the graying sky, their underbellies picking up a faint tint from the orange-gold glow that lingered just above the western horizon, marking where the final glint of the day's sun had winked out.

Lone's steps were unhurried but, in sharp contrast, his thoughts were racing. The sequence of events stemming from the interruption to his night camp back at Coyote Pass (only just last evening, hard as it was to believe!) had come so thick and fast that the interim had left scarcely any time to think at all. Now, suddenly, there was much he was being forced to ponder.

Most immediate, of course, was this pending meeting with the Widow Thorndike and whatever it ended up being about. And what exactly was

Harriet Munro's involvement? And then, on the subject of involvement, how much deeper did he want to get involved with the two Rio Fuego lawmen? He'd already been willing to get drawn in plenty. Some of that, he realized, was an obligation he felt (maybe out of borderline guilt) for his part in the lynching break-up that resulted in Marshal Bartlett catching a fatal bullet. For the time being, Lone had left it with Zack and Steve that he wasn't ready to pin on a badge just yet, but neither would he ride off and leave them in a lurch.

Then, too, underlying it all, was the impetus behind coming here seeking to deal on horses in the first place. It marked his rekindled goal to start up his old Busted Spur horse ranch again, one of the steps aimed toward reining in his drifting ways and trying to come to grips with the ache and the void left in him by the loss of his beloved Velda. Not that the ache would ever go away, he knew, but at least re-focusing on something like the previously disrupted horse ranch dream was a better way of coping than merely trying to smother the restless anger simmering inside him over the freakishly tragic way Velda died—until it one day reached a boiling point that turned into blind, mindless rage.

As this jumble of thoughts walked along with him now, Lone realized that, in a quirky kind of way, these fresh and unexpected involvements here in Rio Fuego were serving their own purpose in giving him something else worthy to focus on. If a bit of horse buying still worked out with the Widow Thorndike, that would be fine. If this somehow met with the approval of his old friend Harriet due to whatever her relationship with the Thorndike woman was, so much the better. And, whether he agreed to temporarily wear a badge or not, if he could further assist Mercer and Steve in bringing their town's current discord under control then he knew that would be the right thing.

By the time he began making his way up the flagstone walk that led to the broad, open front porch of his destination, Lone was feeling less unsettled and looking forward to the "chin wag" session with Harriet later on.

It was Harriet who answered his knock. She greeted him with a smile and a hello, adding, "Right on time."

"I recall you being a lady who appreciates punctuality."

"Indeed. More so than ever after spending the past three years in the Denver court system." Harriet rolled her eyes. "You wouldn't believe the amount of miscommunication and procrastination that takes place there on a daily basis."

Lone grinned. "I'll have to take your word for it since I ain't sure what some of those twenty-dollar words even mean."

Harriet gave him a look. "Save the bumpkin act for somebody else. I know better, remember?"

"If you say so. But what's with this talk of Denver? Last I knew, I thought you had made up your mind to settle in Rainrock?"

"I had," Harriet confirmed. "But a lot can happen in four years, friend. It turned out my success—*our* success—with the Bigbee case gained me a lot of positive attention in legal circles. Attention that resulted in some very attractive offers to join some larger firms in larger settings. The one in Denver simply turned out too good to pass up."

Lone nodded. "I'm happy for you then. Congratulations. But speakin' of the Bigbee case . . . how are the sisters, Roxanne and Rebecca, gettin' on? You keep in touch with 'em since you moved?"

"Oh, yes. Roxanne and I correspond regularly," Harriet replied. "Both girls are doing fine. Roxanne took to running the ranch with amazing competence. It's bigger and more prosperous than ever. Rebecca is doing exceptional in school, growing like a weed."

"That's good to hear. Roxanne take herself a husband yet?"

Harriet eyed him. "Not yet. Though not for lack of suitors who are lined up for two counties. A couple have come close to winning her hand, but none have succeeded all the way

". . . you know darn well that's partly due to you. She was heartsick when you left. For the longest time, she wouldn't even look at another man."

"Well, I'm glad to hear it sounds like she finally smartened up."

Harriet sighed. "I suppose that's one way of looking at it."

Lone had no response to that.

"Getting back to my move to Denver, that was when I first met Amanda," Harriet explained. "She was a law clerk staying at the same boarding house where I took a room. We hit it off right away. She helped me get acclimated to the big city. But by then she had already become involved with Judge Thorndike during his visits to the Denver courts so it wasn't long before they married and she moved away. We made a commitment to stay in touch, though. We got together whenever she came to Denver and she invited me to come visit here whenever I could. Which I did two or three times a year. I enjoyed taking a break from the city and I think my visits helped her make the transition to being *away* from it.

"When word reached Denver about the judge being slain, I immediately caught a train to Ford City and then hired a carriage to bring me the rest of the way here to be with her. I knew she hadn't made any close friends in Rio Fuego, not the kind one needs at such a time. I thought I could fill that need."

"I'd say that makes you a pretty good friend."

"I hope so."

"Speakin' of friends and gettin' back for a minute to you leavin' Rainrock," Lone said. "As I recall, there was a certain young marshal back there who couldn't have been too happy about you goin'."

A flicker of remorse came and went on Harriet's face. "Let's just leave it at saying some things worked out for the better, and some didn't."

Again Lone had no response for that, other than to wish he hadn't brought it up.

"Would you like me to take your jacket?" Harriet asked.

"No, that's okay," Lone declined. In truth, it was a bit warm to keep on the corduroy jacket he'd chosen to wear. But Lone had reasons for not wanting to shed it. One was the short-barreled Colt Lightning revolver in its right pocket; the other was the handful of spare bullets occupying the left. It had seemed inappropriate to wear his gun belt and openly holstered Peacemaker (the Lightning's big brother) to the dinner. But going unarmed altogether hadn't been a viable option either. The pocketed, out-of-sight gun was a suitable alternative.

"This way to the parlor then. Amanda's waiting for us there. Dinner will be announced shortly,"

Harriet said. Following her down a short, wide hallway, Lone noted that she had changed from her earlier attire and was now clad in a well-fitted dress, deep purple in color, sleeveless, with a flowing skirt and one bare shoulder. No matter what the meal turned out to be, she was already a feast to the eyes.

Not surprisingly, the interior of the Thorndike house proved to be richly appointed. There were strong masculine strokes—dark wood, leather, brass—countered by feminine touches mixing in splashes of bright color and delicate trim. The overall balance created a sense of subdued elegance yet still with a homey feel.

When Harriet ushered Lone into the parlor, a dark-haired woman rose from an upholstered chair to greet them. At forty, give or take a year, Amanda Thorndike was still very attractive. She was dressed in a simple black dress with a full-length skirt and a faintly scooped neckline, the bodice snug enough to reveal a full-breasted, somewhat short-waisted figure. Her jet black hair was combed straight back from her forehead and the sides of her face, held in place by a wide, dark-blue ribbon to just behind her ears and then left to fall loosely to her shoulders. Her face was an almost perfect oval dominated by wide-set eyes, lavender in color, that even though presently bloodshot and with dark circles underneath, remained quite striking.

When Harriet was finished making introductions, Amanda let go of Lone's hand and said, "It was good of you to agree to join us on such short notice, Mr. McGantry." Then, a somewhat rueful smile curving her mouth briefly, she added, "Although, keeping in mind the considerable distance you traveled for the initial purpose of meeting with my husband, I guess this wasn't *entirely* short notice after all."

"In any case, I'm appreciative of the invitation, ma'am," Lone told her. "And my journey gettin' here was nothing compared to the journey of loss and grief you're havin' to deal with. Please accept my condolences on that."

Amanda regarded him more closely. "Very gallantly said, sir. Harriet warned me how you liked to pass yourself off as a bit of a primitive while in truth you are a well-rounded and very competent individual. I can quickly see what she meant."

Lone cut a sidelong glance over at Harriet and then brought his eyes back to his hostess. "Could be Miss Munro is layin' it on a mite thick," he allowed. "But I'd have to be primitive *and* kinda simple-minded to argue too hard against bein' described that way, wouldn't I?"

"Just don't let it go to your head," Harriet was quick to remark.

Before the discussion went any farther, a stout, elderly woman wearing a dazzling white apron and a dour expression appeared to announce that dinner was ready. Lone and the two ladies followed her to a spacious dining room located diagonally across the hall. A long, dark walnut table covered with linen nearly as white as the stout woman's apron filled the center of the room. Three places were set near one end of the table. The chair at the head of the table and the place before it were empty. A black ribbon was draped over the back of the chair. Lone and Harriet sat next to each other, Amanda Thorndike took a seat on the opposite side of the table.

The meal spread before them consisted of baked ham, boiled potatoes with creamed onions, and greens in butter sauce. There were pitchers of crystal-clear spring water and cold buttermilk from which to drink. And a fresh-baked, still warm blueberry pie awaited to be enjoyed for dessert.

Once all of this had been served and deemed satisfactory, Amanda excused the cook, Mrs. Gladstone, for the night. She assured her that she and Harriet would see to clearing the table before retiring. The stout woman departed quietly, her expression having never changed throughout.

"The poor old dear," Amanda commented once the cook was gone. "She's taking the passing of Reginald very hard and fighting not to break down. She's been with this household for years, long before my coming. I offered to let her take some time off during this period of grief but she refused, saying she'd rather keep busy."

"That's a common way for some people to help cope in an emotional time," said Harriet. "Though I dare say you haven't been giving her much to keep busy with. In the time I've been here, you've barely eaten enough to sustain a bird. I hope you'll do a better job of putting away some of this delicious fare before us now."

"I'll try," Amanda responded, but only half-heartedly. "I simply haven't had any appetite. Maybe that's my way of coping."

"By starving yourself to death?" Harriet said tartly. "Come on, Amanda, you're stronger than that. Reginald, even in the depths of his worsening pain, was planning carefully and methodically for you to have a good future. I know how hard it must be, but don't you think his efforts deserve you finding a way to move forward and live your future to the fullest?"

Amanda's expression turned brittle. "But do *I* deserve it, Harriet?"

Once the plate of food had been heaped before him, Lone was struck by the realization of how long it had been since he'd had a substantial meal, let alone one as fine as this. As a result he'd wasted not a second digging in with gusto, holding back only enough to keep himself from looking quite like a ravenous wolf. The exchange between the two ladies, however—

and in particular the stridency suddenly present in Amanda's tone—was enough to distract him from his minor feeding frenzy.

When he looked up with a fresh slice of ham dangling off the end of his fork, he saw that the already grief heavy countenance of the newly widowed woman was now also burdened by a look of deep anxiety. Meeting his gaze, she said in a sudden rush, "I'm dreadfully sorry to bring this up in the middle of our meal, Mr. McGantry. I had every intention of waiting until later to discuss it, but I . . . it's a matter of great distress, one that's been tearing me apart on top of my poor husband's tragic death. I finally shared it with Harriet and it was she who gave me hope that you were distinctly qualified to perhaps be of some help."

Beside Lone, Harriet said quietly, "Her problem is a serious one, Lone. And it affects more than just her. It's something I believe you'll take an interest in. In fact, you're already involved to a certain extent."

While Lone was frowning over that statement, Amanda spoke again, saying eagerly, "I'm prepared to make it worth your time and attention, Mr. McGantry. I can pay you well. We can work out payment in horses—since that was your original interest in coming here. Or cash. Maybe a combination of each. Please, at least hear me out . . ."

Chapter Thirteen

Amanda Thorndike's "matter of great distress," once explained, turned out to be a well justified concern. It threw a startling twist into the murder of her husband and gave her added reason for torment over it. In short, she was in a position to swear with certainty that Jaime Rodero could not have done the killing. But her distress came from the circumstances of *how* she knew this. She knew because she had been in Jaime's arms—out in the livery behind the house—all during the span of time within which the judge was murdered.

"I watched him ride away after we parted," she recounted to Lone and Harriet. "I watched until he was nearly out of sight—and that's when Rose Ellison started screaming inside the house upon discovering my husband's body. Jaime was too far away to have heard. So he had no reason to turn back, just like he had no time or opportunity to do the horrible deed he got accused of."

Digesting this, Lone responded, "Yet to the nurse and cook who also saw him ridin' off, it looked like he was fleeing the scene. Way I heard, it sounded like he was leavin' in kind of a hurry."

"Yes. He was," Amanda admitted. "We had fought, you see. He was angry at me because I was insisting that our affair had to end. The whole thing was a dreadful mistake with no real future from the start. Just a foolish, reckless physical attraction that had gotten out of hand during the time Jaime was breaking in Honeydew for me and teaching me how to ride her. I know how shameful that must sound, even worse when you consider I was cheating on a cancer-stricken man. That was why I . . . I finally couldn't continue.

"Jaime refused to understand. He saw the fact that Reginald would be dying eventually as our chance, once enough time had passed, to openly pronounce our feelings for one another. He couldn't accept that the thing between us, like I said before, was just a reckless physical attraction that had no real future, regardless."

"Yet when he was apprehended," Lone pointed out, "he never brought you into it, never mentioned you as an alibi."

Amanda shook her head. "No. He wouldn't. He's far too honorable for that." There was a moment of awkward silence before Amanda spoke again, saying, "Which brings into question my honor—or lack of, as if that's not already established—for failing to step forward in his defense."

"You're stepping forward now," Harriet told her, softly but firmly. "So quit working so hard to run yourself down."

Amanda took a deep breath, let it out slowly. Then: "Everything happened so fast after the murder was discovered. It all started rushing by in a blur. When I heard Jaime had been arrested, I *knew* it wasn't true of course, that it was a terrible mistake, a misunderstanding. And when I realized he was sparing me, not mentioning my name in his defense, I convinced myself it would be okay for me to stay quiet also. Surely there'd be a further investigation and Jaime's innocence would be discovered, I told myself, so there was no need for me to be in a hurry to speak up and bring shame and humiliation to the Thorndike name. And if, God forbid, nothing changed and Jaime ended up facing trial for murder . . . well, *then* I would speak up and make sure it went no farther."

There was another pause and a moment of ragged silence.

This time it was Harriet who ended it. "The problem now, with Jaime having escaped the lynch mob and truly taken flight," she said, "is that if Amanda comes forward at this point little would be accomplished except to bring her humiliation. As long as Jaime is a fugitive, there's no way to corroborate her story. Plus, if he's unaware anything has changed, there's no reason for him to stop running."

"Not only keep running, but possibly running deeper into trouble," Amanda added forlornly.

"What do you mean?" asked Lone.

"He has two cousins in New Mexico, somewhere down near the border. They ride with an outlaw gang," Amanda explained. "They've long tried to convince Jaime to join them. He nearly did at one point, just before hiring on to the JT Connected. His real love is horses. He has a special way with them. But the day Reginald was killed . . . the same day I told him we had to end it between us and we argued, after he'd already been terminated from the JT Connected . . . he said he might as well go ride with his cousins."

"Don't you think that was likely a desperation play to gain your sympathy, try to get you to reconsider breaking with him?" Lone suggested.

"At the time he said it, yes, that probably was the case. I recognized as much," said Amanda. "But now, with all that's happened since to paint him as a murderer and put him on the run as a wanted fugitive . . . I-I can picture him actually going ahead with it. Since he's already been branded a murderer, what would he have to lose?"

"You can see what a bitter injustice that would be," Harriet stated solemnly. "Jaime driven to certain crime, taking up with an outlaw gang, over an act he's totally innocent of . . . not to mention the little matter of the judge's real killer roaming free and no one having cause to do any looking for him."

Lone's gaze drifted slowly back and forth between the two women. Until he said, measuredly, "Okay . . . I see what a complicated tangle all of this is. Where I'm comin' up a little short is how I might fit in. What is it you think I could do to help?"

Harriet was ready with a prompt answer. "You could go after Jaime. Track him down and bring him back so this tangle, as you call it, can get straightened out. Amanda's ready to do her part, tell the truth and withstand whatever backlash comes of it. I'll represent Jaime legally to whatever extent necessary. And then the search for the *true* murderer can commence."

Lone took a drink of buttermilk and wished to hell it was something stronger. "You make that rundown of Rodero sound awful easy," he pointed out. "In the first place, New Mexico is a healthy stretch of real estate and he has a two-day head start—practically three since the earliest I could head out would be tomorrow. And was he to reach the border before I caught up with him, that'd increase the difficulty even more. Also, if his cousins are so determined to get him into their gang, did it occur to you that they might not like the notion of me taking him back *out?*"

Harriet's mouth spread in a sly smile. "The wheels are turning. You wouldn't be putting so much thought into it if you weren't leaning toward saying yes."

"Now wait a minute," Lone protested. "I never indicated anything of the kind. I'm a long way from—"

Amanda cut him short, saying, "I think I know a source, Mr. McGantry, who might provide information that could be very useful in finding Jaime."

Lone eyed her expectantly, waiting for her to continue.

"His sister," Amanda said. "Her name is Lucinda and she and Jaime are very close. She lives on the south end of town. Jaime has been staying with her and her husband since being dismissed from the JT Connected."

Lone nodded. "Her place is where Jaime was arrested followin' the judge's murder."

"That's right. The fact he was there, so easy to find rather than attempting to hide or flee," Amanda said bitterly, "should have been at least some indication to the marshal and his deputies that he might not be as guilty as they were so eager to believe!"

"What's done is done. Let's stick with the sister," Harriet advised, aiming to keep things on track, "and how she might be of help finding Jaime."

Amanda took a short breath and expelled it. "Yes, of course . . . Lucinda is well aware of the cousins. They are family, blood, so she, like Jaime, maintains a certain amount of contact even though she highly disapproves of their ways. Times past, when they have come around trying to lure Jaime to go with them, she has stood up to them and demanded they leave him alone."

"Yet she still maintains contact," Lone echoed. "So what you're thinkin' is that, if she has reason to believe Jaime has now gone off to join the cousins and their outlaw pals, she'd want to stop it bad enough to maybe give me a lead on where to find 'em. Is that it?"

"I believe so, yes," Amanda said. "Especially if we can convince her that if Jaime comes back, we're prepared to present proof of his innocence."

Harriet regarded her. "Do you think Jaime told her about him and you?"

Amanda looked thoughtful for a beat before replying, "I'm not sure. It's something that never came up between us, where he would have indicated if he did. But, like I said, they're very close. I wouldn't be surprised if she knew."

Nobody had an immediate response to that.

Until Lone broke the silence by heaving a sigh and saying, "Well, the way it looks to be shapin' up, if she don't know already—she's gonna be findin' out soon enough."

Harriet's eyes shone brighter. "Then you'll do it? You're agreeing to go after Jaime?"

"I'm agreein' to go talk to his sister for starters," Lone said. "If she's willin' to give me something to go on . . . well, yeah, then I guess you two have talked me into takin' a stab at bringin' him back."

Chapter Fourteen

It wasn't too late in the evening to still go calling. Trouble was, Amanda was uncertain whether or not Jaime's sister or her husband—one Carlos Acuna, who ran a small *restaurante* serving primarily the town's Mexican residents—spoke English. So, since it was for sure that Lone was lacking in Spanish, Harriet agreed to accompany him in case some interpretation was necessary. All she needed was a couple minutes to change from her dinner dress back to her attire from earlier in the day.

The evening air remained pleasantly warm and the distance to Lucinda's address was well within reasonable walking distance. As they navigated the haphazardly-patterned side streets of the residential area, their way was adequately lit by illumination pouring from the windows of the homes they passed. A few sporadic street lamps helped, along with a sprinkle of brightening stars overhead. The moon had yet to make an appearance.

"I guess this is hardly the 'chin wag' session we planned on, is it?" said Harriet as they walked along. "I hope we'll still be able to find time for that before this all concludes. I have much to update you on since last we saw one another.

And, from bits and pieces I've overheard, you haven't exactly been idle during that time either."

Lone cocked an eyebrow. "Uh-oh. More of my 'escapades' you've been keepin' track of?"

"Not so hard to do, really. Especially not when some of them involve the likes of Buffalo Bill Cody."

"That business in Wildcat Hills?" Lone huffed. "It's no secret that Col. Cody don't do much without drawin' attention—But I didn't know my part in that gained much notice. Nor did I mean for it to."

"No. Knowing you, I'm sure that was the case," said Harriet. "But when one keeps one's ears open, you tend to hear bits and pieces of things, like I said. And—again, knowing you—more can then be deduced."

Lone grinned. "I thought things like hearsay and speculation were supposed to be out of bounds for a legal mind like yours?"

"Now who's throwing around twenty-dollar words?"

A corner of Lone's grin quirked higher. "Reckon the company I sometimes keep must've rubbed off on me more than I thought."

They walked a ways farther before Harriet said, "Speaking of keeping company . . . I gather you're still living up to the 'lone' part of your name?"

Lone's grin faded and his expression went

tight. "Way it's worked out," he said quietly.

Harriet cut her eyes over and regarded him more closely. "I-I'm sorry . . . you lost someone, didn't you?"

"I've lost a lot of people, Harriet," Lone responded in a flat tone. "Like you said a while back—sometimes things work out, sometimes they don't. Just as soon not go into it any more right now."

By this point they had progressed nearly to the southern limits of the residential district, populated mostly by Mexican families. The homes in this area had become smaller, boxier structures for the most part, as opposed to the larger wood-frame houses they'd passed prior. Some of these dwellings were made partly of sod or adobe, yet all appeared generally tidy and well maintained.

No sort of house numbering system—or street names either, for that matter—seemed to exist. The Acuna house of Lucinda and her husband Carlos was on a corner lot with a red tile roof and shutters and trim of a matching color, according to Amanda Thorndike, who had had it pointed out to her by Jaime once when they were out riding.

Upon reaching the right vicinity, the attention of Lone and Harriet were first drawn by something else before spotting the markings they were looking for. The something else was a raucous knot of men, eight or nine in number, filling the middle of the street just ahead. As they slowed but continued to advance, the next thing Lone and Harriet saw was that the house the knot was formed in front of had a red tile roof and matching shutters and trim.

"Appears," Lone said, his jaw tightening and his right hand automatically slipping into the gun-heavy jacket pocket, "we ain't the only ones who've come visitin' this evening."

They continued moving forward. The general rumbling murmur of the men's voices grew louder, and the words began to take on some clarity.

"Damn it, Carlos, we ain't lookin' to make trouble for you or your wife. We got nuthin' against you."

"It's that no good, murderin' brother of hers we want. If she ain't hiding the little bastard straight up, then she damn well knows where he is. That's what we want to find out!"

"Everybody knows how you Mexes are all related and all stick together."

"He gutted the judge like goddamn catfish—you can't tell me you're willing to stand up for an ungrateful animal like that!"

Weathering this verbal barrage was a banty roosterish man standing with feet planted wide before the front door of the house, facing defiantly out at the noisy pack. He had some years on him, closer to fifty than forty, his hair thinning on top and some slivers of gray showing in his neatly trimmed pencil mustache. The left sleeve of his shirt was cut off and sewn closed over a stub where the arm ended at the elbow. In the fist of his right hand he was gripping a long fireplace poker.

"You men are not welcome here and have no right to be on our property," the man proclaimed to his tormentors. "Neither me nor my wife have seen Jaime since the lawmen took him away two days ago. Leave us alone and go see them if you want to know what became of him."

"They're the ones who let him get away all over again—why should we count on anything more from them?" somebody shouted back.

"Plus, the best of 'em—Marshal Tom—got killed tryin' to protect the greaser bastard. That puts even more blood on his hands!"

Suddenly the door behind the one-armed man burst open and a buxom woman wearing an off-the-shoulder white blouse burst out. She had a mane of glistening black hair tumbling around the exposed shoulders and flashing eyes almost as dark as her hair. Standing nearly a full head taller than Carlos, the woman reached out over his shoulder and shook her balled fist angrily at the knot of men. Along with the fist shaking came a string of words spoken in Spanish that chopped through the air as rapidly and fiercely as rounds cranked from a Gatling gun.

Lone released a low whistle. "Whew! I don't understand a word she said, but I'm mighty glad I ain't on the receivin' end of any of 'em."

"You bet you are," Harriet assured him. "She spat them out so fast I barely understood half, and each was more blistering than the one before."

But whether or not he fully understood everything said by the woman—whom Lone reckoned clearly must be Lucinda—one of the men who *was* on the receiving end decided he didn't much like it. He was a tall, lanky number wearing a dusty, dented-in bowler hat and a faded blue work shirt with the sleeves cut off at the shoulders. He had buck teeth and an oversized Adam's apple that bobbed up and down in his elongated throat like a gopher caught in a trouser leg. At first glance some might have found his appearance a bit comical, but Lone was quick to note the dull glint of pure meanness in his eyes that signaled nothing to be amused about.

"Here now, gawd damn it," exclaimed this specimen, taking a drunken, lurching step forward. "You better rein in that spitfire of yourn, you pint-sized crip!"

"You tell him, Big Link!" somebody encouraged the surly hulk. "Hell, anybody can see he ain't man enough to handle all that woman. Not nohow."

"Maybe he ain't," growled Big Link in response. "But I don't take no dressin' down like that from nobody—man *or* woman. And 'specially not from no spic hussy who oughta be usin' that mouth for better things in a crib out behind some saloon somewhere."

Carlos Acuna wasn't having any of that, not for a second. Never mind he was a one-armed man facing nine, and the spear point of the nine was half again his size and at least twenty years younger. He charged like he had a regiment behind him, hurling himself forward and snarling viciously through bared teeth, "Filthy *bastardo*!" As he stretched into a long stride, he reached back with the iron fireplace poker and then swung it in a whirring overhand arc as if meaning to split the big man's head like a melon.

But it didn't take long to see there was more than just mouth to Big Link—he'd been in a scrape or two and knew how to handle himself. Despite the drunken lurch he'd demonstrated earlier, he quickly got himself set and was ready for the poker when it blurred toward his head. A second before the iron bar would have struck, Link leaned his upper body sharply to one side, jerking his head out of the way. At the same time, he thrust his left arm up and then outward in a swift, chopping-away motion. The edge of his forearm hit with a meaty thud just behind Carlos's wrist and the inside of the fist gripping the poker. This not only deflected the blow Carlos was meaning to land, but it drove his arm away and down so forcefully it pulled the diminutive man off balance and sent him into a stutter step.

Before Carlos had even the slightest chance to regain his balance, Link instantly pivoted and came around with a sweeping, powerful right hook that landed square on the hinge of Carlos's jaw. The punch drilled in with an explosive pop of meat, muscle, and bone being mashed together. Carlos's feet literally lifted off the ground. He lost his hold on the poker and was sent flying off to the side as if he'd been pitched from a low platform.

An excited, cheering-on ripple ran through the knot of men.

In the open doorway, Lucinda looked on horror-stricken and gasped, "Carlos!"

Seemingly oblivious to any of this, Big Link clomped determinedly after the fallen man. He advanced on him with the menacing focus of a predator who has tasted first blood and now is ready to go for the jugular. Without hesitation, he drew his foot back—just as his battered target was struggling to push up onto his knees and one good hand—and slammed a savage kick into Carlos's ribs. The little man let out a bleat of pain and was sent flopping and rolling across the ground.

More encouraging cheers came from the knot of so-called men.

Another anguished gasp sounded from Lucinda. But then, an instant later, the anguish gave way to anger and the spitfire emerged once again. With a fresh burst of Spanish curses, she launched from the doorway straight toward her husband's punisher. Just as quick, however, two men from the pack sprang to intercept her. She thrashed wildly as they grabbed her and halted her progress. One of them immediately paid for it when four fingers curled into claws attempted to gouge at his eyes, missed, but instead left bloody tracks ripping down his cheek.

"Ow!" howled the injured man. "Hold that clawing bitch, Pete. She 'bout took my eye out!"

"I got her—I think," grunted Pete, hooking Lucinda's arms from behind. "But watch her feet, Bo, or she'll damn sure go after your onions next!"

Right on cue, Lucinda's right foot lashed out, aiming a kick for Bo's crotch. Bo got his hip turned just in time, getting a heel driven into the side of his thigh. He howled again, but not as loud as he likely would have if the heel had struck where intended.

Big Link seemed to take no notice of any of this taking place. He was focused strictly on Carlos, plodding forward again to where the little man had stopped rolling. Reaching him, he stopped and shifted his weight, clearly intending to deliver another vicious kick.

The roar of Lone's Colt Lightning being triggered, the shot aimed skyward, caused everyone in the vicinity to instinctively flinch and then freeze all other motion.

Only Lone moved, striding forward into the space between where the two men were struggling with Lucinda and where Big Link was getting ready to slam another kick into Carlos. He lowered the Colt and swept it in a slow, flat arc covering Bo and Pete. "Let go of the woman, you polecats, or I drop you where you stand." His flinty gaze drilled into them along with the words, and the two men jerked their hands away from Lucinda like she was a hot stove.

Next Lone cut both his gaze and the muzzle of the Colt in the direction of Big Link. "And you, tall man," he grated. "You try swingin' that ox hoof you call a foot in another kick, I'll make you a damn site shorter by blowin' the bottom half of your kickin' pin clean off."

Chapter Fifteen

Everything went still and quiet for a long beat. The only sound was that of ragged breathing.

Then, slowly turning his head, Big Link locked eyes with Lone. His mouth stretched into a buck-toothed sneer. "Tough hombre with a gun . . . same old story. Pukes like you who ain't got the grit to stand toe to toe with a real man always got to make your brave talk behind a shootin' iron and a wheel full of lead. That your story?"

Lone smiled a wolf's smile. "And cowardly slobs like you always have to have a crowd of easily impressed fools to play to . . . yet you still need somebody three-quarters your size to make sure your act succeeds. That *your* story?"

"Try sayin' that without a .44 aimed at my gut," came the growled response.

"We can rush him for you, Link—he can't get us all," a voice from the pack suggested.

"Then you could do as you please with the damn meddler!" somebody added.

Lone's smile widened. "Sure. Have 'em go ahead and try that, Link . . . but, before they do, you might want to explain to 'em how you ain't gonna be able to give 'em much of a show no more afterward on account of I'll burn you down the second they make a move."

Link's sneer faltered.

The voice from the crowd called, "Aw, that's a bluff, Link! He ain't gonna shoot you in cold blood—not in front of all us witnesses!"

But the bold talker from the crowd wasn't the one in front of Lone's gun. Link was. And, looking into Lone's eyes, he didn't see anything in them that looked to him like a bluff.

"Gawd damn it, don't nobody do nothing stupid!" he blurted. "I'm the one handlin' this. Leave it to me!"

Lone's expression changed. Turned flat and cold. "That ain't a half bad idea. Maybe you should be left to handle it at that."

"What's that supposed to mean?" Link asked suspiciously.

Never taking his eyes off the big man, Lone said quietly out the corner of his mouth, "Lucinda . . . come help your man to his feet. Take him back to the house."

In jerky, unsure movements at first, but then quicker and with more assurance, Lucinda did as instructed. Nobody tried to stop her. Carlos helped as much as he could and fought hard not to groan, determined to deprive Link and the others of the satisfaction.

Next, when the pair were on their way toward the house, Lone held his Colt out to one side. Still with his eyes locked on Link, he said, "Here, Harriet, hold this for me . . . if any of the sheep try to stick their noses in, give 'em a fresh whiff of powder smoke."

Looking alarmed even as her hand started to close around the grips of the gun, Harriet said, "You don't mean? . . . no, that would be insane. You can't possibly be thinking—"

"But I am," Lone cut her off as he began shrugging out of his jacket. "Ever since I arrived in these parts, I've been runnin' into clumps of so-called men who can only find courage by mobbin' up behind some blowhard eggin' 'em on. Well, big boy here is one blowhard I'm gonna let the air out of. I aim to show the rest the difference between guts and gut wind."

Suddenly realizing what Lone was proposing, Link's mouth stretched wide with a confident smile. "Mister, you just made the biggest mistake of your life," he boasted as he raised his big, knobby fists and hunched into a fighter's stance. "When I get through with you, there ain't gonna be enough left for that scrawny, no-titted girlfriend of yourn to bother takin' back home. And after I show her what a piss poor excuse for a man she's been hangin' around with, I just might—even though she's, like I said, considerably bonier than I like—treat her to some pleasure from a real man."

The onlookers in the pack guffawed loudly.

Seizing Lone's Colt with a sudden firmness, Harriet hissed, "Go ahead and knock that braying jackass into the middle of next week, McGantry!"

And so it began. Lone raised his own fists and rolled his shoulders to get loosened up some as he advanced toward Link. The latter took a step to meet him and then the two began warily circling each other. Link was wearing a wide grin of bravado, Lone was stone-faced.

Lone had been half expecting (maybe hoping) that his opponent would come in a bull rush, the way many big brawlers tended to favor. But it became increasingly clearer (as already evidenced earlier, the way he'd moved in response to Carlos's charge) that Link had more fighting savvy than a common saloon brawler. In fact, Lone judged by the way he was holding his fists and shifting his feet, it appeared he might know a thing or two about actual boxing. If that held true, then this could turn out to be a more prolonged dust-up than the former scout had anticipated. Lone was thicker through the chest and shoulders, packing more raw power and probably endurance he figured. But with Link's height and reach advantage, if he had the skill and patience to stick and jab and keep moving, it would be damned hard to get to him before he managed to inflict some damage.

They continued circling. Then Link began throwing jabs, proving he did know at least a few boxing basics. He snapped three lefts in rapid succession, held off for just a moment, then flicked out another fast three. Lone blocked all but two. The pack of men cheered loudly for the ones that landed.

The punches had some pop to them, no denying. But they were worth taking for what they showed Lone. Number one, even though a couple slipped through, Link didn't really have what veteran fighters call "fast hands." Number two, the big man didn't know how to properly put his weight behind those jabs in order to give any of them their fullest impact. The big right he held back, cocked and ready to deliver a smashing follow-up when it was time, that would be a different story as Lone had witnessed by the way he'd unloaded it on Carlos. But, for now, Link appeared bent on doing some initial softening up with the jabs.

Okay. So that told Lone what he needed to do to make his move ahead of the pulverizing right coming into play. He kept his expression cold, unchanged. Determined.

He circled some more and waited. Sure enough, Link repeated his jabbing routine. Three fast ones, slight pause, then three more. To the increased cheers of the onlookers, Lone even let an extra one get to him this time. It stung like hell, but that was okay—he damn sure had Link's rhythm now.

They went to circling again. Lone tightened his crouch just slightly, once more waiting. The expected flurry of jabs came. Lone blocked the first two, slipped the third. Instead of leaning back away as part of the slip, however, he uncoiled out of his crouch and drove forward underneath Link's extended left arm. Lone became the one doing a bull rush, slamming a shoulder into the taller man's chest and simultaneously hammering the top of his head up under Link's chin. A strangled yelp got caught in Link's throat. His bowler hat flew off and his teeth clapped together as loud as a whip crack. He was driven backward, his dangerous right fist pounding down ineffectively onto Lone's broad, muscular back.

The two men broke apart. Link stood weaving unsteadily, eyes glassy, blood streaming heavily from his mouthful of broken teeth. When his bleary vision found Lone, he immediately uncorked a wild roundhouse right. Lone easily ducked it, then straightened up and delivered a backhand right to the side of Link's face followed immediately by a left hook to the same spot. The tall man staggered drunkenly but did not fall.

Lone closed on him and they traded a series of heavy blows. The still-dazed Link threw sluggish, windmilling bombs that Lone managed, for the most part, to block or duck. In return, he repeatedly landed shorter but solid punches to jaw and ribs. They went into a clinch. With the battered Link still refusing to go down, Lone suddenly changed tactics. He hooked his left arm up around the back of the taller man's neck and at the same time got a grip with his right fist on Link's belt buckle. Squatting momentarily, he then thrust with all the strength in his legs and arms, hoisting his opponent up, swinging him half around, and slamming him to the ground flat on his back. Along with a great gust of air exploding out of Link's lungs, a groan of despair escaped from the onlookers watching.

But, to give the durable bastard his due, Link still wasn't ready to quit. He clawed the air with his hands and struggled to a sitting position, making frantic sucking sounds as he tried to regain some air. At the same time, he was pushing stubbornly with first one hand and then the other in an attempt to get back on his feet. But he wasn't able.

Lone, himself breathing hard and dripping sweat, leaned over the tall man and, almost gently, shoved against one shoulder and pushed him down flat again.

From out of the otherwise silenced pack of men, a sad, husky voice urged, "Stay down, Link . . . you're licked, man. Fer Chrissakes, have the sense to know it."

Chapter Sixteen

"If you two trusted me enough to want to pin a badge on me," Lone stated, his gaze cutting back and forth between Rio Fuego's newly appointed marshal and his deputy, "then you oughta not find it so hard to trust me on this other matter."

"If you want to talk trust," Zack snapped back, "then why can't I shake the feeling that you're not leveling all the way with us?"

"You wouldn't be callin' me a liar, would you, Zack?" Lone said in a carefully measured tone.

"No, I didn't mean to make it sound like that. But, doggone it, the notion of Mrs. Thorndike somehow thinking Rodero might be innocent and asking you to track him down so's to bring him back for a fair and proper trial with Miss Munro here acting as his attorney . . ." Zack let his words trail off and made a hopelessly frustrated gesture with his hands. "You gotta admit that's a lot for a body to take in. Where would the judge's widow get such ideas?"

"And why," said Steve, "would she care so much about this Mexican kid she barely knew and who seems hell-bent on his way to join a bunch of outlaw relatives—almost like he was looking for an excuse to do that all along?"

Now it was Harriet Munro's eyes that tracked

back and forth between the two lawmen. In a tone almost as frosty as her gaze, she said, "It seems to me you gentlemen are awfully quick to accept—even jump to—certain conclusions, while at the same being rather close-minded to other possibilities and reasonably related questions you might consider asking."

It was just short of ten o'clock, a little over three hours since the disturbance in front of the Acuna house. Zack and Steve had shown up on the heels of the fight between Lone and Big Link, summoned at first by word of a pack of troublemakers roaming the Mexican neighborhood and then spurred all the more by reports of Lone's warning shot. By the time the lawmen got there, the rowdy mood of the troublemakers had been pretty effectively quelled due to seeing their man get whipped. Zack and Steve took note of their identities—all locals known to them—and then sent them on their way. All except Link Remus, a known bully who worked as a bouncer for the Grizzly Den Saloon and had a reputation for instigating almost as many brawls as he then claimed to "break up."

It had been necessary to send for Doc Praeger to tend both Carlos and Link. Carlos suffered damage to his cheekbone as well as a cracked jawbone from Link's smashing right hook to his face. Further, the vicious kick he'd received left him with three badly cracked ribs. All of these would be a source of considerable misery for a while, the doctor explained, but would heal in time as long as the ribs were kept tightly wrapped and Carlos restricted his diet to soft food for the next couple of weeks. Praeger also provided some pain medicine to help him sleep at night.

Link, too, was diagnosed with a couple of cracked ribs, though not as seriously injured as Carlos. Otherwise, most of his damage was to his teeth and the inside of his mouth as a result of the head butt delivered by Lone. The doc also wrapped his ribs and then extracted the worst of the broken teeth he could get at (this bit of dentistry was performed with neither much sympathy or gentleness, considering what was done to Carlos plus the memory of prior patients Praeger had treated after they'd been worked over by Link).

Lone had a couple scrapes and bruises of his own that got treated quickly by cleaning and applying some disinfectant. "Got to keep you healthy," the doc quipped. "You're too good a source for sending business my way."

After things had settled down, when offered the chance to press charges over the incident, the Acunas declined, saying they only wanted it over with and to not be harassed any more in the future. In spite of this, Zack took it on himself to charge Link with disturbing the peace and fined him in the amount of Dr. Praeger's combined fee for his services.

Once a sullen Link had departed and the doctor and the lawmen were preparing to also take their leave, they were somewhat surprised by Lone announcing that he and Harriet would be tarrying a bit longer in order to have the discussion with Lucinda that had initially brought them there. This drew a puzzled, somewhat suspicious look from Zack which Lone countered by assuring the marshal he would get a follow-up explanation after the discussion was completed and some details had been worked out.

This subsequent meeting now taking place in the jailhouse office was Lone's word being kept. Harriet had insisted on accompanying him here after they'd finished their talk with Lucinda.

Given the way Lone had intervened on their behalf, Lucinda and Carlos (though he being limited in his ability to say much due to the injury to his face and the swelling around his jaw) were naturally willing to sit down with their visitors and listen to their proposal regarding Lucinda's brother Jaime. Lucinda, who spoke and understood English quite well, had immediately been keen on the idea of retrieving Jaime before he got in deeper trouble with the outlaw gang. She was at first less receptive to the idea of bringing him back for trial, but Harriet's assurance she would serve as his attorney managed to change her mind. Otherwise, Harriet pointed out—whether as part of the outlaw gang or not—Jaime would remain a wanted fugitive on the run from the law.

The final thing to be resolved with Lucinda, the main purpose in seeking her out in the first place, had been to determine if she could provide any useful information to help Lone locate her brother. It turned out that yes, she had such information. But there was a catch to her handing it over. A big one. She insisted on accompanying Lone to go bring Jaime back. She would *lead* him to the outlaw stronghold but would not reveal the location otherwise. A good deal of arguing over such an arrangement had ensued, but in the end, Lucinda won out. She not only could serve as Lone's guide, she pointed out, but she would also be useful as an interpreter and would have considerable influence on convincing Jaime to come along once they caught up with him. Carlos, Lucinda's husband, had sat mute through all of this, indicating no feeling one way or the other. Lone had a hunch his silence had to do with more than just his injured jaw—it was the acquiescence of a man who'd long ago accepted the odds against winning any argument his fiery wife felt strongly about.

And now, seated confidently on a wooden chair hitched up before the marshal's desk, another strong-willed woman was attempting to set things straight regarding motives behind the plan to re-apprehend Jaime Rodero and bring him back to stand trial. "As far as Amanda Thorndike 'barely knowing' Jaime Rodero," she was continuing, "you seem to be overlooking the weeks they spent together while Jaime—under direction from Judge Thorndike himself—was breaking in a special gelding for Amanda and then teaching her how to ride. In that time, she feels she got to know Jaime quite well and found him to be an exceptionally kind and gentle person. It is on that basis she now questions how such a gentle soul could commit such a brutal act as the one he's accused of."

Zack Mercer listened attentively from his seat behind the desk and then formed a deep frown. "Mrs. Thorndike obviously has every right to feel how she wants. But that's a mighty skimpy nail to hang your hat on," he said. "I been around long enough to have seen more than a few so-called 'gentle' folks who could turn just as nasty as anybody else when they lost their temper."

"That's right," chimed in Steve. "Wasn't more than a year ago that Mrs. Herring, a rancher's wife living off a ways to the east—sweetest ol' gal you'd ever want to meet—up and stove in her husband's head with an iron skillet one evening at the supper table. He complained 'cause she'd burned the fried chicken she served him. Made her mad."

"That's a charming little tale," Harriet allowed. "But I fail to see how it applies to Jaime Rodero."

"It's widely known that Rodero was mad at Judge Thorndike for having him fired from the JT Connected," Zack told her. "There were witnesses to previous times he had angrily confronted the judge—one of 'em being the man who used to sit in this very chair."

Harriet promptly countered, "And a man, I will point out, who gave his life trying to keep Jaime safe for a proper trial. Don't you see how, if it was important to Tom Bartlett then, then it remains just as important now? And, not to put too fine a point on it, it is the kind of thing that was even more important to Judge Thorndike. He spent decades presiding over trials that sometimes involved the worst of the worst—but he nevertheless wholeheartedly believed they had the right to their day in court . . . *that* is where Amanda gets her same belief and what's behind this 'notion,' as you call it, of hers to see Jaime gets nothing less."

At no time had Amanda's deeper motives been revealed, either to the Acunas or to the lawmen. That was an Ace waiting to be played at the proper time, if one was able to be brought about.

But for the moment, Lone could see by the faces of Zack and Steve—just as it had been with Lucinda Acuna—that Harriet's way with words was making an impact. The marshal demonstrated this by replying, albeit somewhat grudgingly, "You're right in what you say, Miss Munro. Twice we fought off lynch mobs to try to make sure Rodero got a fair trial—once here at the jailhouse and a second time out on the trail. With, as I guess you know, some help from McGantry. If it came to that again, we'd do the same thing all over. But that don't make it something I'd look forward to."

"I have no doubt you and Steve would do the right thing," Lone said. "But, if it eases your minds any, was I to succeed in haulin' Rodero back, I could go ahead and deliver him over to Ford City like you was intendin' before."

Zack's eyebrows lifted. "Yeah, that'd be a good idea. You get word to me you're on the way, I'll notify the marshal in Ford to be on the lookout for you."

"Uh-huh. That might be a whole lot better than actually bringing Rodero here," Steve agreed. "But word is bound to spread, regardless, about Lone going after him. Especially with Jaime's sister in on it too. That would be enough, all on its own, to keep the pot simmering around here. We all saw again tonight how too many fools are still in an ugly mood over the recent happenings. And if word gets around that you're planning to be Jaime's lawyer, Miss Munro, I'm afraid that will make you mighty unpopular in the eyes of those kinds of idiots."

"I appreciate your concern, Deputy," Harriet said. "But I'm quite capable of taking care of myself. This will hardly be the first time I have represented an individual and been viewed unfavorably for it."

"Besides," Lone growled, "ain't it the job of you two rascals to see that her bein' 'unpopular' still better not mean no harm comes to her? Yeah, I know, me pinnin' on a deputy's badge would have given you better coverage for that kind of thing. But, blast it, ain't there no other *men* in this burg you can call on to back your play until things simmer down?"

"Take it easy. You're the one who'd better simmer down before you blow a gasket." A corner of Zack's mouth quirked up a little. "It so happens we *have* lined up a couple good men to serve as temporary deputies. And I got a telegram shortly after you were here earlier informing me that a US Marshal out of Santa Fe is coming in with the pack of dignitaries arriving for the judge's funeral. So that will help give us extra coverage and ease our load quite a bit."

"That sounds better," Lone harrumphed. Then he asked, "What about those other fellas from that list of names I gave you? You made a move on them yet?"

"No, we haven't. Not yet," Zack said. "For the time being, we're just keeping a close eye on 'em. We've narrowed it down to Merl Brown as likely being the 'Brown' whose name you heard mentioned the other evening at Coyote Pass. He was seen huddled with Hollister and Reece Dooley earlier that afternoon in the Morocco Saloon. Him and the rest are all locals who—since they don't know they've been identified in any way—got no reason to rattle their hocks away from here. That's why me and Steve decided against 'fronting them until the judge's funeral is over and all those highfalutin mourners have left. With the mood still running hot all through town like it is, ain't hard to figure there'll probably be those who try to bring it to a boil all over again when word spreads we're arresting suspects in the killing of Marshal Tom. We want to avoid the risk of that while all those big-wigs are present."

Lone nodded. "Reckon that makes sense. Long as you're confident those skunks won't try to hightail it on you."

"We are," said Steve. "But the one loose end remains the hombre they called Trent. We haven't been able to get a line on him yet. When we *do* start collaring the rest, though, we figure they'll spill on him quick enough."

"Seems like a reasonable expectation," Lone agreed.

At which point Harriet spoke again, addressing the two lawmen and saying, "It sounds like you gentlemen have put a lot of thought into the host of problems facing you and have put together a plan for competently dealing with them. There is, however, one matter I haven't heard mentioned at all."

Zack cut a sidelong glance at Lone and then brought his eyes back to Harriet. "I'm probably going to regret asking . . . but what is it?"

Harriet smiled wanly. "If we're right and it turns out Jaime Rodero is innocent of killing Judge Thorndike, then that means the real murderer remains at large . . . I know your plates are already full to overflowing, but that's the one more thing I suggest you keep in mind."

Chapter Seventeen

Lone and Lucinda Acuna rode out early the next morning with minimal fanfare. Only a silent, somber-looking Carlos was on hand to see them off. Before mounting the magnificent Palomino stallion left behind by her brother, Lucinda warmly embraced her husband and kissed him gently, cautiously due to his bruised, swollen face.

Lone had said his goodbyes the previous night. To Zack and Steve upon leaving the jailhouse, and then Harriet and Amanda Thorndike a little later. Walking Harriet back to the Thorndike house had provided the chance for another brief snippet of their chin wag.

"There's so much more I want to hear about what you've been up to since last we saw each other in Rainrock, and things I want to tell you in return," Harriet was saying. "Yet our chance to spend time together seems to keep getting interrupted."

"There's nobody keepin' us from talkin' now," Lone pointed out.

"No *body* perhaps," Harriet countered. "But the fact you plan on riding out early tomorrow morning with Lucinda means you need to get some rest tonight. It's already quite late and you're still operating on an awfully short ration of sleep as it is. I feel guilty enough asking you to once again head into potential danger. The least I can do is not put you at any disadvantage by keeping you up jabbering with me."

Lone grinned. "In the first place, you're not forcin' me to do anything I ain't willin' to do. And jabberin' with you is worth losin' a piece of shuteye any day of the week."

"There you go being gallant again. Too much of that might clash with your otherwise rugged persona, but I can't say I personally find it unappealing." Harriet paused and cocked one finely penciled brow. "On the other hand, considering your recent display when it came to dealing with Big Link, I guess your ruggedness remains safely intact."

"I'm glad you're not holdin' it against me for failin' to knock him into the middle of next week, like you asked," Lone quipped.

Harriet made a face. "I guess that was a rather unseemly request coming from someone who advocates on behalf of legal policies and procedures, wasn't it?" Then she paused and her mouth curved into a sly smile. "I have to admit, though, that seeing you pick that big ox up and slam him to the ground—that felt nearly as good as winning a big court case!"

Recalling that exchange as he rode away from Rio Fuego this morning, Lone suppressed a quiet chuckle. Though he'd thought of Harriet Munro often in the years since last they saw each other, he'd almost forgotten what a feisty side she had. Yes, there was a bit of a high-class air about her and she sometimes overdid it with her strict, lawyerly demeanor—but underneath it all was a core of plain toughness. She had to be tough, fighting to make her mark in what was generally considered a man's field, especially in rugged frontier towns like Ogallala and then Rainrock, the places where she'd first hung out her shingle.

According to what she'd said when explaining about her move to Denver, it had been her success with the Bigbee case in Rainrock—a matter in which she'd enlisted Lone's aid and how they first met—that had solidified her place among both her peers and those in need of legal representation. Hearing this, Lone was equal parts proud and pleased for her.

Reflecting more on the Bigbee case as he rode along stirrup to stirrup with Lucinda Acuna, it occurred to Lone there were certain similarities between that situation and this current one that Harriet had once again brought him into. Back then, the fugitive from a murder charge had been a young woman by the name of Roxanne Bigbee. As now, the victim was a prominent, well-liked and respected individual, a rancher, and the locals were hell-bent on seeing the ungrateful Roxanne hang for the deed. In truth, she *had* killed the man, one Alston Bigbee by name; her adoptive father. But Harriet's efforts, with the help of Lone, revealed that Bigbee had been a twisted monster who'd been abusing Roxanne sexually for years and it was when he'd begun turning his attention to her younger sister that she took fatal action to stop him. When these facts came out, a ruling of justifiable homicide resulted, granting the two sisters full ownership of the Big B ranch that, according to Harriet, they were now running quite successfully.

This current situation differed, of course, in that Jaime Rodero *hadn't* killed anybody. At least not yet. The first challenge was to catch up with him before he joined his cousins' gang and became foolishly involved in activities that would brand him a criminal nevertheless. Then would come the challenges of convincing him to return to Rio Fuego so he could stand trial and be cleared—not to mention the lingering matter of rooting out the real murderer.

For the time being, Lone reckoned he had his hands plenty full with the task of running down Rodero and fetching him back. Though he'd balked at the idea at first, he had to admit (but only to himself, and still grudgingly even then) that having Lucinda along would likely prove beneficial when it came to convincing her brother that returning with them was a good idea. But that didn't mean she would necessarily have any such sway with the cousins or the rest of the gang if they decided to be uncooperative about giving up a new recruit. There, Lone had a hunch, was where the greatest difficulty might arise.

That same morning, only a few hours after Lone and Lucinda rode away from town to the south, Hank Birchfield rode north to the remote JT Connected line shack where Eli Trent was staying to nurse his wound. Birchfield carried a sack of coffee and other supplies with him, but more than that, he also carried some news. Some troubling news.

"Ah, am I glad to see these," proclaimed Trent, seizing the supply sack as soon as Birchfield came through the door and pulling from it a bag of coffee beans. "I'm a whiskey-sipping man by day, but first thing in the morning, I sure like me some good coffee. And not to complain, old friend, but the beans left behind in this storage bin are mighty damn stale. No matter what else you got in the sack, first thing I'm gonna do is pound up some of these babies and set 'em to brewing."

"You go ahead and enjoy the coffee," Birchfield said, making no attempt to hide a frown. "But I got something else to hand over that I don't reckon is such a welcome thing."

"And what would that be?" asked Trent, forming a frown of his own.

"It's that damn meddler McGantry," Birchfield spat. "He's up to something—I don't know exactly what—but I don't like the sound of what I do know."

"Quit beating around the bush then. Cut to it," demanded Trent. "What do you know and what about it's got your hackles up?"

"Okay. For starters, you remember how Rose told us he's some kind of old friend to that lady lawyer who's tight with the Widow Thorndike, right? Well I reckon that got proved out plain enough last evenin' when he was invited to take dinner with the lawyer gal and Mrs. Thorndike."

"So they must have gone ahead and talked some horse business, in spite of what we figured," said Trent as he spread some coffee beans out on a clean bandanna, preparing to crush them.

"Be nice to believe that. And maybe I could, if the dinner had been the end of it," replied Birchfield. "But afterward, McGantry and the lawyer took a stroll to go pay a visit to Jaime Rodero's sister."

Trent had folded the coffee beans inside the hanky and was raising his heavy revolver, getting ready to use its butt to do some pulverizing. He paused, scowling. "Rodero? You mean the Mex me and the boys tried to fit with a hemp necktie? What business did they have with his sister?"

"You tell me, and we'll both know. Whatever they had in mind, the first thing they ran into when they got there was a pack of rowdies who'd showed up to harass the sister about knowin' where her brother had run off to. McGantry broke things up with some gunplay."

"Barging in again. Once more playing the big hero," Trent sneered.

"And that ain't all," Birchfield continued. "Before the law showed up to finish clearin' everybody away, McGantry went toe to toe with the leader of the mob—an hombre by the name of Link Remus. Big Link is a double tough local thumper, works as a bouncer at one of the downtown saloons and ain't nobody can ever remember him bein' beat in a one-on-one fight. But McGantry did. Whaled the tar out of him by all reports and did it pretty handily to boot."

"You sound like you wish you was there to cheer the sonofabitch on!" Trent said bitterly, starting to hammer the cloth-wrapped beans.

"I'm just tellin' you how it was told to me, damn it. It's the talk all over town this mornin'. I got it from Rose just a little while ago." Birchfield made a sour face. "She's back waitressin' at the Swede's place again now, in case you didn't know. Moved back into her old room up above too. With the judge gone, Mrs. Thorndike didn't waste no time tellin' Rose her services at the big house was no longer needed."

"So much for loyalty and appreciation," grunted Trent.

"Woulda been different—like so many things—if the judge had stayed healthy and had a say in the matter," declared Birchfield. "But that's okay. Cold-hearted bitch Amanda has got her day comin'."

Trent stopped hammering, satisfied he had the beans sufficiently ground up. "If the judge had stayed healthy, Rose wouldn't have been nursing at the house to begin with. Too damn bad, though, she wasn't still there last evening to have maybe overheard some of the talk that led to those two busybodies, McGantry and the lady lawyer, going to visit the sister."

"Trouble is, we might still have a pretty good idea even without her bein' there. I got another piece to tell."

Trent gave him a look. "Shit. What else?"

"First thing this mornin'," the ranch foreman explained, "McGantry and Rodero's sister, Lucinda, her name is, rode out of town together. Headed south."

"South. Toward Mexico," Trent muttered. "Where everybody figures the Rodero kid made his run for."

"Uh-huh."

"You know, old friend, I told you how grateful I was for you bringing these fresh coffee beans and all. But you're sure as hell doing your best to ruin any enjoyment I'm gonna get out of 'em!"

"I told you that at the start. You think I *like* havin' this news to share?"

Determined to get some good out of the beans he'd prepared regardless, Trent dumped them into a pot of water and then thumped the pot down on top of the stove in which he had a fire already crackling against the morning chill. Turning back to Birchfield, he said, "So what does the talk around town say McGantry and the sister are up to?"

"Nobody knows for sure. Speculation has it they must be goin' after Rodero."

"What the hell for? Would the sister be part of wanting to bring him back to hang?"

"No. But if he can dodge any more lynch mobs, the kid will be facin' a trial before that could happen. Remember how it works? So, with the lady lawyer involved, what seems to fit is that she maybe is gonna stand up for Rodero in court. Talk has it that's the kind of thing she's had success at."

"But what chance does she have of pulling off such a thing in this case?" Trent wanted to know. "The way you and Rose have it set up—and with the cook backing up Rose seeing the Mex fleeing away—everything is stacked pretty tight against him. What could that lady lawyer have to sell it as being any different? And if the lawyer is so tight with the judge's widow, where does *she* fit in? You'd think she'd have more reason than anybody to hate the dirty skunk who has everything pointing to him as being her husband's killer. What kind of friend is the lawyer if she's aiming to try and get the killer some kind of break?"

"I don't know," wailed Birchfield. "I can't make sense out of any of it. All I know is I don't like it. And, for some reason, it all seems to hang on that goddamn Mexican pup. If the little bastard was dead like he was supposed to be, I don't figure any of this would be takin' hold."

"What kind of crack is that?" Trent snarled. "You blaming me for—"

"Back off!" Birchfield cut him off sharply. "I ain't blamin' nobody for nothing. If I was, I'd start with that meddlin' McGantry bastard. Every since he showed up, he's been the poke in the spokes to everything we had rollin' along smooth. And it looks like he's gonna continue to be . . . leastways he will if him and that *puta* sister of Rodero's succeed in bringin' her brother back. I say again, for some reason—and I'm blamed if I can reckon how—that noose-cheatin' horse lover seems to be the key to whatever it is they're cookin' up."

"I don't have to tell you again *my* feelings on McGantry," said Trent. "Nothing I'd like better than to personally set his sun—that'd stop his poking into anybody's spokes permanent-like."

Birchfield grunted. "Too bad you're laid up from his bullet. Otherwise—"

This time it was Trent who did the cutting off. "Hold on there, mister. Who says I'm 'laid up'? Yeah, my shoulder's stiff and sore, but it so happens your girlfriend did a pretty dang good job of patching me up. I've managed my business with worse, let me tell you. What's more, it's my left shoulder took the damage. My right arm and hand are what I do my gun work with."

"You also lost a lot of blood," Birchfield reminded him. "And one day ain't much time to build your strength back up."

"My horse didn't lose no blood or strength. He's plenty fit to take me wherever I need to go to do whatever I need to do," Trent said stubbornly. "What notion did you have in mind when you spit out that 'otherwise'? You want I should go after McGantry?"

Birchfield's brows pinched together. "Well . . . yeah. Can't say it didn't cross my mind. Since whatever's bein' cooked up seems to hinge on that Mex pup bein' brought back. If McGantry and the sister was to not make it far enough to fetch him . . ."

"Be my pleasure to end that big Nebraskan's fetching days once and for all." Trent's expression turned shrewd. "But it's gonna cost you."

"Goes without sayin'," Birchfield said earnestly.

"If our plans work out, you know I'll have the means to treat you right."

Now Trent looked thoughtful. "You say those two headed out first thing this morning? That'll make it four hours or so before I can get to their starting point. And 'headed south' takes in a pretty wide swath through territory I'm not familiar with. No closer idea to where they might be aimed?"

Birchfield shook his head. " 'Fraid not. How are you at trackin'?"

"Fair. There's worse, but there's plenty who are better."

"And it happens, I know one. Rides for our outfit," said Birchfield. "An ornery, eagle-eyed old rascal who used to scout and snipe for the Gray. He can track a puff of milkweed through a snowstorm. Name's Bone Harper. Don't much like nobody who ain't part of the JT Connected, especially if they're a Yankee. I tell him McGantry is a Nebraskan who fought for the Blue and is up to no good for our brand, Bone will run him down for you and gladly help hold him while you do your worst."

"All I need is for him to help do the running down. I can handle the rest," Trent said confidently.

Birchfield nodded. "Alright. Done and done. About a mile due west of the town is a rock formation called Rabbit Rock. You can't miss it.

Be there in an hour and a half, Bone Harper will be waitin'."

The pot on the stove began to spit and bubble and give off a tantalizing aroma. Trent cut a glance over at it and smiled. "I'll be there. Primed with good coffee and raring to go."

Chapter Eighteen

Lone and Lucinda rode at a steady, miles-eating pace through the morning. Their mounts—her tall, proud Palomino called Conquistador and Lone's equally tall, durable Ironsides—could have held up to being pushed harder but for the time being they were making satisfactory progress. Also for the time being, Lone let Lucinda set both the pace and the course. The latter, after all, was one of the main reasons for agreeing to her participation in this. In addition to hopefully being a persuasive voice when it came to convincing her brother to return with them, she also allegedly had knowledge on where to locate the gang it was believed he was on his way to join.

Lone wasn't crazy about riding blind toward an inexact destination yet unless or until some better option presented itself, putting his trust in Lucinda seemed the surest, fastest way to achieve what he was setting out to accomplish—at least as far as catching up with the fugitive Rodero. From there, he expected to be playing a more direct role. In the meantime, if at some point he got a clearer sense of where they were headed or gained enough of the girl's trust so that she revealed more, then he might sooner feel like less of a mere tag-along. As someone who'd spent so much of his life scouting and tracking either on his own or in the lead of others, this present circumstance of being the follower was more unsettling than he would have guessed. He accepted it, though, as a temporary and necessary means toward the desired end.

The route they traveled was by turns over well-defined roads and trails, sometimes across open country. Lucinda seemed sure in her bearings, aiming mostly due south with a slight western slant. The terrain varied between flat, grassy expanses and stretches of choppy hills with a smattering of rock outcrops and low buttes. Always in sight, off in the western distance, was the rise and fall of the mighty Rockies as they reached down to eventually merge into the Sangre de Christo range.

The day was bright and still, no breeze and only a few cloud wisps to offset the steadily increasing heat poured down by a white-hot sun. They stopped to water the horses once at mid-morning and then again at noon when they broke briefly for a bite to eat in the shade of some aspen and birch trees on the edge of a spring-fed pond. Their meal consisted of a shared tin of peaches and ham sandwiches as prepared and packed for Lone the previous night by Amanda Thorndike.

During the morning ride, Lone and Lucinda had conversed very little. Both had been lost in thought and quietly intent on the undertaking they were joined in. The prior evening when the notion of going after her brother and getting him to come back for trial had first been brought up, Lucinda was very animated and fluent in discussing it. Lone realized now that most of this, once the Acunas thanked him heartily for his handling of Big Link, had been exchanges with Harriet. It was somewhat understandable, Lone supposed, that Lucinda might feel more comfortable talking with another woman, particularly one who was a lawyer offering to defend Jaime. While Lone had never been particularly big on making small talk just for the sake of it, it nevertheless occurred to him that this trip would surely seem to go quicker and be less awkward if he and Lucinda took to trading words somewhere along the way.

Almost as if reading his mind, she spoke up now, rather abruptly, in the middle of their respite. "Since you are generously providing our lunch," she said, "I will prepare the meal when we make night camp. That is, unless you have no fondness for Mexican food."

"Nope. Mex food is fine by me," Lone told her. Then, grinning, he added, "Matter of fact, ain't too many foods that don't appeal to me."

Lucinda smiled. "I guessed as much. You are a big man and do not have the look of one who has . . . how you say . . . a 'picky' appetite."

"Guilty as charged," Lone conceded.

"Although my Carlos is not a big man, his appetite—aye-yi!—is like that of *two* men his size." Lucinda rolled her eyes. "I tease him and say that if he had both arms complete, I wonder how much more it would take to fill him up. And then I tell him what a good thing it is that he runs a *restaurante* or I don't know how we would stay in groceries."

Since she had brought it up so casually, Lone felt safe in inquiring, "How is it he lost his arm, if I may ask?"

"Many years ago, to a Comanche war lance," Lucinda answered solemnly. "Carlos and my father were among the first settlers to the area around what is now the town of Rio Fuego. It was only a mission and a small village back then. Comanche raids were common, seeking to steal horses and women. That was before the Army established a post at Fort Garland. In a final defiant raid before the Army secured the territory, my father and Carlos's first wife were killed. Carlos lost his arm saving my mother from being abducted."

"That's quite a story. I regret asking a question that caused you needing to recount all of it," Lone said.

Lucinda shook her head. "No need. It was long ago, and Carlos and I have had many happy years since."

"Well one thing is for certain—your husband

has lost none of his bravery in those years. The way he tore into that entire pack of troublemakers last night all on his own was something to see."

Lucinda frowned. "That was not brave, that was *stupido*! What good did he think he was going to do with only a piece of iron in hand? We had a gun in the house. He should have taken it out with him in the first place to confront those drunken lobos."

"That might've been smarter. Then again, it might've worked out for the worse," Lone allowed. He paused before venturing a faint grin. "I also seem to recall another individual who looked ready to jump into the fray with nothing but a couple fists she was wavin' around while hollerin' what sounded like some mighty unflatterin' words. How good an idea was that?"

"Paugh!" Lucinda huffed in response. Scowling, she took a bite of her sandwich and chewed it very aggressively for a minute. Then: "Very well. I lose my temper sometimes, and when I do, neither my actions nor my tongue behave in a wise manner. Still, that doesn't excuse Carlos's recklessness. You Anglos have a saying, do you not, about two wrongs failing to make a right?"

"Indeed we do."

Lucinda's gaze turned shrewd. "Furthermore, one might even say that your actions—intervening against the same superior numbers—was not the wisest of decisions either. Though I must add that it turned out, thankfully, to the benefit of Carlos and me."

"Like you said . . . sometimes I lose my temper," Lone replied. "And, by the way, I *did* have a gun."

"Which you soon discarded," Lucinda was quick to remind him, "and then went out of your way to goad that big *puerco* Link Remus into a fist fight that could have gotten you as badly injured as my Carlos."

Lone popped the last of his sandwich into his mouth, washed it down with a swig of canteen water, then rose from where he'd been sitting propped against a birch trunk. "Expect we could come up with more bad habits to jaw over," he said, "but don't you reckon our time would be better spent gettin' back on the trail?"

"To be sure," Lucinda agreed.

In a matter of minutes, they were once more in their saddles and again making dust toward the south. The afternoon grew hotter as they rode, still with no breeze or appreciable amount of clouds to counter the blazing sun. The course Lucinda was now setting was almost exclusively across open country though the terrain was only moderately broken.

"Don't worry. There will be plenty of water along the way," Lucinda assured Lone at one point.

Now that the conversational ice had been

broken during the noon break, they talked intermittently as they rode along. Lone felt himself growing more at ease with the Acuna woman. She certainly wasn't hard on the eyes, she was an excellent horsewoman, and she seemed totally confident in knowing where they were headed.

But it continued to rankle Lone some that he *didn't* know. Not yet.

Chapter Nineteen

They rode steady until dusk, finally stopping to make night camp at the base of a grassy slope with a spine of low, jagged rocks running along its crest. A thin stream of water trickled down from a break in the rocks, wearing a teardrop-shaped area on the edge of the flat where a shallow pool had collected over time before the stream continued on its way. A clump of brush and a handful of cottonwood trees stood a dozen or so yards off to one side of the pool and it was before these that Lone and Lucinda unloaded their gear.

While Lone tended the horses, Lucinda got a fire going and started supper. She browned taco shells in a frying pan and then folded them around generous scoops of spiced shredded beef and pork she had brought along, already prepared, in a canning jar. She served these with seasoned rice, also previously prepared. To drink along with this, she insisted Lone try a cup of strong-brewed coffee sweetened with brown sugar. The fare was all very aromatic and proved every bit as delicious as it smelled.

When Lone tried to praise Lucinda for the meal, she declined accepting the compliment directly, explaining how she had merely assembled the ingredients prepared and packaged for their trip by her husband. Upon hearing this, Lone declared, "Well if this is a sample of what Carlos serves in his restaurant, then I know where I'll be takin' my meals for as long as I remain in Rio Fuego after we get back."

"And you would be most welcome if you did," Lucinda told him. "My Carlos is not one to forget a debt, and your intervention on his behalf makes him very beholden to you."

Lone waved a hand dismissively. "Let's not get into that again. You and your husband have both thanked me plenty when all I really did was what any right-thinkin' fella would have—or *should* have—done in my place."

"Unfortunately," Lucinda said somberly, "Rio Fuego as we left, it seems to have grown short of such men. An ugly, dangerous mood has taken hold. Too many decent men who in their hearts know better, are getting caught up in it and no longer acting, as you say, in a 'right-thinking' manner."

Lone took a sip of his coffee. "Yeah, I gotta admit I saw those same signs. But don't discount the good men still there who will find a way to get that mood tamped back down. Zack Mercer and Steve Leonard, the two lawmen, they're workin' hard to get a handle on it. And your husband, unless I miss my guess, still has a voice of influence."

"Yes, he does. Not as strong a one as he once did, alas . . . times change, memories fade. Too many these days, especially the young and impetuous, look at him, as well as his remaining peers from back in the early, even wilder times, and see only tired-looking old men. They do not realize or appreciate the struggles and the battles such men went through to help make what is taken for granted in the present. They do not understand how well earned those tired looks are . . . or how much wisdom is still contained behind them if anyone took the time to look deeper."

Listening to her, studying her in the flickering campfire light as she spoke, Lone came to realize a number of things. First off, here obviously was a very thoughtful and wise woman in her own right. The "young and impetuous" she mentioned, he strongly suspected, very much included her brother Jaime. And finally, but by no means least, was the fact that this was a woman wholly devoted to and in love with her husband.

Once again, almost as if reading his mind, she pinned him with a very direct gaze and said, "Pardon me if I carry on a bit too enthusiastically about my husband, Mr. McGantry. My temper again—it angers me that so many are so dismissive of him and others like him who sacrificed and endured all that they did to give Rio Fuego its birth."

"You got no call to ask pardon from me or

anybody else for your feelin's," Lone responded earnestly. "Not a blasted thing wrong with givin' credit where it's deserved. And ain't a man alive—leastways not none with a brain in his head—who wouldn't plumb bust over havin' a woman speak up for him like you do for your Carlos."

"That is kind of you to say." Lucinda smiled. "But if we are being candid, tell me this: Have you not wondered about the union of Carlos and I? He being an older, rather plain-looking man with physical limitations and I barely half his age and generally considered—to say it as immodestly as I can—quite attractive? Trust me, I am well aware it has raised more than a few eyebrows and caused the empty clucking of tongues attached to rude minds."

"Okay," Lone said measuredly. "It ain't something I pondered on to any great extent but, if I'm bein' honest, I gotta admit it crossed my mind to wonder some about it at first. Didn't take long bein' in the presence of the two of you, though, to tell that your feelin's for each other was about as deep and solid as any I ever ran across. With that goin' on in the inside, didn't see where what was on the outside mattered much."

Lucinda's smile remained. "You speak with a simple eloquence, Mr. McGantry. It is a shame more people don't see and feel about things with your clarity."

"Careful now," Lone said with a crooked grin. "You start throwin' around words like 'eloquence' and 'clarity,' you'll soon be soundin' like my lawyer friend Harriet. I have a hard enough time keepin' up with some of her lingo. You can already snow me under with your Spanish. No need to start doin' it in English too."

"I think you are being too self-deprecating."

"There you go again. Now you're just showin' off."

Lucinda's smile turned into a short burst of musical laughter. "Very well. I promise to choose my words more carefully. But before we finish talking about Carlos and me, there's more I want to explain."

Lone reached and took the pot off the coals at the edge of the fire, poured himself another half cup of coffee. "I don't feel I'm owed any more explainin'. But go ahead if it suits you."

"In a manner of speaking," Lucinda proceeded, "it coincides with what you said a minute ago about what is on the outside not mattering when one feels strongly enough on the inside. You see, I fell madly in love with Carlos when I was eleven years old and have never stopped feeling that way since. Not for a moment. That was when he returned after an absence of being cared for and healed by Army doctors and then staying away until he was ready to accept and learn to function with a missing arm. My father had many friends when I was little so I had no clear memory of Carlos from that earlier time. But I had, of course, often heard the tale of him fighting alongside my father and rescuing my mother from a dreadful fate. Because of that, in my mind's eye I had him pictured as a hero of magnificent proportions . . . and when I first saw him upon his return, I never saw anything less.

"It was at that moment that I knew in my heart I would one day marry him. I told him boldly how I felt and, as I grew into womanhood, I made him feel the same about me. It was, not surprisingly, considered scandalous by many. There were those who expected it would have been more logical for my mother and Carlos to have sought solace in one another. But, like me, my mother devoted her heart solely to one man—my father—and when he was gone, there could be no other for her. That is how she was able to understand how I felt about Carlos. So, with her blessing and that of our shared god, Carlos and I went ahead and fulfilled my girlhood dream. Raised eyebrows and wagging tongues be damned. Other than being unable to have issue of our own, we have never had any regrets."

When Lucinda was finished relating these things, Lone was at a loss for how he should respond.

Reading his awkward silence, and apparently even sharing a bit of how he felt, Lucinda then added, "I-I'm not sure why I felt it was important for you to hear all of that. It is not something I have ever detailed to anyone before . . . I can only imagine it has something to do with you having about you the same kind of heroic aura as my Carlos."

Lone reacted with a start. "Whoa. Hey now. I got no claim to havin' no 'aura' or to bein' any kind of hero."

"I hardly meant it as something offensive," Lucinda was quick to say. "And it is really not up to any person to judge how others view them. The way you intervened last night, your willingness to risk danger in this attempt now to try getting my brother away from Mano's gang of bandits—without even mentioning, as I have learned in the interim, how you previously freed him from a lynch mob . . . these are not the incidental, non-heroic deeds of just a common man, my modest friend."

"No," Lone argued, "what they are is a series of misfortunes a fella runs up against and ain't got no choice but to react to. No need to make more of it. Don't make me no doggone hero."

Lucinda smiled slyly. "Then how do you explain why—though you foolishly appear to pay no attention—your friend Senorita Harriet looks at you with the kind of admiration one has for such as I am describing? Or does her look perhaps convey an even more personal feeling?"

Lone barked out a short laugh. "Now you've really veered off course. You sure your husband ain't mixed some locoweed into the seasonin' for some of the food he's been feedin' you? Me and Harriet are friends, yeah. Hell, just *acquaintances* is probably more accurate. Until yesterday, we hadn't seen each other in near four years. But I think I know her well enough to say the only thing she looks at with admiration the way you mean is her set of law books."

Lucinda's smile stayed in place. She added a one-shoulder shrug. "Believe as you will. But I think your short-sightedness is making you act the loco one."

"You sure they were here?" questioned Eli Trent, wearing a doubtful scowl as he swept his gaze over the clearing in front of the birch and ash trees. "I don't see sign of a campfire or anything."

" 'Cause there weren't none. I never said there was," grumbled Bone Harper in response. "I said they stopped here a spell, probably 'long about noon. If they ate while they rested, it musta been cold vittles. But they was here, the signs are plain."

As advertised, Harper was an ornery old cuss with a Southern twang and a perpetually sour attitude. He could have been anywhere from middle fifties to middle sixties in age. Tall and lanky, well befitting the "Bone" monicker, with a thick, tangled beard, mostly iron gray in color but shot with streaks of white and stained reddish brown from tobacco juice around the corners of his mouth. Above the beard poked out a long, bulbous-tipped nose and bracketing it was a pair of piercing, slate-gray eyes. Atop his head perched a battered, misshapen, faded gray Confederate cavalry hat.

"Well if they nooned here," said Trent, thinking out loud as he lifted his gaze to consider the descending gloom of dusk, "then that leaves us still a half day behind. Damn, I was hoping we would have gained more on them than that."

Harper frowned. "Way they been hoppin' on and off heavier-traveled roads and trails made it slower and trickier to spot where they made the changes. Not sure if they was doin' that a-purpose, or if it just suited their aim. But looky"—he extended one long, scarecrow arm, pointing—"they headed off cross country from here. They continue to open ground and we get a good jump in the mornin', we can do some gainin' then."

Trent followed the aim of Harper's pointing finger, though not really seeing whatever trail sign the old Rebel saw. He reached up and absently massaged his wounded shoulder, which the long day of riding had caused to bother him more than he'd reckoned on. Or would admit. Nevertheless, he wouldn't deny that stopping and being out of the saddle for a few hours—and indulging in some generous doses of "pain duller" whiskey during that time—was a welcome thought.

"All right," he said to Harper. "Let's break out the gear and make our night camp here. Then we'll get that jump in the morning, like you said, and give 'er hell tomorrow."

Chapter Twenty

Lone and Lucinda rose with the sun next morning and were back in the saddle again after a simple breakfast of more brown sugar–sweetened coffee and the rest of Amanda Thorndike's ham sandwiches.

After Lone's dismissal of Lucinda's suggestion about Harriet Munro seeing anything more in him than as a friend and ally (though he did ponder the ridiculous notion a bit further later in his bedroll) they had talked a while longer around last night's campfire. At Lucinda's prodding, he gave her a quick rundown of his past—how he'd been orphaned as a nameless infant when his parents, the McGantrys, were massacred by Indians; how the Army wives at Fort McPherson had collectively raised him and eventually sifted out the name "Lone" after growing weary of always referring to him as "the lone survivor of the McGantry massacre"; how he'd grown to become an Army scout and tracker for many years, and then a drifter until recently deciding to re-start the small horse ranch he'd been forced to abandon a few years back.

Talking about himself in such a manner wasn't something Lone made a habit of or felt very comfortable doing. But since Lucinda had been so open about herself and he'd grown increasingly at ease around her, the telling wasn't too much of a chore.

Afterward, Lucinda said in her thoughtful, perceptive way, "Yes, the name 'Lone' suits you. Even in the presence of others there is a sense of . . . remoteness about you. I believe that accounts for much of your strength, and that may be a good thing. But at the same time, it makes me feel sad for you."

"Don't," Lone told her. "I got friends I can count on when I need to. The rest of the time I've grown plenty comfortable with bein' on my own."

That was a lie, though. It had been true enough for most of his adult life. But it changed a year or so ago when he fell in love with Velda. Now, since he'd lost her, the being on his own again might be bearable but it sure as hell wasn't comfortable. It felt empty in a way it never had before . . . only those weren't feelings he was ready to share, no matter how at ease he felt with Lucinda.

A number of long, stringy clouds had moved in during the night, pushed by a gusty breeze out of the northwest, making the new morning quite cool and implying the coming day wouldn't be as hot as yesterday. As they rode out, Lucinda aimed them at slightly more of an angle toward the mountains. They stayed to open country, no more roads or trails. The terrain grew gradually choppier, with fewer trees and more frequent outcrops of rock. They saw a few clumps of cattle here and there and even a small herd of sheep, but never caught sight of any houses or outbuildings nor any sign of other riders.

Somewhere around midmorning Lucinda announced she judged they must have passed into New Mexico by now. Lone nodded, sensing that seemed about right. The day warmed pleasantly, stringy clouds continuing to slide along overhead and soft wind gusts rippling the long grass around them.

When they stopped for their noon break, Lone brought up something that had been worming around in his head since last night. Swallowing a bite of cold burrito (since they'd decided to forego building a fire in order to keep their stop relatively brief), he said, "When you were talking before about us fetching your brother back, you mentioned a name—Mano. I take it he's the leader of the outlaw gang you figure Jaime is aimin' to hook up with?"

Though she tried to hide it, Lucinda seemed momentarily startled by the question. It appeared she hadn't realized she'd let the name slip and was regretful that she did. Faced with it now, however, she had no recourse but to go ahead and discuss it. "Yes," she said reluctantly. Then, a sudden bitterness in her tone overcoming her reluctance, she added, "Mano Manolito—'Mano the Merciless' he likes to proclaim himself."

"Sounds like a real charmer," Lone quipped.

"Paugh!" Lucinda's upper lip curled in disgust. "He is a petty thief and a bully who has somehow browbeat a pack of lesser fools—like two of our cousins, alas—into being led by him into doing his dirty work. He himself is a fat coward who hides behind the ferocity of his enforcer, a man called Escobar, and Mano is only merciless when Escobar does the bloodletting for him."

Lone grunted. "Doesn't sound that different from the leaders of too many countries all through history."

"What?"

"Never mind." Lone waved a hand dismissively. "How is it you know so much about him?"

"Largely through my *stupido* cousins on the occasions they have come north to visit," Lucinda answered, disdain in her voice. "They sing the praises of Mano's daring deeds along the border, supposedly striking at will on either side and laughing in the faces of both the Rurales and the Anglo lawmen who try to thwart him. The cousins do this to make themselves look brave and daring, of course, largely in order to woo impressionable young women and sometimes to attract followers from among young men like Jaime."

"And Jaime's never been tempted to become a follower?"

"Never before, no. Not until the false charges against him and the threat of a lynch rope chased him away and gave him no choice." The bitterness was back strong in Lucinda's voice. "The truth, as it filters up from the border and not spoken by those as brash or foolish as my cousins, is that Mano's gang is really little more than a ragtag bunch who barely manage to keep themselves fed and clothed. And their 'daring deeds' are mostly raids on weak targets that yield only meager results. The single fact from it all seems to be the fierceness of Escobar and his strange devotion to Mano—this is what holds the gang together, the fear of Escobar going after any who dare to try and defect."

Lone expelled a breath. "Don't sound like it bodes well for your brother, does it? Or our attempt to yank him out."

"The young fool! He knows better," Lucinda said, "but his fear of the rope is clouding his brain."

"That ain't exactly unreasonable—fearin' the rope, I mean." Lone set his jaw, the muscles at the hinges bulging visibly. "So it sounds like it'll boil down to us havin' two jobs once we catch up with him. One, we gotta convince Jaime he'll get a fair deal if he comes back. That'll fall mostly to you. Two, we gotta get him out past Mano's pet rattler Escobar . . . guess who has the luck of the draw for that part?"

They heard the gunshot only a couple hours after riding out from their noon stop. It was the unmistakable boom of a rifle, rolling over the choppy hills from somewhere close by.

Lone and Lucinda drew rein sharply, his hand dropping automatically to his hip and thumbing the keeper thong off the hammer of the Colt holstered there. Lucinda's head snapped this way and that, eyes searching, long mane of hair switching back and forth across her shoulders. The sound came from somewhere near, but the rise and fall of the surrounding hills made its direction less clear. Lucinda held her tongue but her gaze fell questioningly on Lone.

The former scout held up one hand, palm out, motioning her to stay quiet. A gunshot out in open country could mean many things. It could be trouble, but it also could merely be a hunter or maybe just a ranch hand aiming to cut down a varmint.

Lone concentrated, ears pricked sharply for another shot or any other sound that seemed not to belong. There was nothing but the sigh of a wind gust. At least, Lone told himself, a single shot was a lesser sign of trouble and more likely meant a hunter or varmint shooter. Then he heard the voices. Vaguely at first. But getting louder and being spewed more rapidly. Angry voices.

Lone focused on the shaggy crest of a hill he judged the voices to be coming from behind. He nudged Ironsides in that direction, gave a jerk of his for Lucinda to follow him. Just short of the hill's peak, he reined up again and dismounted. He pushed his hat off his head, letting it dangle down across his shoulder blades by the chin strap, and ascended on foot the rest of the way to the top. Lucinda held back, remaining in her saddle.

At the crest, Lone dropped to a knee and parted the fringe of long grass to peer cautiously down the opposite slope. There were four people down there in the middle of a ruggedly-etched trail, angrily accosting one another. Slightly off to the right in Lone's point of view were two men on horseback. Directly down in front of him, not quite a half dozen yards from the horsemen, two people were standing beside a broken-down buckboard. The rig's left rear wheel, on the side facing Lone, had worked its way off the axle and was lying on the ground. The pair who apparently had been its occupants before the accident consisted of a young boy who looked to be about twelve and a slender young girl, maybe six or eight years older. By their resemblance to each other, Lone judged them to be brother and sister. The girl was standing partially in front of the boy, as if meaning to shield him from the two riders. But the boy kept trying to push around her—and in his hands he was holding a double-barreled shotgun.

"If that little brat tries aimin' that blaster at me again," Lone heard one of the horsemen threaten harshly, "I'm gonna come take it away from him and stick it in his ear!"

The boy shouted in return, "If I aim it at you again, I won't miss, and there won't be enough left of you to stick nuthin' nowhere!"

In spite of himself and without knowing the full story of the situation, Lone couldn't help but grin at the kid's display of moxy.

After sweeping an arm to push her brother back again, it was the girl who spoke next, saying, "If you two Bluethorn scoundrels dare lay a hand on my brother or me, you will be sorry! You will answer not only to my father but I will swear out charges against you with Sheriff Buford Peale!"

The second horseman threw back his head and laughed mockingly. "Sheriff Peale—that drunken old sot? He knows better than to try and bother any Bluethorn men. Hell, he couldn't stay on his horse long enough to even make it out to the ranch."

"And if that lazy ol' man of yours was worth anything," said the man who had threatened the boy, "he wouldn't be sendin' you two out to do his business on a fallin'-apart wagon in the first place."

This riled the boy all over again. "You leave our pa out of this, you! The only reason he ain't—"

"Never mind, Ben," the girl cut him off. "We don't have to explain anything to the likes of this pair!"

The two horsemen exchanged looks.

Then, turning back to the boy and girl, the hombre who'd spoken ill of their father said, "You know, you two are bein' mighty unreasonable, not to mention damned ungrateful. Me and Red go out of our way to stop and offer to help and all we wanted was a little friendliness in return."

"The kind of friendliness you wanted is revolting enough to make my stomach turn," the girl returned hotly. "You can get all of that you want from the saloon slatterns in town—where you just came from, by the whiskey on your breath that I can smell from clear over here!"

Lone could see the rider's face twist into a menacing sneer. "See what I mean? You sassy-mouthed little bitch!"

The other man, the one referred to as Red, said, "You know, there's ways to shut that sassy mouth of yours, missy. And there's ways of *teaching* you how to be friendly, too." He emitted a nasty laugh. "Hell, when me and Tom get done with you and you find out what you been missing, you won't want to *stop* being friendly."

The boy tried to lunge around his sister but she held him back.

The rider called Tom jabbed a finger. "And if that little bastard thinks he has a chance of stoppin' us with the one barrel he has left in that scattergun, we'll teach him a damn hard lesson he'll never forget!"

Lone had seen and heard enough. He dropped back, grabbed up Ironsides' reins, and swung smoothly into the saddle. Over his shoulder, he said to Lucinda, "There's trouble brewin' for a couple kids over yonder. I need to go give 'em a hand. You might want to hold here 'til we see how it plays out." And then he gigged the big gray up and over the crest of the hill.

Chapter Twenty-One

The faces of the four people down on the rugged trail all turned at the sight of Lone descending the slope toward them. The expressions of the boy and girl turned cautiously hopeful. The look on the mugs of the two horsemen, by contrast, immediately showed annoyance and narrow-eyed suspicion.

Lone checked down Ironsides as he reached flatter ground and called ahead in a cordial tone, "Afternoon, folks . . . I won't say *good* afternoon on account of I see you've got yourselves a problem. Anything I can do to help?"

The one called Red answered, "No, we're takin' care of it just fine, stranger. Thanks for askin', but you can go ahead and continue on your way."

From closer range now, Lone made a quick study of the speaker and his partner. Both had the look of work-worn, standard-issue cow hands. Red was of average height, somewhat squat in build, with a ruddy, weathered face and predictable rust-colored hair poking out from under his battered Stetson. The other one, Tom, was similar in build though taller, with a hawk-beaked face and a notably darker complexion that hinted at him having some Indian blood in him.

Lone pooched his lips thoughtfully and raised

a hand to brush the knuckles along his jawline before replying to Red, "Now that's a curious thing. You see, I was watchin' from up on the hill for the past couple minutes and I couldn't help but notice how you and your partner ain't got down off your horses at all. That's the curious part. You say you're takin' care of this problem . . . how does that work without gettin' your asses out of those saddles?"

Red's face went tight and his lips peeled back. "You're a real observant cuss, ain't you? And kind of a mouthy one too."

Tom was quick to add, "What's more—and I hope I'm wrong about this, for his sake—but he's also got the look of somebody who ain't smart enough not to stick his nose into other people's business."

"What do you say there, young Ben?" asked Lone, taking his eyes off the two wranglers only long enough to flick a quick glance over at the boy. "These hombres been any help with that busted wheel?"

"Far from it," Ben answered.

Continuing to address the boy but still without taking his eyes off Red and Tom, Lone said, "Uh-huh. And am I right in reckonin' that the rig belongs to you and your sister?"

"To our father, yes." It was the girl who answered.

"Uh-huh," Lone said again. "So if I was to

ask the two of you if you wanted me to lend a hand and you said yes, then nobody could claim I was stickin' my nose in where it wasn't wanted. Right?"

"Now just a goddamn minute, you!" blurted Red. "*I* say you're stickin' your nose in—and if you know what's good for you, you'll pull it back out in a mighty quick hurry."

With deceptive casualness, Lone's arm lowered and all at once the heel of his right hand was resting on the butt of his Colt. "You keep brayin' noises like that in my direction, mister," he grated, "there's only one thing I'll be inclined to pull."

Meeting Lone's flinty gaze, Red went very still. A nervous tic bounced a couple times under his left eye.

But on the other side of him, Tom puffed up boldly. "Stranger, you must have been riding out in the sun a little too long. You really willing to buck two-to-one odds over a couple raggedy-ass kids and a busted-down wagon?"

"Appears you don't figure odds no better than you read people," Lone replied. "I make it that me and my new pal Ben calculate out to even odds."

A corner of Tom's mouth lifted tauntingly. "Now I know you're loco if you're counting on that pup to side you. He can barely lift that blaster he's got hold of. Plus, he was shaking so bad when he fired off a round a couple minutes ago that all he accomplished was blowing a hole in the grass on the side of the hill."

"I don't see him shakin' now," Lone said calmly. Then, after just a half beat's pause, he added, "And for sure I don't see no sign of my partner shakin'."

Red suddenly decided to show some bravado again. "What the hell you talkin' about—what 'partner'?"

"That would be me," spoke up a new voice.

Halfway down the slope of the hill, at an angle behind Red and Tom but visible to Lone out the corner of his eye, Lucinda had descended on foot. She stood there now, feet planted wide, holding a long-barreled pistol trained steady on the pair of Bluethorn riders.

Ever so slowly, Red and Tom slid their eyes as far as they could to one side and then swiveled their heads carefully the rest of the way until they were able to confirm Lucinda's presence and the fact she had a weapon aimed their way.

"A minute ago something was mentioned about bein' out in the sun too long," Lone drawled. "Don't it seem like a good idea for you fellas to get on back to the shade and comfort of whatever bunkhouse you crawled out of?"

Red and Tom swung their eyes back to him and for a handful of seconds, there was an uncertain tension rippling in the air.

Then, abruptly, Red expelled an audible breath and his shoulders sagged. "To hell with it, Tom," he spat. "We got enough of an ass-chewin' due for gettin' back late as it is. No sense makin' it worse . . . not over a piss-ant deal like this. Come on, let's pull foot and head for the Bluethorn."

Red wheeled his mount away. But Tom lingered long enough to fix Lone with a hard glare, saying, "Alright. But I ever cross paths with you again, mister, I guarantee you won't get off so easy."

Lone smiled. "I'll be sure to remember that. And here's a guarantee from me—I hear of you varmints botherin' these kids anymore, you damn betcha our paths will cross again."

The pair put spur to their mounts and quickly disappeared in a dust haze.

As they faded from sight, Lone nudged Ironsides up closer to where Ben and his sister stood watching him. Looking down at them, the former scout said, "You youngsters okay?"

"We are now. Thanks to you," answered the girl.

Lone grinned. "Oh, I don't know. You two were standin' your ground pretty strong before I showed up. Especially Ben there with his shotgun."

The boy blushed a little. Then, squinting up at the big man on the big horse, he asked, "How did you know my name?"

"Heard your sister say it before I came down the slope," Lone told him.

"We're the Ritters," spoke up the girl. "Ben and Sue Jean."

Up closer now, Lone saw that she was a bit more mature than he'd first thought. Still no more than nineteen, he judged, but her fresh, pretty face and the supple curves filling out her simple cotton dress held the promise of a full-fledged woman getting ready to bloom very soon. The vulgar way that Red and Tom had been talking about treating her sparked a heightened rage in Lone and made him wish he hadn't let them off so easy.

As for Ben, he was every bit the typical, rambunctious, tow-headed boy. Freckles under the rose tint of sunburned cheeks, blue eyes eager to learn and be astonished, wheat-colored hair the same shade as his sister's smoothly brushed tresses but in his case a wild, cockle burr–like growth.

Lone pinched the brim of his hat to the Ritters. "Pleased to meet you. My name's McGantry, Lone McGantry. Long story on the 'Lone' part, but it's what got handed me." He turned to acknowledge Lucinda as she came walking up. "And this here is my friend and partner, Lucinda Acuna. Gettin' back to passin' out thanks, reckon she's owed a big one for makin' an appearance when she did. I don't know that those two rannies would've been quite so quick to back off if they hadn't found themselves starin' down the muzzle of a third gun."

Lucinda arched a brow. "Did you children know those men—those pieces of trash?"

"Only in passing. Never had call to speak with them before, and hope never to again," said Sue Jean. "Their names are Red Ansel and Tom Block. They ride for the Bluethorn brand, a big spread that borders our property to the east. Silas Blue is a rough old cob himself, but he would not approve of the way those two were acting. I will make sure my father lets him know the first chance he gets."

"Where is your father?" Lone wanted to know.

Sue Jean and Ben exchanged looks as if silently questioning how they should answer. Sue Jean turned back to Lone and said, "He's waiting at home. He's temporarily laid up. The axe slipped when he was chopping wood a week or so ago and he cut a bad gash in his foot."

"We lost our ma to pneumonia last winter," Ben interjected solemnly.

"The doc says Father's foot will heal okay," Sue Jean continued. "But only if he doesn't try to do too much on it. That's why Ben and me went alone into town for supplies. We were on our way back when the wagon wheel fell off."

"How much further to your place?" asked Lucinda.

"Only a couple more miles."

Lucinda looked at Lone. "Can you fix the wheel?"

Lone swung down from his saddle and squatted to more closely examine the damage. After a minute, he straightened up and said, "Yeah, I can get it back on. Then, with some nursin' along, I think it should last a couple of miles okay."

"We'd be even more in your debt." Sue Jean's tone was achingly sincere.

"Save that to see how successful I am. I don't claim to be no great shakes as a wheelwright," Lone replied.

"Aw, I know you can do it," proclaimed Ben.

Lone grinned at him. "Well, in order to even get started, I'm gonna need a long sturdy sapling or tree branch to use as a lever for liftin' the wagon axle. I spot a stand of trees up ahead that looks like it oughta provide something that'll work. While I go get that, how about you hike up over this hill and fetch Miss Lucinda's horse for her. It's a big, beautiful Palomino."

"Sure thing," said Ben. He leaned his shotgun against the side of the buckboard and started off. After a couple steps, he stopped and turned back, frowning. "When I fired that first barrel off into the grass, I meant to do that. It was a—a warnin' shot. It wasn't 'cuz I was shakin' and couldn't lift the gun like that lyin' Red Ansel claimed!"

" 'Course not. I knew better than that all along," Lone assured him.

The boy beamed a wide smile then turned back and went trotting up the slope.

Chapter Twenty-Two

Judd Ritter was a tall, rawboned, sandy-haired man just short of forty. He'd been standing on the front porch of the Ritter cabin, leaning on a crudely fashioned crutch and gazing out anxiously when his children came rolling into the front yard on their wobbly-wheeled wagon in the company of two strangers, a man and a woman. When he heard the story of what had happened, why they were running late enough to cause him worry—all explained to him in an excited rush by Sue Jean and Ben—he was immensely grateful and welcoming to Lone and Lucinda.

By contrast, when he heard the part about the actions of Ansel and Block and some of the things they had said to his daughter, a smoldering anger clearly gripped him. "Silas Blue has been warned more than once about that pair of lowlives due to the trouble they've caused in town and even among other men in their own outfit. Why in blazes he keeps them on, I don't know. But I won't be going to him with another complaint—I'll be paying a personal visit straight to those boy-os."

"Remember your bad foot, Father," Sue Jean admonished him sternly.

"Don't worry, child, I'll make sure I'm healed well enough to handle the job. But when I am, *they* might be the ones getting around on crutches for a while."

Ben listened to this with an excited gleam in his eyes.

Lone fully understood the father's ire and intentions, and there was a solid intensity about the man that made him seem capable of backing up his words. But, at the same time, he was a father and a hardscrabble type honed mainly by raising a family and laboring to turn this small spread into something he could rightfully call a ranch. Red and Tom were more the hard *case* types. Hardly top of the line in that category, but nonetheless regular scrappers (by Ritter's own assessment) and gun-toters to boot. Lone could only hope that, when the time came, Ritter didn't let hot-headedness rule to the point where he put himself in a position of being outnumbered and outgunned.

Having concerns along those lines, Lone said, "You reckon there's any chance those polecats might not wait for you to look 'em up and instead make the first move by comin' 'round to test out your feelin's?"

Ritter spat disdainfully. "They don't have the stones to brace a man straight up that way."

"Good to feel sure about such things," Lone allowed. "But if you are, then I reckon me and Miss Lucinda will go ahead and be on our way."

"No," wailed Sue Jean in protest. "Father, after

all the help these good folks have been to us, surely we owe them the hospitality of a hot meal and the offer of a roof over their heads tonight before they continue on."

Ritter's eyebrows lifted. "By gol, the child is right. Where are my manners?" His gaze swept over Lone and Lucinda. "Our fare is simple but plentiful. There's a pot of fresh ham hocks simmering in on the stove, and only just a short time ago I peeled a batch of potatoes and chopped some greens to fry up with 'em. Like I said, there's plenty to go around. We'd be honored if you would stay and take supper with us."

Now it was Lone's turn to lift his eyebrows. "I gotta admit, you make those ham hocks and 'taters sound mighty temptin'."

"And," Sue Jean added, "unless a certain party did some thumb-sampling like he was warned not to"—here she cast a meaningful look toward Ben—"there is a blueberry pie, baked just yesterday, in the warmer box."

Ben thrust up both of his thumbs. "You don't see no berry stains, do you? I believed you when you said you'd cut 'em off if I stuck 'em where they didn't belong."

Everybody had a chuckle over that, although Sue Jean blushed furiously.

"Okay. You have definitely got me swayed," said Lone. He looked at Lucinda. "What do you say?"

"You've only got a couple hours of daylight left before you'll need to stop and make camp anyway. Might as well stay the night here, get a good night's rest and start fresh in the morning," Ritter encouraged.

Lucinda arched a brow. "Is there any chance a hot bath might be available as part of the proceedings?"

"By gol, that can surely be arranged," declared Ritter. "We got a big copper tub in the washroom, with clean towels and bars of soap at the ready. The stove's hot, won't take no time to heat up a couple pails of water."

Lucinda smiled. "In that case, consider me 'swayed' every bit as strongly as Mr. McGantry."

Bone Harper emerged silently from a chest-high wall of shadow-mottled brush and stepped out to one side of where Eli Trent sat on a broken, flat-topped chunk of boulder, one of many scattered along a ridge overlooking the Ritter ranch. Trent gave a start, his head snapping around and the cigarette nearly dropping from a corner of his mouth.

"Jesus Christ," he muttered. "You move like a damn ghost."

Harper's beard split apart with a wide grin. "That's the general idea."

"Well it's not supposed to be the idea when it comes to *me*. Jesus," Trent said again. "What if

I'd spun and plugged you, creeping up on me like that?"

Harper's grin stretched even wider. "You jumpy, Cap'n?"

"No. But still . . . I could do without this damn wind whipping about."

With sunset, the gusting breeze of the day had picked up steam and was now lashing the land with much stronger, more frequent gusts. A coinciding drop in temperature was making it bite like sharp teeth and was driving the ache in Trent's shoulder steadily deeper, making him touchy and irritable.

"Wind like this works in a body's favor when you're doin' a close-in look-see like I just done," said Harper. "Though I can still get such a job done, even when it's dead quiet. I can be dead quieter—dead bein' the keyword. What made me such a good sniper back in the war. I could slip up on a Yank close enough to count the frayed threads on his shirt collar and he'd never know I was there . . . until he was past never knowin' nothing no more."

"I thought snipers picked off their targets from a distance?"

"Did a whole bunch that way, too," Harper confirmed. "But hell, they's plenty who can plunk from a ways off. I liked to challenge myself every so often to do it close in, right under the noses of other blue bellies."

"I'm duly impressed," Trent said dryly. He flipped away his cigarette butt and it caught in the wind, swirling away in a shower of sparks. "But I didn't bring you along to hear about your past accomplishments. What did you see down there? Is it them?"

"Sure enough is. Just like their tracks told me," answered Harper. Then, frowning, he added, "You don't mind me sayin', Cap'n, you might oughta be careful with them cigarettes. It's gettin' dark enough now so that a glowin' tip or 'specially a match strike could be seen plain from down below—'specially to a sharp-eyed hombre like that McGantry is supposed to be."

"That might be true if he had any call to be on the lookout. But he has no reason to suspect anybody is on his back trail," Trent argued. "So quit worrying about me and my cigarettes and tell me what you saw down there."

Harper sighed and squatted down to get out of the wind. "Well, like I said, it's them sure enough. First I checked the barn and found that Palomino Jaime Rodero used to ride stabled there. No mistakin' that critter—I 'spect his sister is ridin' it now. There was also a big gray stud in there with the 'Mino, must be McGantry's."

"It is. I saw him ride it into town after the meddlesome bastard busted up our play at Coyote Pass." Trent's tone was bitter.

"So then I skinnied up to the house and did

some peekin' through the windows," Harper continued. "They must've finished supper not too long ago. I saw the Mex gal, Jaime's sister—Lucinda, is her name—doin' dishes with a younger gal in the kitchen area, and a couple men and a boy was sittin' in the parlor part. I didn't see no other woman, like a wife or mother to the kids. I recognized Lucinda from her husband's restaurant in Rio Fuego where I go to eat sometimes. Damn, she is one hot tamale all on her own! She's got a set of—"

"Spare me the editorials," Trent cut him off. "What about McGantry—was he one of the men in the parlor?"

"Bein's how I never met McGantry, remember, I can't say for certain. But one of 'em was a big, rugged lookin' son wearin' a buckskin vest. I reckon that was him. The other fella had some heft to him too, but he looked more a farmer type. Plus he had some kind of binged-up foot all wrapped in a thick bandage."

"Yeah, the one in the buckskin vest was McGantry," said Trent with the same bitterness.

Harper lifted his battered Confederate hat long enough to dig into his unruly mop of hair and scratch his scalp. Dropping the hat back in place, he asked, "So now that we've caught up with 'em, how you figurin' to 'front 'em?"

Trent ground his teeth. He pulled a dented pack of ready-fashioned cigarettes from inside his coat, extracted one, hunched his shoulders against the wind and struck a match to light up. Harper looked on disapprovingly but Trent didn't notice and the old Rebel held his tongue.

Exhaling a plume of smoke, Trent finally responded, "Damned if I know. If I knew what to make of the stopover here with these ranch folks, it would be different. I figured to catch up with that nosy Nebraskan out in the open. But what the hell's with this? If McGantry and the sister are aiming to corral Rodero and haul him back, you'd think they would want to keep kicking up dust steady in order to close the gap on him as quick as they could, not tarry along the way."

"Judgin' by the sign back on the trail," said Harper. "I read it that somebody from the ranch here had trouble with their buckboard. You can see it still parked down there in front of the house with a tilted wheel. I'm thinkin' maybe McGantry and Lucinda must've come along and gave 'em a hand. Then I could see where they followed along, probably to make sure the wheel made it the rest of the way okay. If all that took enough time, it would've been pushin' dusk. So it could be the family, bein' grateful and neighborly, invited 'em to stay and take supper and bed down for the night."

"Grateful and neighborly," sneered Trent. "Don't that kind of shit make you want to puke? What's more, it would mean that damn McGantry rode up, stuck his nose in somebody else's business again, and got treated like a hero for it! That makes me want to puke even more."

Harper shrugged. "Some of that was just speculatin' on my part."

Trent dragged hard on his cigarette then jetted the smoke out his nostrils. He dragged hard again only this time held the smoke. Until he let it trickle out around the next words he spoke. "On second thought, maybe this ain't so bad after all. Closing in on McGantry out in the open was bound to have been tricky. But now we got him bottled up nice and tight, right down there in front of us."

Harper scowled. "Now hold on a second. Boss Birchfield made it clear I was comin' on this ride-out to scout, not do no shootin'. Though I ain't against it, not if you need me to join in. But I hope you ain't thinkin' to start blastin' away at McGantry while he's in there with that innocent family, are you? A couple of 'em are just young 'uns. That'd stick mighty tight in my craw, even if I wasn't in on the trigger pullin'."

"For Chrissakes, I ain't *that* cold-blooded," Trent rasped. "Leastways, I ain't ever had to be yet . . . but I sure like the idea of somehow making my move on McGantry while he's cornered down there, rather than letting him get back out in the open again."

Harper's heavily whiskered face pulled long in

thought. Then he said, "How about this . . . in the mornin', when they're fixin' to head out, they're first gonna have to go into the barn and fetch their animals. Right? What if we was to lay for 'em in there? That way we'd have 'em isolated away from the family and you could cut McGantry down before he ever knew what hit him."

Trent's eyes went bright in the pre-moon gloom. "By God, that ain't a half-bad idea. In fact, it's a damn good one! It could work out real slick."

"We could go on down now and take up our positions," Harper suggested. "Ain't nobody from the house likely to be goin' to the barn any more tonight. And the sooner we settle in, if that's how we're gonna do it, the sooner we can get out of this blasted wind."

Trent stood up. "By God, Bone man, you should have been a general, not just a sniper. Maybe the South would have won that lousy war!"

"Some of us ain't gave up on it yet," Harper said somberly.

"Whatever you say." Trent clapped him on the shoulder. "Let's drop back and get our horses. We'll leave 'em tied at the rear of the barn and have them ready for a fast getaway after I've made my strike."

Harper nodded. "Shoot and scoot. That's the sniper way . . . works most every time."

Chapter Twenty-Three

The first time he thought he saw something, Lone wasn't quite certain. He was sitting in the parlor, talking with young Ben and his father while the women finished up in the kitchen. Lone was settled in a comfortable cowhide easy chair, Judd Ritter was occupying a similar one off to his right; Ben was sitting cross-legged, Indian style, on a thick, woven rug on the floor before the fireplace. Ritter was actually doing most of the talking, telling how he was determined to one day turn his modest ranch into something substantial he could leave his children. Lone was impressed by how, even with the recent passing of his wife, the man remained so devoted to his dreams and his family.

The layout of the Ritter cabin consisted of a large rectangular main room with the kitchen and dining area at one end and the parlor and fireplace at the other. There was a washroom and two bedrooms (one for Ritter, one claimed by Sue Jean) on the back side. Ben slept in a loft over the parlor.

The chair Lone had been gestured into after supper happened to be centered on the front window, allowing him to gaze out at the howling night while he listened to Judd Ritter relate his plans. The former scout couldn't help but reflect on the good fortune of things working out so he and Lucinda were here inside this night rather than out in that buffeting wind. He'd endured a hell of a lot worse in his years on the drift, but he never minded an alternative touch of comfort when one was available.

It was while Lone was absently gazing out and feeling glad he wasn't on the other side of the window that he first saw what looked like a quick burst of tiny sparks up on a distant ridge. It was there and then gone so fast he wasn't sure he'd seen anything at all. He concentrated on the ridge but saw nothing more. The way some of the wind gusts were causing the cabin to creak and shudder, he told himself, it must have been just a trick of light on the shivering window glass.

Lone continued to watch, however. After a full minute and more, up at the same spot, another small but longer-lasting flash of fire appeared—the unmistakable flare of a partially shielded match being struck. Lone willed himself to stay very still and relaxed in his chair, not show any outward reaction. Now a tiny red dot—the tip of a cigarette being puffed—began to glow periodically up on the ridge.

Somebody was up there looking down on the Ritter cabin. Watching.

But who? And why?

Lone's thoughts immediately jumped to Red

and Tom, the two Bluethorn rannies who'd caused trouble on the trail earlier in the day and ended up eating crow for it. Judd Ritter had been convincingly confident they lacked the backbone to bring any retaliation straight on, but that didn't mean they were above seeking payback in some slipperier way. Yeah, sizing them more in hindsight, Lone saw little doubt they had the makings for a yellow-bellied strike. Maybe running off or injuring some stock. Maybe a fire or a fouling of the well. Possibly a rock or some lead sent through a window. Lone didn't figure the pair for aiming to seriously hurt or kill anybody, but that didn't mean they might not do so inadvertently out of recklessness.

There was the possibility that whoever was up on that ridge might *not* be Red or Tom. Could be a lookout for rustlers. But it seemed Ritter would have mentioned something if they were having a rustling problem hereabouts. Lone's gut told him the Bluethorn troublemakers were still the most likely candidates for the presence he'd spotted. Regardless, whoever it was had to be up to no good. Nobody having a legitimate, harmless purpose would be lurking out there on a night like this.

The next question facing Lone was how best for him to react. He didn't want to alarm everybody unnecessarily nor did he want to put on any kind of display that might let the ridge watcher know he'd been spotted. What Lone needed was a reasonable excuse for slipping away to do what he did best—get outside and go on the scout.

He rolled it around in his head for a minute and came up with something he thought would be acceptable. When Judd Ritter stopped talking long enough to re-light his pipe, Lone stretched as if working out some kinks and then stood up. "That supper was so good," he announced, "I'm afraid I made a downright pig of myself. I'm feelin' plumb bogged down."

"Maybe it was that third piece of pie," Lucinda quipped from over by the sink. "Surely the mound of potatoes and ham hocks preceding them had nothing to do with it."

Lone gave her a look. "I'm admittin' my excess and payin' for it, okay? What I need to do is walk some of it off."

Sue Jean looked around. "You're not going out for a walk in that fierce wind, are you?"

Lone smiled and told her, "I been out in the wind before. In fact, it's partly the wind makin' me want to step out for a few minutes. My horse Ironsides, you see, he gets kinda skittish in a blustery conditions like this. 'Specially bein' in a strange barn and all, I'm thinkin' I oughta go check on him, settle him down some if need be."

"I can go check on him for you, Mr. McGantry," offered Ben.

"I appreciate that, son. But if he's fussin', he'll

respond best to me," Lone replied. "Besides, like I said"—here he patted his stomach—"I need to walk off a little of my overindulgin' anyway. So you folks carry on visitin', I'll be back directly."

Instead of going to the front door, though, Lone turned and headed for the door to the washroom, which led on out to the privy in back. Over his shoulder, he said, "I, er, got another piece of business to tend to before goin' to the barn."

In the washroom, after closing the door behind him, Lone immediately went to where he had earlier left his saddlebags and possibles pack when he came in to wash up himself once Lucinda was finished with her bath. From the saddlebags, he withdrew his backup Colt Lightning. This he tucked in his belt and in his pocket went a box of extra cartridges. His gun belt was hanging on a peg out in the main room, Winchester Yellowboy leaning against the wall next to it. Walking around armed while a guest in the Ritter home had hardly been called for and there'd been no logical way to explain doing so now for the purpose of going to check on his horse. On the other hand, going unarmed to confront an expected pair of skulkers was even more illogical to Lone's way of thinking. So the backup Lightning would have to suffice as a suitable trade-off.

The wind walloped him as soon as he stepped out the back door. The drop in temperature since sundown made the sting of the gusts even sharper. Lone stood just outside the closed door for a minute, letting his eyes adjust to the darkness and willing himself to ignore any physical discomfort, the way he'd learned to do under far harsher conditions on more than one past occasion when he'd been caught deep in Indian territory. The thing was to focus on the task at hand, on getting done what needed doing.

The moon wasn't up yet, but the stars in the darkening sky were starting to glimmer bright enough to pour down some meager illumination. Lone saw that a scattering of pine trees and scrub oaks ran behind the cabin and stretched all the way to the barn about sixty yards away. He could use those for cover, he decided, to make it as far as the barn. From there, he could circle wide then ghost slow and careful up through the high grass and bramble to the point on the ridge where he'd spotted signs of the watcher.

Once in the trees, Lone paused for a couple minutes to give the ridge another close study. He saw no further match strikes or glowing cigarette tips to indicate his man was still there. But neither did he see any sign of departure. The sneaky sonofabitch was still skulking out there somewhere—and Lone meant to find him (or them) and get some accounting for whatever was going on.

Lone went in motion again, moving down through the line of trees until he reached the barn. The weathered structure rattled and groaned in the wind. Lone could hear Ironsides whicker softly from his stall on the inside, sensing his nearness even in these conditions. Lone smiled and said under his breath, "Just take it easy, boy." Then he continued slipping along the back side of the barn.

He reached the corral at the far end. The enclosure was empty. All horses were on the inside, the cattle were out grazing. Lone could make out a few lumpy shapes not too far off, huddled together against the gusts, chuffing and lowing once in a while as if in protest.

Lone was just beginning to slip through the corral rails, meaning to angle across and out the other side as he proceeded on his wide swing before hooking around onto the ridge. He froze. There was movement on the other side of the corral, just outside the rails. Movement of something or somebody that didn't belong, was out of place.

Then he heard voices. Talking low and tossed around some by the wind, but still clear enough for Lone to make out.

"This oughta do plenty good. These posts are nice and sturdy and there's a fringe of grass alongside for our cayuses to chaw on. We'll tie 'em up and leave 'em ready for ridin' off quick-like, soon as you finish your gun work in the mornin'."

"Suits me. It'll be good to get out of the saddle for a while and even better to get out of this damn wind."

The movement and voices merged into murky shapes. Two men on horseback. Lone squatted low and pressed motionless against a post. He watched as the pair dismounted and began tying their horses. Although Lone couldn't determine any clear features, he could tell that one of the men was the right size to match either Red or Tom from earlier in the day. But the other appeared considerably smaller and spindlier than Lone remembered either being. And his voice had a distinct Southern twang that was also a mismatch.

"I got a full canteen here, Trent," said the spindly one. "If you bring that vittles sack, we can chow on jerky and biscuits once we get settled inside. Won't be hot coffee and bacon, but it'll fill our bellies and we'll be by God comfortable while we're eatin'."

"Suits me," the other man said again. "And when this is over, my bony friend, the first decent-sized town we come to I'll treat you to the biggest full-course meal we can find!"

Lone felt a shiver of recognition and then instant rage course through him. That voice. And the name that had been used—*Trent!* As impossible as it seemed, the facts were right there on the other side of the corral. One of the skulkers over there was none other than the mysterious Trent, the leader of the lynch mob from back at Coyote Pass and the ambusher who had gunned down Slick Hollister and tried to kill Lone in the street of Rio Fuego! He and the other man had to be the source of the signs Lone spotted up on the ridge. They'd worked their way down here now to . . . Lone could only figure they must have trailed him and Lucinda from Rio Fuego for the purpose of finishing off Lone, either as retaliation for interrupting Jaime Rodero's necktie party or to keep him from identifying any more of the would-be lynchers. Or both. It didn't really matter. Just like it didn't matter who the spindly man was. From what he could see of him, Lone was pretty sure he hadn't been part of the Coyote Pass lynch mob. But he was aligned with Trent now, so that made him an enemy all the same.

Lone closed his hand around the Colt Lightning in his belt but otherwise remained motionless. Even though a part of him wanted badly to rush out and start pouring lead at that goddamn Trent. But no, not just yet. Out here in the relative open, in the dark and with their horses right there handy, there was the chance, albeit small, they might manage to scatter and make a getaway. Better to be patient, play it smart. If they were going inside the barn, then that held promise of being able to corner them a lot tighter.

Lone replayed in his mind the snatches of conversation he'd overheard. *". . . We'll tie our cayuses up and leave 'em ready for ridin' off quick-like, soon as you finish your gun work in the mornin'. . ."* That made it plain enough. Their plan was to wait inside and stage an ambush—Trent's specialty—when Lone and Lucinda came for their horses in the morning. An ambush on Lone primarily, but there was little doubt they'd include Lucinda, too, if she got in the way. The scurvy back-shooting bastards! The blood pulsing in Lone's veins was suddenly as cold as the wind pulsing against his face.

He watched the men slip between the corral rails and then enter the rear of the barn through a narrow-hinged door off to one side of the wide double doors that swung open for stock to pass in and out of. Lone stayed still for a while longer, making sure neither of the men came back out for anything. While he waited, he pictured the layout of the barn from when he'd gone in there with Ben to put the horses away. The stalls where they'd left Ironsides, Conquistador, and the buckboard horse were near the other end, the front. Down this way he recalled seeing three or four additional stalls, empty, and a couple open-ended bins for grain or other storage that also looked mostly empty.

Lone tried to reason how the ambushers might think. If it was him, he reckoned that for now, he would lay back closest to where he could make a quick exit in case something unexpected happened and he had to pull out and come up with a change in plans. If things stayed quiet until morning, *then* he would move up closer to where he intended to strike. So if Trent and his partner figured similarly, that meant Lone's best approach for slipping inside undetected until he was ready to surprise and get the drop on the intruders was to retrace his steps and enter from the front.

Acting on that decision, he eased away from the corral rail and turned to start back along the side of the barn. The wind howled, and the structure creaked and groaned in response. That was good. Lone was capable of moving Apache quiet, but a little cover noise wouldn't go unappreciated . . .

Chapter Twenty-Four

He found them just like he figured he might, burrowed deep in one of the storage bins near the rear of the barn. They not only were obliging enough to act as he'd anticipated, but they helped guide Lone to them even more directly by wrapping themselves in a soft glow of illumination within the bin. Seeing this upon first slipping inside at the front of the barn, Lone paused to puzzle on it some before moving toward it. Was it possibly a trap? In the end he decided that no, what it must be was simply a lantern—probably one they inadvertently found hanging on the wall after they'd entered—with its wick set very low to provide the intruders some meager and temporary light. Deep in the bin, with its high wooden divider walls, there was no risk of it being seen from the house or anywhere outside. Only after entering the Stygian nighttime blackness of the cavernous barn did it stand out as a distant soft glow.

Lone thought back on the beacon candle Trent had left in the dark hardware store to guide his escape. Lone's mouth curved in a wolf's smile. The tricky bastard might not know it, but at the moment he was leaving another beacon light—only this one wasn't going to serve in his favor.

Lone moved stealthily down the length of the barn's center aisle, Colt Lightning extended out at waist level. The musty mingled scent of horses, straw, grain, and dust filled his nostrils. All around him, the building continued to shudder and moan from the wind. Ironsides whickered softly as Lone passed behind his stall, but the big gray seemed to sense that something was afoot he needed to stay quiet about.

Lone got within a few feet of the bin's divider wall and stopped. He could hear the men talking on the other side of the tightly fitted horizontal boards.

"Yessir," the twangy-voiced Southerner was saying, "we get done feedin' our faces, we can stretch out on a couple of these plump feed bags and snooze dang near as comfortable as on a bunkhouse cot."

"I suppose that's one way of looking at it," Trent allowed. "But me, I'm not going to rest in complete comfort until I finish with McGantry. That big meddlesome bastard has been a thorn in my ass for too long. I aim to—"

He was cut short by the sight of Lone stepping around the corner of the divider wall and planting himself square in the open mouth of the bin. He swept the muzzle of his Colt in a flat arc and said, "Speakin' of thorns, I got six of 'em in the wheel of this cutter, Trent. They're kinda dull, but they sink in real deep. You don't want a taste, both of you get your hands up—grab those ears!"

The scene inside the bin was pretty much what Lone had expected and what the piece of conversation he overheard had painted. There were a dozen or so grain sacks stacked against the inside wall of the bin. Two of them had been pulled down for the men to sit on; a third lay flat between them with a bandanna spread open on it to hold some biscuits and pieces of jerky. The only thing Lone had guessed wrong was the source of the throbbing light they were wrapped in. It didn't come from a commandeered lantern but rather from another of Trent's stubby candles propped up on the edge of the bandanna.

"Real cozy," Lone muttered. "Lot cozier than the nearest jail cell I aim to see you slapped in."

"You'll see me in Hell first," Trent grated, even as he raised his hands, curled into claws, up on either side of his head.

Lone made the mistake of focusing a little too tight on him—the *known* danger—and not quite as much as on his wiry partner. That gave the latter a split second of having Lone's eyes flicked away from him, and in that split second he made a desperation move. Shouting "No Yank sonofabitch is gonna put me behind bars!" Harper slapped away the candle and pitched himself backward off the feed sack.

Everything plunged into blackness.

Lone immediately opened fire, swinging his

Colt in a sweeping motion meant to cover the width of the bin as he triggered three rapid rounds. Then he twisted away, threw himself to the floor of the barn aisle and went into a roll angled off toward the opposite side. Return fire erupted from the bin. Tongues of yellow-gold flame licked out in brilliant, momentary flashes. Lone fired again, aiming at those flashes, then rolled some more knowing that his muzzle flare had targeted his position in return.

He also knew that the men in the bin would be hunkering low and finding some cover behind the filled feed bags, while he was caught out in the open with staying in motion his only chance to keep from catching a bullet. What was more, he only had two rounds left before he'd have to reload.

More shots poured out of the bin, aimed low but still whining above Lone's head and smacking into the barn wall somewhere behind him. He aimed a shot at one of those muzzle flashes and got the satisfaction of hearing a responsive yelp of pain as he pushed off into another roll.

"Aww, the Yankee sonofabitch got me!" wailed the twangy-voiced Southerner. "Four years of dodgin' blue-belly bullets all through the war with nary a scratch, and now this—But I ain't done yet, Yank! I'll take you to Hell with me 'fore I go!"

"Shut up and keep shooting!" barked Trent.

"That meddlesome cur has near run himself out of bullets . . . ain't that right, McGantry? That wheel full of dull thorns is running pretty dry, ain't it?"

"It might be—if I was dumb enough to bring only one gun!" Lone hollered back. And then, in a show of bravado, he triggered his final live round.

This promptly earned him a hail of return lead. But, again, the slugs sailed high and wide, hammering hollowly into the barn's inner walls. Rolling away from these, Lone all of a sudden bumped up against the end of the divider wall of an empty stall. It bit painfully into his shoulder, but it was a welcome stab of discomfort because it meant he had now gained some cover of his own and a position from which he'd have the chance to reload. By his reckoning, his series of rolls had taken him across and away from Trent's bin at a sufficient enough angle so that the depths of this stall on the opposite side of the aisle ought to be safely out of the line of incoming fire.

"Aww, damn," Lone heard the Southerner groan, weaker this time. "He got me good, Trent. I'm bleedin' out fast . . . looks like I might be makin' that trip to Hell ahead of him after all."

"Don't fold on me yet," Trent snapped before triggering a pair of fresh rounds in Lone's general direction. One gouged into the aisle floor short of Lone's stall, the other whapped loudly against the divider wall. Having scrambled deep into the stall, Lone smiled grimly as he thumbed reloads into his Colt with practiced speed and dexterity.

That's when he heard Trent say, "You might be done for, you old Rebel, but I'm not—Hang on long enough to cover me, damn you!" Then came the scraping and thumping of running feet as Trent made a desperate break.

Lone snapped shut the cylinder of his Colt and shoved to the front of the stall. He damn near rushed into the requested cover fire slammed out by Bone. But these shots, triggered by the finger of a dying man, were wilder than ever. High and low, coming nowhere close to Lone yet still presenting a threat that the next one *might*. And, beyond the flashes of these shots, Lone caught sight of a different kind of brightness—a vertical sliver of murky gray that marked a glimpse of outside starlight as Trent bolted through the barn's back door!

Emitting a roar of frustration and rage, Lone barged out of the stall with his Colt extended at arm's length, spitting hot lead in a tight grouping centered on Bone's muzzle blasts. Three claps of thunder rapped from the Lightning in such rapid succession it sounded like a single rolling boom. There was a final gargling cry from within the bin and then the old Rebel sniper was done shooting forever.

Lone broke into a run toward the sliver of

outside light still showing from the back door left hanging ajar. When he reached the opening, Lone paused for a moment, not wanting to rush out too recklessly in case Trent was anticipating exactly that and had a bullet ready to plant in him. Crouching down low, the former scout peeked cautiously around the edge of the door frame. Outside, the clear sky was awash with stars now, pouring down muted silver-blue illumination over the corral. No bullet slammed in from Trent. Instead, Lone's searching gaze fell on the varmint as he was struggling to free and mount one of the horses he and his partner had left tied just outside the confines of the corral.

Lone pushed out through the doorway and snapped off a quick shot. His bullet struck the upright post the horse had been tied to, hitting with a loud *whack!* right on the heels of the gun blast. This startled the horse just as Trent was starting to plant his foot in a stirrup. The animal reared up and spun away, nearly dumping Trent to the ground. He staggered but managed to stay upright, cursing aloud, then twisted half around and hurriedly triggered a round in Lone's direction. It missed by more than a foot and Lone promptly returned fire, sending another slug that chewed into the corral railing directly in front of Trent.

This sent the man bolting in desperation. He turned and ran toward the wide-open graze land out behind the corral. Fleeing blindly, as fast as his pumping legs could carry him.

Lone didn't hesitate to take off in pursuit. Racing across the breadth of the empty corral, up and over the railing, and on out into the pasture dotted with bulky lumps of sleepy, bewildered cattle. Ahead, Lone could see Trent dodging in and out among the animals, could hear more of his harsh cursing as he bumped against some of them. Twice, he twisted around as he ran and fired wildly back at Lone. The first attempt sailed high; the second one didn't go anywhere because the gun's hammer fell on an already spent cartridge with merely a metallic clink. Hearing this even above his pounding feet and chugging breath, Lone smiled a wolf's smile. He'd been keenly aware that he was again down to only one live round—but now he knew that was one more than Trent.

Over the span of choppy grassland, the two men continued running—one in flight, one in pursuit—covering a hundred yards, then more. Lone could see he was gaining on Trent, but the stubborn bastard wasn't making it easy. It crossed Lone's mind to spend the Colt's final round and try to bring his quarry down. But the gap between them remained great enough to make hitting a running target while he himself was also running too much of a gamble. If he missed, he would have only cut down the odds he felt he currently had working in his favor. He was convinced he could outlast Trent, damn it, and when he did, having that live round still in the chamber might prove most effective at that point.

And then, suddenly, everything took a drastic turn. Trent all at once vanished. One second he was there, a murky shape bobbing and weaving up ahead—and then he dropped from sight as if the earth had swallowed him! Surprised and somewhat stunned by this, Lone checked his forward momentum to almost half. What the . . . ?

It was only when Lone heard a yelp of alarm from Trent, followed by a loud splash and a rapid series of lesser ones, that he realized what had happened. Somewhere up ahead there was a stock watering pond or creek and, in the meager starlight, the fleeing man hadn't seen it until he was literally right on top of it and had plunged headlong into the water.

Lone resumed running, drawn by the sounds of more frantic splashing and sputtered curses. He quickly reached the source of these, coming to a twisting creek, not particularly wide but cut deep and with sharp banks on either side. Skidding to a halt on the near edge, Lone looked down and saw that Trent had righted himself in the four-foot-deep water and was scrambling madly to gain purchase on the opposite side in an attempt to claw his way up the muddy bank.

Lone didn't hesitate. He launched himself from the lip of the bank where he'd momentarily halted and landed on Trent with jarring impact. Both men fell back into the water at its deepest point in the middle of the channel. Lone still gripped the Colt in his right fist, his intent having been to hook his left arm around Trent's face and head and club him with the gun. But the plunge into the surprisingly cold water combined with Trent's instant wild flailing resulted in Lone failing to get his arm locked the way he'd meant to. Trent, soaked and slippery with mud, twisted away and whirled half around with a smashing elbow to the side of Lone's head.

The former scout was rocked, nearly losing his footing on the slick, sucking floor of the creek. When Trent tried to slash again with the elbow, Lone got his forearm up in time to block it. The two men struggled against each other, Trent trying to pull loose, Lone fighting to hang on to him. They were jammed so tightly together Lone was unable to swing the Colt in order to deliver a telling blow. Trent tried kneeing him in the groin, but the creek mud sucked at his foot and the resistance of the water slowed the effort enough to allow Lone to easily twist at the waist and take the diminished impact on his hip. In retaliation, he rammed forward and smashed his forehead hard against Trent's nose and mouth. There was nothing diminished about that blow.

Trent fell away so sharply he was jerked from Lone's grasp and dropped under the surface of the water. Lone immediately plunged after him. Submerged, they struggled anew. Lone grabbed at Trent's legs, trying to restrain him but Trent kicked with such fury that he knocked the Colt from Lone's grip. Cursing inwardly, Lone grabbed and clawed more intently at the churning legs until he seized a fistful of pantleg and then reached higher to clamp onto his opponent's belt buckle. From there, he essentially *crawled* the rest of the way up the length of Trent's body until they were face to face again in their struggle. They went into a series of gator rolls, all the while savagely pummeling and gouging at one another.

They broke surface together, gasping for air yet immediately starting to throw fists. But the arms of each were growing slower and heavier from exhaustion. Lone sensed he had the edge, though. He had more raw power to begin with, plus the head butt had taken its toll on Trent, especially the way his breathing was now impaired by the smashed nose.

The durable bastard had one last trick, however, aimed at turning things in his favor with finality. Leaning back from a glancing right hook that luckily only grazed the point of his chin, Trent suddenly squatted down and dropped his shoulders and head below the surface once more.

Lone immediately took a step forward, ready to dive down after him again, when Trent burst back up like a sounding whale. Fat drops and rivulets of water streamed off his abruptly rising face, catching glints of silvery starlight. And there was also something else that glinted in that same light—the menacing, six-inch blade of the knife Trent had reached down and snatched from his boot!

Trent lunged forward instantly, swinging the knife in a vicious cross-body slash meant to lay open Lone's guts. Lone pulled back, his reflexes as sharp as ever though his movement slowed somewhat by the mud and waist-deep water. He escaped the blade by less than an inch.

"Hop away all you want, you sonofabitch," sneered Trent through his mangled lips. "But you're one thorn I'm gonna cut out *permanently!*"

He came again, swinging the knife first in a forward slash then immediately reversing and whipping it back the other way. Lone eluded both attempts, back-churning wildly. But at the same time, he assessed Trent's fighting style, his skill. What was more, Trent was sucking air harder and harder, blowing bloody strings of snot every time he exhaled.

Grunting fiercely each time, he came again with the double slash. First forward then quickly in reverse, leaning into it more aggressively each time. His knife fighting skills were little more than rudimentary.

After dodging the latest flurry, Lone got set. He once again dodged the next forward slash. But then, instead of continuing to back-churn in anticipation of the next one, he hurled himself forward. Extending his arms and reaching with both hands, he clamped iron grips on Trent's forearm as it was poised for a split second across the width of his torso before starting back in the follow-up slash. It never made that second swing.

Lone threw himself against Trent with bull force, pinning his arm against his ribs and driving him back. As they jammed tight together, the two combatants found themselves face to face once again. And once again, without hesitation, Lone drew back his head and slammed his forehead hard into Trent's already smashed face. The victim fell back with a strangled cry and disappeared under the surface of the water.

Lone went down with him, refusing to let go of his double grip on the knife arm. Even in his half-stunned agony, Trent struggled frantically to break free. They turned over and over in thrashing gator rolls, scraping the floor of the creek, kicking up a thick cloud of silt and mud. They struck bottom hard enough during one of the turns to momentarily knock loose Lone's grip.

Trent wasted no time trying to take advantage

of this by twisting his knife hand around and attempting a desperate thrust with the weapon. But he misjudged how close he was to the bottom. His thrust was denied by his hand getting snagged in a tangle of muck and debris on the creek floor. Half a second later the body of a still thrashing Lone, reaching and clawing to regain his hold on the knife arm, bore down on Trent and inadvertently drove him the rest of the way to the bottom with the knife he clutched now turned in such a way that its full six-inch length was plunged straight into his black heart.

Chapter Twenty-Five

Young Ben was the first to spot a battered, bedraggled Lone plodding back across the corral. His shout drew the others out the back of the barn and they all came rushing to greet Lone. Judd Ritter and Sue Jean were holding lanterns; Ritter was also gripping a Winchester in his other hand. The distraught features of Lucinda were sharply etched in the light given off by the lanterns. The wind seemed to have lessened somewhat but was still gusting strong enough to send Lucinda's thick mane of ebony hair rippling straight out from the side of her face.

"Good God, man, what happened?" Judd Ritter blurted as they all reached the former scout. "We heard all the shooting coming from the barn, but by the time we got out here you were nowhere to be found."

"Two men," Lone husked in response, "followed us from Rio Fuego. It was me, mainly, they were after. To kill . . . they were settin' up an ambush in the barn. I expect you found one of 'em still in there?"

"Yes. Dead. Where's the other one?"

Lone jabbed a thumb over his shoulder. "Out there, in your graze land. Layin' beside the creek. Tried to get away . . . he's dead as well . . . I was too damn tired to try draggin' him in right now."

Lucinda stepped close and placed a hand on his arm. "What about you? Are you all right?"

"A little beat up is all," Lone told her. "And I think I might've swallowed about half of that damn creek . . . but my worst pain comes from losin' my trusty Colt Lightning in the muddy bottom."

"We need to get you in the house," Sue Jean said. "Out of those wet clothes and dried off. I'll make some strong coffee or broth to help warm you."

"Go with coffee," her father instructed. "You know where the cooking rum is. Add in a generous splash of that."

Lone grinned crookedly. "How about skippin' the coffee and just goin' with a cup of rum?"

"Whatever," Ritter responded tersely. "While all of you are tending to that, I'm going to take the horse one of those polecats left tied over yonder and ride out to bring in that other body. Whoever he was and no matter his intentions, I can't abide leaving him out there all night for the coyotes to start picking at."

"Hard to argue," Lone said, albeit grudgingly.

Two hours later, they were all gathered in the Ritter parlor. Lone was dry and warm, dressed in a spare change of clothes from his saddlebags. His boots were drying beside the cookstove.

It was closing on midnight. The wind was still gusting outside.

In the time since Judd Ritter had re-joined them after retrieving Trent's body, Lone and Lucinda had related with full candor the story behind the journey they were on. This included an explanation of why Trent and his anonymous partner were out to kill Lone—to make sure he couldn't identify any members of the Coyote Pass lynch mob that resulted in the death of Marshal Bartlett and also, apparently, out of a hankering for personal vengeance on Trent's part. Something that *wasn't* included in the telling, of course, was any mention by Lone of Amanda Thorndike's true motive behind wanting Jaime Rodero brought back.

"So I hope you can see," Lone was saying now in summation, "how this incident tonight could put us in a real bind, time-wise. If me and Lucinda have to tarry here and deal with your local sheriff over these killings it might cost us a couple days, maybe more. Critical time if it allows Jaime, an innocent man at this point, to get sucked deeper into the activities of Mano Manolito's gang and have his innocence and reputation ruined beyond repair."

"He is highly vulnerable at this point," added Lucinda. "He has been chased and nearly lynched twice. He feels he can no longer trust the proper authorities. They have falsely branded him an outlaw, so what does he have to lose by truly becoming one?"

"Joinin' up with Mano the Merciless would sure enough make him an outlaw," Ben said, a touch of excitement in his tone. "We've heard about Mano and his raids all down along the border. A lot of people are afraid his gang might swing up into these parts some day."

"Never mind that," said his father impatiently. Then, aiming a frown at Lone, he asked, "So what is it you're suggesting about our situation here? I've got two dead men on my property—you expect me *not* to tell the sheriff?"

Lone heaved a sigh. "No, I can't ask you to do that. For God's sake, believe me when I tell you how sorry I am to have brought this to your doorstep. If I'd had the slightest idea those two were on our tail, we never would have stayed here and risked draggin' you into it."

"I do believe you," Ritter said. "But that don't change the fact that—"

He was cut short by Sue Jean suddenly blurting, "Rustlers!"

All eyes swung to her.

Sue Jean lifted her chin and stood ready to explain further. "Those men were evil and they were intruders. Intruders on our property, Father, just like you said. If they'd shown up here looking to steal some of our cattle and you caught them in the act, you would have shot them. You've shot at rustlers before."

Ritter scowled. "What's your point, girl?"

"I know all falsehoods are a sin, but would it be such a terrible fabrication to claim that these men *were* rustlers? What they were seeking to do was actually far worse," Sue Jean pointed out. "So, for the sake of serving the greater good by allowing Mr. McGantry and Lucinda to proceed without added delay in trying to help her innocent brother, would it be so bad to say that pair got shot as would-be cattle thieves?"

"Shot by me?" her father questioned.

"It's something you *would* do—have attempted to do—isn't it?" Sue Jean said. "In the end what harm will be done? You think Sheriff Peale will go to the trouble of mounting an investigation, not take your word for it? Either Ben or I can go into town and bring him out to hear our story and take custody of the bodies. He'll have them buried in the town's boot hill, and that will put an end to the whole ugly business."

Lone was shaking his head before she was done talking. "No, I can't go along with that. I can't expect your pa to own up to a couple killings he had nothing to do with. And I especially don't want you kids dragged into such a big lie you'll have to carry with you from now on."

"Not so fast, not so fast." This came, surprisingly, from Ritter. His scowl had shifted to a deeply contemplative look. "Give me another minute," he said, "to let it sink in what a devious mind my daughter has. I never before had a clue . . . but, now that it's been revealed, I gotta say what she's proposing maybe ain't such a bad idea. In fact, it might be beneficial in more ways than one."

"How so?" Lone asked.

"Well. First off, it would prevent further delay for you and Miss Lucinda and allow you to still be on your way in the morning. That's the main thing. I'm still indebted to you for what you did on the trail this morning to help my kids." Ritter's expression darkened. "I don't want to think how far those drunken curs might have gone otherwise . . . that's the other thing, the other potential benefit. For us. If word gets around that I cut down a couple of rustling skunks—which, as Sue Jean said, I wouldn't shy away from if the need was there, and so have no qualms about claiming such in this instance—it might send a useful message. To rannies like Ansel and Block or any others who might be inclined toward making trouble for us and what's perceived to be our puny little spread. The message being: Puny or not, it's risky to mess with the Ritters."

"Damn straight!" declared Ben.

"Watch your mouth, young man!" his father and sister responded in unison.

And so from there, the matter was settled. Everything was agreed upon in accordance with the plan suggested by Sue Jean. After that, a few hours of much-needed sleep was eked out by everyone. In the morning, shortly past sunrise, goodbyes and expressions of gratitude were exchanged all around and then Lone and Lucinda took their leave.

Chapter Twenty-Six

"I have every right to be angry with you, you know, for the way you slipped out last night to confront those bad hombres without giving me any indication what was going on."

Thus spoke Lucinda almost as soon as they were out of sight from the Ritter ranch.

Lone looked over at her as they rode along stirrup to stirrup. He said, "I been wonderin' if I might hear something about that."

Her dark eyes, under knitted brows, flashed to meet his. "In other words, you expected to because you knew you deserved it and felt guilty for *not* telling me."

"Now hang on. I never said all that," Lone objected. "Like I already explained, I wasn't a hundred percent sure what I'd spotted up on that ridge. I wanted to check it out before alarmin' everybody, in case it turned out to be nothing. And I didn't see no way to let you in on what I was up to without cluin' the others. Besides, I figured that—worse case—it was probably those drunk jackasses Red and Tom out to do some chousin' as cowardly payback for gettin' their tails stung earlier. No way in hell I was expectin' it to be that ambushin', lynch-happy Trent havin' dogged us all this way."

"Do you really think his whole motive was to get revenge on you?"

"From the talk I overheard between him and whoever that partner he brought along was, Trent was definitely harborin' a grudge against me," Lone replied. "As to whether or not it was his only motive, I can't help but wonder if he wasn't also out to eliminate me as a witness to the attempted lynching of your brother that got the marshal killed as part of it. I told you before how Trent cut down one of the other lynchers to make sure he wouldn't talk."

They rode on for a ways in silence. Lucinda's expression became that of someone lost in brooding thought.

The morning was cool and mostly clear. Last night's wind had finally abated but it left behind numerous long, stringy, murky clouds it had dragged in from the northwest. The terrain they were riding over remained mostly a pattern of grassy, choppy hills with frequent rock outcrops and scattered clusters of trees. Off to the west, the Sangre de Christos loomed ever closer.

At length, and somewhat abruptly, Lucinda spoke again. "The man who was with the one called Trent . . . I recognized him."

That lifted Lone's eyebrows. "You did?"

"Si. He was very fond of Mexican food. Whenever he was in town, back at Rio Fuego, he came to eat at my husband's *restaurante*. His name was

Harper. They called him 'Bone,' though I do not believe that part was his true Christian name. You Anglos and your habit of so often assigning 'nicknames' . . . anyway, does any of that mean anything to you?"

"No. Can't say it does."

"Something more. Harper worked for the JT Connected."

"You mean Judge Thorndike's outfit?"

"The same."

Lone pulled rein on Ironsides. Suddenly he became the one scowling in thought. "Now *that* is damned interesting. Interesting and a mite curious," he said. "How does a JT Connected wrangler fit with a snake like Trent—what would make him come along on a vengeance ride?"

Checking down alongside him, Lucinda said, "Perhaps he was part of that same lynch mob Trent headed up. Giving him reason to also want to make sure you did not identify him along with the others."

Lone shook his head. "Trouble is, I'm pretty sure Harper *wasn't* part of that mob. I couldn't make out any of 'em by sight, but I heard their names called, and Harper wasn't one of 'em. Plus, when the shootin' broke out there was a lot of shoutin' back and forth and I never heard that distinctive twangy voice as part of it."

"Si. Then how he fits with Trent in following you here is most curious."

"Why is it," Lone wanted to know, "you didn't mention about recognizin' him before this?"

Lucinda shrugged. "It did not seem necessary for the Ritters to know. I felt the more anonymous the men who died on their property remained, the easier it would be for them to get over."

"Reckon maybe you're right. Kinda shrewd thinkin' on your part," allowed Lone. They gigged their mounts back into motion again.

They hadn't gone far before Lone said, "I know you want to stick to open country in order to keep eatin' up miles. But somewhere between here and the border we oughta pass close enough to some town where we can afford a quick stop. I'm wantin' the chance to buy a new backup gun to replace my Colt Lightning that I lost back there in that blasted creek mud."

"How many guns do you need? You already have one on your hip and a repeating rifle booted to your saddle."

Lone cut her a sidelong glance. "In case you forgot, we're on our way to face an outlaw gang run by a he-bull calls hisself 'the Merciless' . . . if I'd had more time before we took off, I might've considered tryin' to scrounge up a Gatling gun to strap on my back."

"I cannot tell whether or not you are being serious."

"I don't make a habit of jokin' about guns," Lone assured her.

She regarded him. "Still on the subject of guns, then—of using them—tell me something: Back there, when we were getting ready to leave the Ritter ranch, you insisted on going into the barn by yourself to bring out our horses. Ben offered to help but you wouldn't let him. Why?"

"The bodies of those two men were in there. He didn't need to see that again."

"While you were in there, alone, there was a gunshot. You came out saying you shot a snake in one of the stalls." Lucinda's gaze continued to be very direct, probing. "But it was something else, wasn't it?"

"You're doin' the telling."

"I'm asking."

Lone sighed. "All right. I put a bullet in Trent's carcass. Still a snake, so I wasn't exactly lyin'. But it occurred to me that, no matter how much of a lazy drunk the local sheriff is supposed to be, he might still notice and find it fishy that one of the 'rustlers' Ritter is gonna claim to have shot and had only a knife wound in him. So I planted a slug where the knife slice was, just to make sure no suspicion got raised about it. It was a necessary but kinda cold-blooded thing to do. I figured it best not to be spelled out too plain."

"And you call me shrewd."

"You are . . . what I am is thorough."

• • •

They pushed steady through the day, stopping only at brief intervals to let their mounts blow and drink. The miles fell away. They remained in their saddles and kept riding while eating a noon meal of jerky and biscuits. The sky cleared and the sun beat down hard and hot. The land rolled on, essentially unchanging.

Late in the afternoon, Lucinda announced, "We will be coming to a town shortly. Beatrice Springs. You should be able to find a suitable gun dealer there."

True to her word, just before sundown they came into sight of the town. It lay on the grassy bottom of a broad, shallow natural bowl with tree-stippled hills on three sides and a jagged red-rock ridge along the southwest rim. The modest cluster of buildings appeared laid out in an orderly grid of five or six criss-crossing streets.

They drew rein and paused to gaze down from the crest of the north slope. "We made good progress today, more than making up for our stop with the Ritters. Looks like a good spot for night camp right over there," said Lucinda, pointing to a stand of aspen and cottonwood trees about twenty yards to the west. "I will stay and set up while you go down and conduct your business. We are close enough now so that I think it best we do not draw undue attention by going into the town together."

"Close enough to what? Draw attention from who?" Lone wanted to know.

Lucinda's face took on an odd, almost sad expression. "I will explain when you return," she said.

Lone's first inclination was to argue, not wait but demand to know now what she'd meant by the puzzling remark. But he held himself in check. He was harboring a secret, after all, he reckoned she had a right to one as well. Especially if it was only for a short time longer. He'd trusted her this far. He was in too deep to balk at this juncture.

"Alright," he said in a flat tone. "Shouldn't take long. I'll be back as quick as I can."

"Please do." Lucinda's mouth curved in a faintly apologetic smile. "Bring back some potatoes if you can—to go with the leftover ham hocks Sue Jean sent with us. I'll have a pan of water boiling and ready."

"Potatoes it is," said Lone, then swung Ironsides down the slope.

Chapter Twenty-Seven

After unsaddling and picketing Ironsides, Lone carried his bundle of purchases over and deposited it on the ground next to the crackling campfire. It was full dark now, the town down in the basin he'd just ascended from a shadowy mass with tiny yellow dots twinkling in its midst.

Lucinda sat waiting beside the fire, cradling a cup of coffee in her palms, the pulsing light given off by the flames making her bold facial features even more exotically lovely in the shifting shadows. Her eyes lingered on the large bundle for a beat then lifted to Lone. "Either you brought back a great many potatoes . . . or perhaps you *did* find that Gatling gun you were longing for."

Lone grinned. "Somewhere in between. Yeah, I got plenty of potatoes. And while I wasn't able to score a Gatlin', I did pick up some extra firepower. But first, I been smellin' your coffee all the way up the hill and I sure could use a cup while I'm spreadin' my wampum."

Lucinda promptly poured a cup and handed it to him. After a cautious sip of the scalding brew, Lone set the cup on the grass next to where he squatted and untied the thongs on the canvas-wrapped bundle. The first thing he withdrew was a lumpy sack that he held out to Lucinda.

"Potatoes. Already peeled and cooked, all you got to do is heat 'em up."

As Lucinda began adding the spuds to the pan in which she had ham hocks simmering, Lone spread open the canvas all the way. The firelight flickered over an array of gun metal.

Lone plucked up a short-barreled revolver, saying, "This is for you. It's a Model 2 Smith & Wesson, .38 caliber. Folks call it a 'Baby Russian.' I ain't sure why. It's a good, reliable gun. I'd've rather got another Colt Lightning, but the fella only had one and I'm keepin' that for myself. I got you a box of cartridges for this, too."

Lucinda dropped the last potato in the pan and gazed somewhat uncertainly at the gun Lone was extending to her. "But I-I already have a gun of my own," she said.

"Yeah, I saw it when you pulled it on Red and Tom. A Walker Colt converted for cartridges. Big ol' horse pistol powerful enough to knock down a wall or stop a chargin' buffalo. But it's a relic. Apt as not to blow up in your hand. Plus it's too big and bulky for you." Lone pushed the Baby Russian closer. "This suits you way better. Won't break your wrist when you shoot it and will stop anything you're likely to be usin' it on."

Lucinda took the gun.

"How good a shot are you?" Lone asked.

"Fair. My brother taught me."

"Ever shoot anybody?"

"Of course not."

"Could you—if you had to?"

Lucinda's eyes swept to him and a dark fire flared deep within them. "If it were someone threatening me or mine—yes, without hesitation."

Lone nodded. "What I wanted to hear."

While Lone took some bigger gulps of his cooling coffee and the potatoes began to bubble in the ham hock juices, he revealed the rest of his purchases. There was, of course, the replacement Colt Lightning—not brand new, but well broken in and maintained; it settled into his grip like it had always belonged there. But the item that had given the bundle most of its bulk turned out to be a double-barreled Greener shotgun. The big blaster was also second hand though equally well maintained. In addition to extra cartridges for the Lightning and the Baby Russian, there were two boxes of 12-gauge Blue Whistler loads for the Greener.

"You look like you are planning to go to war," Lucinda commented.

"Not necessarily planning—but ready, if it comes to that," Lone countered. Then he took a final item from the spread-open canvas and held it up, a loaf of fresh-baked bread wrapped in waxed paper. "But, one way or the other, I'd sooner do it on a full belly."

Finished displaying his wares, Lone drained

the remainder of his coffee and then stepped to the edge of the camp to wash up a bit before eating. A towel, a wooden bowl to pour some canteen water in, and a bar of tar soap from his possibles pack served his needs. He stripped to the waist for these ablutions, then gave his shirt a good shaking to dislodge some of the trail dust before shrugging back into it and his buckskin vest. When he returned to the fire, Lucinda had heaping plates dished up and ready for each of them.

As they began to eat, Lucinda said, "Excuse me if it is something you don't wish to talk about, but I couldn't help noticing, by the many scars on your body, that it appears you already have been to war. Many times."

Lone smiled. "Many battles maybe. But only one war . . . the long, ongoin' one that amounts to survivin' out here on the edge of the frontier."

Lucinda regarded him. "But you wouldn't have it any other way, would you? *Not* being out on the edge of the frontier, I mean."

"No, I reckon not," Lone admitted as he chewed a forkful of juicy ham hock. "Seems to be where I fit in the best. Accordin' to what some folks keep pointin' out, these wide-open spaces are what suits this 'lone' thing they seem to think I work so hard at."

"I don't believe that. That this 'lone thing,' as you put it, is contrived in any way. But it *does* suit you, just like these wide open spaces. You are who and what you are. It's that simple."

Lone shrugged. "You seem to see it clearer than most. Maybe even me. All I know for sure is that it's how things have had the way of turnin' out."

This line of talk suddenly stirred in Lone fresh thoughts of Velda. Not that thoughts of her were ever very far from his consciousness. Velda, the one piece of his past that had marked the closest he'd ever come to no longer being alone; not ever again. But then an errant bullet from a pair of drunk, arguing cowboys in an adjacent room had ended it all by ending her life. What hadn't ended was more shooting by the pair until the two fools succeeded in also killing each other—not only robbing Lone of the love of his life but also robbing him of any chance to avenge her. No such act would have done anything to bring Velda back, of course, or fill the empty space that would walk beside him for the rest of his days. But at least it might have quenched the unsatisfied rage boiling deep in his guts, at times barely contained.

Lone didn't know what showed on his face but he was abruptly aware of the way Lucinda was looking at him, silent, eyes a little wider than they'd been just a minute ago. He stabbed a piece of potato with his fork, popped it in his mouth and chewed it aggressively before saying, in a carefully measured tone, "But all this talk of bein' alone don't hardly fit the here and now, does it? I've got you beside me for good company at present . . . and somewhere up ahead, though representin' not such good company I expect, is the passel of border desperadoes we're on our way to visit. So I don't see me bein' lonely anytime soon."

Lucinda managed a wan smile. "No, I guess not."

Lone ate some more. Then: "Speakin' of what's up ahead, you said something before about bein' close enough to draw attention. You ready to fill me in now on what you meant?"

Lucinda dropped her eyes for a moment. When she lifted them, she met his gaze very directly. "Si. It is time you knew. Past time . . . I-I am sorry I kept it from you to begin with."

Lone waited for her to go on.

"My husband's *restaurante*, you must understand, gets visited by many travelers, not just Rio Fuego locals. Those who come from the border and farther south bring word of relatives and acquaintances who remain living down there, as well as general happenings. We certainly do not rely on just the reports from my *stupido* cousins"—here a stern scowl—"when they make their visits.

"From such travelers, just a day before my brother was falsely arrested and taken away, we learned news of Mano's gang. Remember how

I told you they were, in truth, merely a ragtag bunch who raided minor targets? Well, it seems that something moved them to aim higher and they successfully robbed a rich Anglo bank. Their take was significant enough to draw serious attention from a most unwelcome source—the Texas Rangers, who previously did not pay them much heed."

A corner of Lone's mouth quirked up. "Havin' those boys sicced on you is *not* a welcome thing for sure."

"Si. As Mano quickly found out. That is why," Lucinda continued, "he led his gang north in an attempt to find safe haven away from the border."

"Where? How far north?" Lone wanted to know.

Lucinda's eyes again dropped for a moment before answering, "Less than a day's ride from here. There is a spur of small mountains that jut out away from the eastern edge of the Sangre de Christos—the Tantos, they are called. Up within them there is a generally forgotten and mostly abandoned old mining town called Hernando Heights. Those who seek it out are men who want to drop from sight everywhere else. The inbred family of a stubborn, leftover miner named Binder is there to provide a degree of protection and supplies to meet their basic needs for the time they are there."

"Jesus Christ," Lone groaned. "Other than

bein' closer than I thought, what we're ridin' into sounds worse by the minute."

Lucinda had no response.

Lone eyed her. "Is that why you didn't tell me sooner—you thought maybe I'd be less willin' to go through with this?"

"No. I knew better than that. You quickly make the impression of a man who finishes what he starts," Lucinda said. "My hesitation for not being more exact about our destination before this was due to . . . well, I feel bad about admitting now, a lack of full trust in the motives of you and Lawyer Munro. I *wanted* to believe all that you were saying, how you were seeking to help Jaime and everything. Yet it sounded almost too good to be true. And I saw how friendly you were with Rio Fuego's new marshal and deputy—the same men who put my brother in irons and took him away in the first place."

"And also the same men who risked their lives to protect him," Lone was quick to point out. "To the point that one of them, the former marshal, paid permanent-like for takin' that risk."

"I am well aware of that," Lucinda conceded. "I am also aware of how deep the grief over Marshal Bartlett's death was, and how it increased the ugly mood already gripping the town due to the judge's murder. And at the center of both—because the marshal died protecting him, exactly as you said—was my brother. Knowing the lengths some would be willing to go to in order to get their hands on Jaime again, is it so hard to understand my suspicions over what you and Harriet were offering? No matter how badly I wanted to believe them?"

Lone could hear the earnestness in her tone, feel the intensity in her words. And he realized that, in her place, he likely would have harbored the same suspicions, felt the same reluctance to buy in too fast and too completely.

Whatever showed on his face was enough for Lucinda to continue without a verbal response from him. "My Carlos, I should say, never doubted you. He encouraged me to trust the two of you. So I agreed. Though I had reservations, I respected his instincts and, as I have already said, I *wanted* to believe in what was being proposed. I decided that, after spending some time with you on the trail, I would be able to make a final judgment on your sincerity, your honesty. Though I have done nothing to deter or delay our progress so far, had I not become convinced your intentions were honorable, I would have taken us on—how you say—a 'wild goose chase' that would have failed to lead either to Mano or my brother."

Neither of them spoke for several beats.

Until Lone said, "Well, I'm glad to hear I earned your trust." He paused again and his mouth fell into a lopsided grin. "On the other hand, maybe a wild goose chase don't sound all that bad—not compared to how you described where we're gonna end up tomorrow instead."

Chapter Twenty-Eight

As Lucinda said, the Tantos Mountains were a minor offshoot of the main Sangre de Christo chain. On sight, they were a jumble of low, jagged, sun-bleached peaks that, to Lone's eyes, looked drab and unappealing even without knowing what lay in store somewhere up within them.

He and Lucinda reached the foothills right at noon. The day was another hot one, no breeze, the sun hammering down from high in the center of a cloudless sky. The terrain over the past few miles of their approach had grown rockier, more rugged. The grass was shorter, nubbier, and though trees had grown sparse, there were numerous bunches of thick, ground-hugging bramble brush.

"Here is where we may need to call on your scouting and tracking skills," Lucinda stated as they drew rein to let the horses blow and to gaze up at the peaks rising before them. "I have been told that the original main route up to the town, an old wagon road, is still open and evident to the trained eye. But more specific than that I cannot say."

Lone lifted his canteen and held it out to her. While she drank, his eyes continued to scan out ahead, and he said, "We'll keep ridin' along the bottom here for a ways then. If there's the remains of a wagon road, I should be able to spot it. How far up is the town, any idea?"

"Not very far, was my impression. The mining, for as long as it lasted, took place higher up."

Lone took the canteen back and frowned before raising it to take a drink for himself. "If the trail is open and the town ain't very far up, what keeps Rangers or other lawmen from goin' in and haulin' out some of the owl hoots holed up there?"

"My understanding is that the Binders make sure the town is clean whenever posses or any such come around. They have lookouts posted with a warning system. At first sign of anybody who looks like the law," Lucinda explained, "those who don't want to be seen are warned and take to predetermined hideouts up in the old mine shafts."

"Pretty slick," Lone muttered. He tipped up the canteen, took a long pull. Lowering it, he said, "Well, I'd say we don't look like a standard pair of law dogs. So that might work in our favor on first gettin' looked over."

"What *do* we look like?" Lucinda asked.

Lone smiled. "Why, that's easy . . . I'm a double tough hombre on the run for a whole raft of nasty doin's, and you're my wildcat of a woman who's crazy about me in spite of my wicked ways."

Lucinda arched a brow. "How long have you been carrying around that fantasy?"

"Must've read it in one of those rootin'-tootin' dime novels," Lone told her. "But if it helps keep us from gettin' plugged on sight . . ."

He swung down from his saddle and, now that the horses had cooled some, gave each of them a good watering from his hat. After re-hanging the canteen from his saddle horn, he stepped back to his saddlebags and rummaged for a moment until he pulled out a folded item of colorful cloth. This he held out to Lucinda, saying, "Here. I picked this up for you when I was in town last night."

Lucinda looked puzzled.

"It's a poncho—or *serape*, I guess maybe you would call it."

Lucinda shook it open but continued to look puzzled. "I do not understand. There is no bad weather. The sun is shining, and it is, in fact, very hot. This will only make it hotter."

"Yeah, I'm sorry about that part," Lone said. "But here's the thing . . . I got to thinkin', even before you gave me the rest of the details on this shithole we're gonna be ridin' into . . . by all reports, this is a mix of plenty bad hombres we'll be minglin' with. Yeah, your brother and cousins will hopefully be part of 'em. But we don't know how soon we're gonna get to them or how much sway they'll have when we do."

Lucinda's puzzled look started to show impatience. "You're being awfully vague, McGantry. What are you trying to say?"

Lone scuffed his feet in the dust like an ill-at-ease schoolboy. "Don't take this wrong now, but you're a, uh, well, a pretty full-figured gal. I don't mean you're the flaunty type or anything, but you sorta can't help it. That white blouse you're wearin' don't leave no doubt you're a woman, and a real attractive one to boot. We go ridin' into a camp of lowdown polecats, like as not half drunked-up, who maybe ain't been around nothing but hog ranch females in who knows how long . . . well, the sight of you might trigger complications we surely don't need on top of the kind we're already expectin'."

Lucinda gave a little laugh. "You're blushing!"

"Doggone it—do you see my point or not?"

"You want me," Lucinda replied, smiling impishly, "to wear the *serape* in order to diminish my curves so none of the human *puercos* we run into might be uncontrollably tempted to paw me and cause you to have to shoot them. Is that it?"

"That's the general idea, yeah," Lone grated.

"Was that so hard? Why did you not just say so?"

They found the wagon road only a short time later. As advertised, it appeared quite passable and even had wagon ruts that looked fairly recent. This made sense, Lone reasoned, considering the report of how the Binders provided for their "guests" during their stay—supplies to do so had to be hauled in.

The road ascended at a steady but mostly easy incline, making occasional sharp twists and narrowing now and then but always remaining wide enough for wagon passage. The rock walls to either side alternated between stretches of high, flat slabs and low, weather-rounded shoulders. Bramble brush grew thick out of every crack and crevice.

They climbed for more than two hours. The sun reflecting off bare rock increased the heat, especially in the narrower, high-walled stretches, to an oven-like level. The horses worked up a lather, their riders dripped with sweat. Finally, as the sun dipped toward late afternoon, the higher rocks began throwing some shadows that offered brief, somewhat cooler patches.

Lone called a halt in one of these. He and Lucinda drank and then wiped their faces with water-soaked bandannas. Even in the shade, perspiration popped back out on their foreheads almost immediately. Once again, after the horses had blown and cooled some, Lone watered each of them out of his hat.

Swinging back into his saddle, he said, "There'd better be some water in Hernando Heights. We're draining ours pretty fast."

"There's bound to be." Exhaustion was heavy

in Lucinda's tone. "We just need to *get* there."

They gigged the horses into motion once again.

Three-quarters of an hour later, they heard the first of the strange whistling, flute-like sounds from up ahead. Moments later, from farther away, came a second one.

"I'd say we've been spotted, and the Binders' signaling system is at work," said Lone.

"It's an eerie sound," remarked Lucinda. "It almost sends a chill down my spine—which, in this heat, should be welcome. But not under these circumstances."

Lone thumbed the keeper thong off the hammer of the Colt riding on his hip. "Yeah. I know what you mean."

A hundred yards farther, the trail took a bend to the left, and as they rounded it, a man came in sight standing on a rock slab off to the right. He looked to be only about twenty or so, hatless, clad in a baggy, homespun shirt and trousers of the same murky gray material. A mop of long, greasy, scraggly black hair sat atop his head and wispy, wiry strands of the same hung under his lower lip, apparently an attempt at a goatee. His eyes were muddy brown, close set, and dull looking. Hanging from a leather thong around his neck was a slotted, hand-carved wooden tube—the source of the musical sounds they'd heard, Lone guessed. The youth on the rock also held a Henry repeating rifle resting casually on one bony shoulder, with the barrel angled across the back of his neck.

"Whoa up thar," he called in a nasally voice.

Lone and Lucinda pulled rein and gazed at him expectantly.

"What bidness ye folks got up this way?" he asked.

"We're on our way to the town, Hernando Heights," Lone answered.

The specimen gave a quick, hard shake of his head. "Ain't called that no more. It's Binderville now. My unc, Pap Binder, he re-named it. He's the mayor. Hell, he's pract'ly the governor of these here mountains. He decided he didn't want it called by no spic name no more."

Lone sensed Lucinda stiffen a little in her saddle, but she held her tongue. He was quick to say, "We don't give a hang what it's called. We just want to get there and find a place to clean up and rest for the night."

The specimen's eyes narrowed. "Ye ain't the law, are ye?"

"Do we *look* like the law?" Lone snapped in response.

"I ain't sure what ye look like. We don't usually get man-woman pairs. And my, ain't she a purty one? Even if she is—"

"Mister," Lone cut him short, "is it your job to stop folks and talk 'em half to death before lettin' 'em on by? We want to get movin' and get somewhere in out of this damn heat. Is that so hard to understand?"

"All right, all right," the specimen relented. "Go ahead on. Ye'll be met a ways farther by my brother, who'll take you the rest of the way in." He scowled. "Best watch yer sassy mouth with him, though, he can be a mite prickly his own self."

Two hundred yards more and the trail flattened out, reaching ahead with smooth, conical rocks resembling giant eggs piled on either side. In the middle of the flat passage waited a man on horseback. Appearance-wise he was cut from a similar bolt as the earlier lookout. Same greasy, stringy hair, same close-set dull, mud-colored eyes, same murky gray homespun clothing. Some differences, in addition to sitting a horse, was that this one looked to be a couple years older, had a slight reddish tint to his hair, no pretense of a goatee, and a battered, tobacco brown hat was pulled down almost to his ears. Instead of wielding a rifle, he had a six-gun holstered high on his waist, worn butt forward over his left hip for a cross-draw.

Lone and Lucinda reined up once again.

Brown Hat eyed them. "Ye got bidness in Binderville?"

"Ain't likely we'd ride all the way up here if we didn't," Lone answered. "We're lookin' for a place to stay for a while."

"Ye runnin' from the law?"

"If we was, would we be dumb enough to admit it?"

"Ye might be."

"Are *you* the law?"

Brown Hat seemed to have to think about that. Then: "Maybe. Close enough for hereabouts."

"Then while we're here, we'll plan to abide by *your* laws. Fair enough?"

Brown considered some more before asking, "What's yer name?"

"Trent," Lone said.

"That all?"

"It's enough."

"What about the gal?"

Lone's patience was wearing thin. "For Christ's sake, are you the local census taker too—or what the hell is this all about?"

Now Brown Hat really had to think. "What's a census taker?"

"Never mind," Lone growled. "Either draw that hogleg you're packin' and try to stop us, or get the hell out of our way. 'Cause I'm tired of jawin' out here in the heat and I'm goin' into town to find some goddamn shade!"

With that, he dug his heels into Ironsides and the big gray surged forward with Lucinda and Conquistador right in his tail. Brown Hat had to wheel his mount frantically out of the way to keep from getting bowled over.

Chapter Twenty-Nine

Binderville, formerly Hernando Heights, was about what one would expect for a mostly abandoned old mining town. Weathered buildings—made largely of stone and adobe, a few of warped gray wood—arranged in a haphazard manner. Streets dusty and empty. A pall of despair and defeat hanging over it all.

The exception, when reached, was what passed for the "downtown" section arranged around a lopsidedly-shaped plaza of sorts. Whatever pulse the town had left, Lone sensed, throbbed from here.

Dominating the plaza was a large, three-story stone building. While the structure itself was wind-pitted and sun-bleached to a milky white, the wooden shutters bracketing its first-floor windows and the rather ornate wooden door propped open to one side of the front entrance all showed a recent coat of maroon paint. In contrast, the shutters of the second and third-floor windows were faded to a dull gray; some hung crookedly on their hinges and a couple of the third-floor windows had none at all.

But perhaps the most eye-catching first-floor feature, at least from the outside, was the sign nailed over the front entrance. It was a long one-by-twelve plank, whitewashed, with sloppily painted black lettering that read:

HOTELL—SALOON—GENRUL STOR

Probably worth noting, Lone mused, that the only word spelled correctly was "Saloon."

At any rate, as he and Lucinda came trotting into the plaza, still at a pretty good clip after blowing past Brown Hat, the building and its sign drew them to it. As they checked down at the hitch rail out front, where four dusty, hard-ridden nags were already tied, Lone said, "I make this a good place to start finding out some answers."

"I am sure," Lucinda replied dryly, "with your charm and patience you will have no trouble finding those eager to provide them."

As if to emphasize her sarcasm, Brown Hat came galloping into the plaza in their wake. He slowed his horse for a moment, favoring Lone with a smoldering scowl. Instead of proceeding on to where they were getting ready to dismount at the hitch rail, however, he swung his animal sharply off to one side and kicked it again into a gallop headed toward an adobe building across the plaza, one that had the look of at one time having been a mission church.

"See? There goes the first citizen you so smoothly won over," Lucinda remarked.

Lone scoffed. "Him? Whatever the peckin'

order around here is, I'm bettin' he don't amount to a hill of beans." He shrugged. "But whether he does or not, I gotta start sellin' my double tough, take-no-shit-off-nobody image somewhere, don't I?"

Despite looking somewhat dubious, Lucinda said, "I suppose. If you say so . . . Mr. Trent."

They entered the stone building, Lone carrying the Winchester Yellowboy loosely in his left hand, the keeper thong still slipped off the hammer of the Colt riding on his right hip. Stepping out of the afternoon sun and into the confines of the building's thick stone walls provided an immediate wash of welcome coolness. They found themselves at a center point of the interior. Immediately ahead, an open stairway climbed to the upper rooms. To their left was the dim, smoky, noisy saloon portion; to their right the quieter, more brightly lighted general store with a visible aisle leading off between stacks of merchandise piled high on either side.

"Let me guess which side you are inclined to go in search of answers," remarked Lucinda.

Lone gave no reply, simply turned and walked into the saloon. Lucinda followed.

Though the sour hybrid odor of sweat, spilled booze, and burned tobacco assailed their nostrils immediately, it took a little longer for their eyes to adjust to the smoky, murky dimness. Lone could make out a rudimentary bar—planks nailed across the tops of wooden barrels stood on end—along one side of the rectangular room. A lone drinker stood with his elbows resting on the plank about three-quarters of the way down. Spread out across and down the length of the rest of the room was a scattering of various sized and shaped tables and chairs. Toward the back, two of these tables had card games going on, shadowy-faced men hunched over their pasteboards on the fringe of yellowish light circles pouring down from lanterns suspended above the field of play. Frequent grumbling and cursing came from the players as they slapped down their cards and shoved their money back and forth.

Lone pushed up to the bar. At first he didn't see anyone on the other side until a gruff voice said, "Strangers in town, eh? Don't recall seein's ye 'round before."

Lone looked down and saw a very short, stout woman standing there. Her chin barely rose above the level of the plank's surface. She had iron gray hair pulled carelessly into a bun and a broad, fleshy face lined by dozens of deeply seemed wrinkles. A smoldering hand-rolled cigarette hung from one corner of her mouth.

When he got past his surprise, Lone responded, "We just now rode in. That's why you haven't seen us before."

The woman craned her neck and looked over toward the entrance. "Ye mean yer alone?"

"That's right. Just the two of us."

"I can see that. What I mean is, didn't nobody meet ye on the trail and ride in with you?"

"Escort us in, you sayin'?"

The woman scowled. "Don't be flingin' big words at me. They shoulda been a couple young fellers met ye back on the trail. One of 'em shoulda rode ye on in. That's the way it's done around here."

"Yeah, we met a couple jaspers on the way in. Guess they didn't explain the rules clear enough," Lone said. "We told the second one—some long-winded galoot in a brown hat—that we could manage by ourselves and rode on past."

"Brown hat . . . that'd be Archie." The woman frowned. "I'm surprised ye got by him. He's usually a mite prickly when it comes to dealin' with folks."

"Oh, he didn't abandon us completely," Lone told her. "He followed us in. When he got here, he cut across the plaza to a sort of church lookin' building across the way."

"So he went to report to Pap."

"Who is 'Pap'?" asked Lucinda, speaking for the first time.

The woman gave her a look. "Boy, ye are new around here, ain't ye? Pap is Pap Binder, he-bull of the whole show around here."

"Mayor and governor and Lord High Hoople of all he surveys, eh?" quipped Lone.

Now the woman shot him a look. "Ye best take the snottiness out'n yer tone if'n ye know what's good fer ye, bub. Pap hears you crowded past Archie 'thout bein' brought in proper-like he ain't gonna like it. He's bound to be comin' over to 'front ye about it. Ye get off on an even worse foot by failin' to show proper respect, I wouldn't want to be in yer boots."

The solitary drinker from down the bar came sauntering up. He was a thin, hard-looking number with a wedge-shaped face and brooding eyes. A black-handled hogleg rested in a silver-trimmed black leather holster slung low on his hip. "There gonna be trouble, Hester?" he asked the stubby woman.

Lone turned to face him. "Why? You lookin' for a piece of some?"

The wedge-faced man stopped short. "Take it easy, mister. More trouble is the last thing I want. I already got a wagon load followin' me around. All I want to know is if Pap is on his way here in one of his black moods so if he is, I can take a bottle and find someplace else to be."

Hester frowned around a puff of her cigarette, saying, "I don't know what to expect fer sure, Brick. Pap ain't likely to be pleased hearin' Archie got crowded past. But special doin's like is scheduled for in the mornin' usually puts him in a mighty high mood. So maybe—if this stranger can keep a respectful tongue in his head—he won't get too riled."

"I don't go out of my way to be disrespectful to nobody," said Lone. "But that cuts both ways. Bein' stood out in the bakin' hot sun answerin' a string of pointless questions don't rate as showin' respect *to* me. So I reacted in kind."

"Yeah, well that's yer story," Hester countered. "But how it rates to Pap's way of thinkin' is what counts. There's what ye need to keep in mind if ye knows what's good fer ye."

From one of the card games going on across the room, a man called, "Hey, Hester! How about a couple fresh pitchers of beer over here! Winnin' all these hands from this bunch of amateurs is makin' me plumb parched."

Hester dropped her cigarette butt on the floor and ground it underfoot before turning to waddle in the direction of the shouting man. "I'm comin', I'm comin', ye thirsty thirsty rascals. There better be a good tip left on that table at the end of yer game for all the runnin' I'm doin' to serve ye. If there ain't, the next time ye come 'round I'll be puttin' bar rag squeezin's in yer drinks!"

When she was out of earshot, Brick said to Lone and Lucinda, "She means it, too. Only catch is, I don't think she uses a bar rag to wipe down much of anything in this dump."

Lone smiled wryly. "Good thing it has at least a

few high-class customers like us to keep it from hittin' rock bottom, eh?"

Brick returned his grin. "Yeah. Good thing . . . my name's Brick Holland, by the way."

"I'm Trent. My lady friend is . . . Lola."

"Trent," Brick repeated with a nod. Then, pinching his hat: "Pleasure's mine, Miss Lola."

Lone placed his Yellowboy casually on top of the plank bar. "So what's the story on this Pap character who might be on his way to skin some bark off me? He really that much of a holy terror?"

Brick thumbed back the brim of his Stetson. "He's a rough old cob, no doubt about it. Him and his two sons, Mase and Romer, keep a mighty tight squeeze on things around here. Even the hardest of the hard cases who come here to light for a spell tend to toe the line during their stay."

"Then it's probably best you amble on back where you were. Or better yet, have Hester fetch you that bottle and go enjoy it somewhere in peace," Lone advised him. "Been a pleasure talkin' with you. But if I'm in for the rawhidin' it sounds like might be comin' my way, you bein' caught in our company might not be a smart thing."

Brick eyed Lone up and down. His eyes flicked to the Yellowboy for a moment, then back to the former scout. "On second thought," he drawled,

"I think I'll stick around. Might be a show I don't want to miss."

"Suit yourself," Lone allowed.

"In that case, speaking of shows," said Lucinda. "What did the old woman mean before when she spoke of 'special doings' scheduled for in the morning."

Brick's face scrunched into an uncomfortable expression. He turned his head and thrust his chin toward the middle of the room. "Over there," he said. "That poor bastard is set to be the main attraction."

Lone and Lucinda turned their heads and their eyes followed the line of his pointing chin. What they saw, previously unnoticed in the gloomy center of the room away from the lamplight over the gaming tables and the lantern burning softly behind the bar, blurred by the layers of tobacco smoke hanging belong the ceiling like wisps of fog, was a thick, flat-faced support beam with a man lashed to it. The unfortunate was stripped to the waist and barefoot. His torso was streaked with dirt and numerous scrapes and cuts, partially scabbed over with dried blood. He appeared to be unconscious, his head hanging down so his face couldn't be clearly seen; but enough of it was visible to show it was bruised and battered. A rope was wrapped around his waist and tied loosely to the beam. Both of his arms were yanked to full extension above his head, wrists bound together and the binding hung over a railroad spike pounded into the beam. Suspended in this manner, even with his legs fully extended, only the balls of his feet touched the floor to support his weight. When his legs tired and sagged, such as now, all of his weight hung on the wrist bindings and his painfully stretched arms.

Lone didn't make the connection right away.

Not until Lucinda suddenly caught her breath and gasped, *"Jaime!"*

Chapter Thirty

Brick Holland's forehead puckered into a ladder of deep seams. "You know that hombre?" he asked.

Lone grabbed Lucinda by the arm, partly to brace her and partly to hold her back from rushing to her brother. "Our paths have crossed," he told Brick in a flat tone. "Not necessarily in a good way . . . but, damn, that don't mean I like seein' him done like this."

"I know what you mean," conceded Brick. "But be careful about saying it too loud."

"If he's the main attraction for tomorrow, what the hell's left after he's already been put through this?" Lone wanted to know.

Brick looked around to make sure Hester was still back at the card table, having served the pitchers of beer and sticking around for a minute to trade barbs with the men. "It's something they call the Choosing Ceremony. I ain't exactly sure what all it involves. But it's a big bust-out, everybody's mighty excited. The whole town's expected to turn out—leastways all who are part of the Binder clan." Beneath a conspiratorial scowl, his eyes darted back and forth between Lone and Lucinda. "You realize they're all crazier than a nest of cockroaches feasting on locoweed, don't you? A tainted harvest traceable back to one original sick seed, if you know what I mean."

Lone grimaced. "So what did this fella hangin' over there on the post—Jaime Rodero, we know him as—do to rile the clan so bad?"

Lucinda twisted around and gripped the plank bar, her knuckles turning instantly white, unable to bear looking at her brother without rushing to try and comfort him.

Answering Lone, Brick said, "Yeah, Rodero is the same name he gave here. What he did was, he, uh, dipped his cup in somebody else's punch bowl . . . dipped it all the way up to the wrist maybe, depending on how many of the accusations against him you choose to believe."

"You've been real friendly and open, Brick," Lone said through clenched teeth. "But I ain't hardly in a mood for riddles."

"Awright! The young fool got caught dallying with one of the Binder women. Is that plain enough?" Brick cast another quick glance in Hester's direction before continuing. "It's one of Pap's most strictly enforced rules and it's made crystal clear to every buck showing up here—hands off the clan gals. Even worse, the one Rodero got tangled up with was Betty Belle, youngest daughter of Mase, Pap's oldest son, and already promised to marry one of Hermoine's boys. Hermoine, that's Pap's widowed sister-in-law who runs the general store next door. Hester, the charmer you've already met running things here in the saloon, she's his *other* widowed sister-in-law."

"Jesus," muttered Lone. "The old boy for sure believes in keepin' it all in the family."

"Yeah. *Everything* is kept in this family," said Brick wryly. "Seems one of the only ones who don't hold very strictly to that practice is none other than little miss Betty Belle. Truth be known, it was more likely her who initiated the dallying Rodero got involved in. Betty Belle's got a real hunger to try out new outsiders when they first show up for a stay in Binderville. Me and plenty of others can attest to that—we were just lucky enough to dodge her or at least not get caught if we weren't able to. Seems young Rodero wasn't so lucky."

Before the discussion could go any farther, there came the low rumble of voices and the sound of shifting, jostling bodies from outside the open front entrance. A vaguely familiar voice said, "Yeah, them's ther horses. They's still inside." A moment later, there was a heavy clumping of boots and then three men came striding in.

Lone turned leisurely to give them a once-over.

There was no mistaking which one was Pap Binder. He walked ahead of the other two, a tall, heavyset man well into his sixties who pushed his massive gut boldly out in front of himself, like it was a weapon or a shield. He was hatless, bald on top with stringy white hair trailing down onto the back of his bull neck and bushy sideburns nearly obscuring his ears. His face was fleshy, florid, nothing remarkable about its features. His attire was baggy, pin-striped trousers stuffed into high-topped boots. Bright red suspenders held them up, hooking over his thick shoulders encased in a shirt made of the same murky gray material as the lookouts back on the trail wore.

Speaking of lookouts, the brown-hatted one, Archie, had come in with Pap, though lagging several steps behind.

The third arrival bore a strong resemblance to Pap, obviously one of his sons. Equally tall, about thirty years younger, stocky build though running more to muscle than fat. Thick brown hair with a faint reddish tint, same facial features but with a brooding scowl that looked like it seldom lifted. He, too, wore a gray homespun shirt, along with denim bib overalls having only one strap hooked over a beefy shoulder. Around his waist was strapped a gun belt of worn, cracked leather but with a gleaming, ivory-handled Colt riding high in the holster.

"Ye thar, stranger," Pap addressed Lone in a booming voice. "Ye the feller was rude to my grandson out on the trail and then came bargin' on into town 'thout hearin' the rules and not bein' led in proper-like?"

Lone eyed him some more, taking his time responding. He could feel Lucinda go rigid beside him and had a pretty good hunch she was staring daggers at the he-bull. He was aware that the chatter around the card tables near the back of the room had gone quiet. He was also aware that Brick Holland had sidled several steps back down the bar.

Lone gave a jut of his chin toward Archie, then said to Pap, "Is that your grandson there in the brown hat?"

" 'Tis indeed."

"Is he some kind of official representative of your town?"

Pap's shaggy brows furled. "He's a Binder, ain't he? All Binders represent Binderville!"

"Okay. If he'd've explained any of that and mentioned how there was rules and laws to follow," Lone said, "instead ploppin' himself in the middle of the road askin' pointless questions, then I might have treated him different . . . on the other hand, I ain't so sure even then. The notion of bein' led anywhere, like a dog on a leash, don't set real easy in my gut."

Pap cocked his head. "Oh. So ye think yer special, is that it? Kinda ornery and inny . . . inder . . ."

"Independent, Pa," said his son, supplying the

word the old man was struggling to spit out.

"Yeah—independent," Pap growled, like the word put a bad taste in his mouth. "Wal, ye can get that notion out'n yer head right quick, bub! In my town, on my mountain, ain't nobody calls they own shots. *I* set the rules and *I* got the final say on what's what . . . and one of my rules, and this kind of a new one on account of I never had call to lay it down before, is that I don't cotton to bein' glared at by no woman the way that one of yern is doin' right now!"

He looked over at his son and said, in a very stern and businesslike manner, "Be sure to remember that one, Mase, and see it gets added to the official list."

"Got it, Pa."

While that exchange was taking place, Lone glanced over at Lucinda and saw that, sure enough, her eyes were throwing enough heat Pap's way to melt a pewter spoon. He gave her a subtle nudge as a signal for her to try and ease up some.

Pap's eyes cut back to Lone. "Now then. Yer here. Not in a way I like very much but, since some things have been ironed out more clear, maybe we can get past that bad start and reach an understandin' fer goin' forward."

"Let's hope so," Lone agreed. Then, jabbing a thumb to indicate Jaime hanging on the support beam, he added, "I take it there's an example of somebody who *didn't* reach a proper understandin'?"

Pap chuckled. "Ye got that right, bub. Smart of ye to notice. We can talk more about him in a minute. Ye came at a good time. If ye're still here tomorrow, ye'll be on hand to see some special doin's where he's concerned . . . but first, let's finish talkin' about ye and yer woman. What brings ye to Binderville and how long ye figurin' to stick around?"

Lone's mind was racing. The situation as it stood before them now was considerably different than what he and Lucinda had expected to be faced with. Yet the story they had concocted for dealing with Manolito would, to Lone's way of thinking, still fit this change. In fact, in a bitterly ironic way, it might actually fit even better. There was still the unaddressed matter of where *was* Manolito and his gang, but that would have to wait its turn. First things first, as the old saying went.

Lone flicked another quick glance at Lucinda, hoping she could continue to hold herself in check and would be savvy enough to keep up with the bit of improvisation he was about to launch.

Meeting Pap's shrewd gaze full on, the former scout said, "I think we both know what usually brings folks to Binderville, don't we? My woman and me rode in here plannin' on goin' with that same line—that we were lookin' for a place to lay low for an indefinite amount of time and we heard this was the place where arrangements could be made to do that sort of thing."

Pap's face scrunched up. "Ye're slingin' around a lot of big words, and I don't like that. Cut to it—If ye ain't here fer the usual reasons, what are ye up to?"

Lone tilted his head to once again indicate Jaime. "Him. We came lookin' to fetch him back with us."

"That lowdown piece of trash?' blurted Mase, stepping part way around his father. "Ye sayin' ye're friends of his?"

"Not hardly." Lone gave a firm shake of his head. "We came to get our hands on him and haul the skunk back to fulfill an obligation."

"I warned ye about them big words," Pap growled. "Ye sayin' ye came to collect a debt? Money?"

"No, nothing like that." Lone hung his head for a moment and acted as if reluctant to go into more detail. Then: "Look, this is embarrassin' for my woman to have me talk about . . . and I don't know what this wretch has done wrong here . . . but back where we come from, he left a baby growin' in a young woman's belly. No marriage. The gal in trouble is my woman's sister and, though I don't understand why, the poor vulnerable thing thinks she's still in love with this rat and wants him back to be a husband and father."

There was a long moment of seemingly stunned silence. Pap, Mase, and Archie just stood gaping at Lone. Slipping a quick glance over at Lucinda, Lone was relieved to see that she appeared to be going along with his act, hanging her head as if in shame.

Then, all of a sudden, Pap threw back his head and roared with laughter.

Chapter Thirty-One

Once the old man stopped cackling long enough to catch his breath, he thumbed tears out of his eyes and said, "Ye'll have to pardon me, Mr. Independent. I ain't makin' light of yer trouble or yer woman's shame. I purely ain't. But what ye just told us about yer dealin's with this scoundrel is too much of a coony . . . colly . . ."

"Coincidence, I think is the word yer searchin' fer, Pa," said Mase, who had remained pointedly somber during Pap's outburst of laughter.

"Yeah, that's the one," Pap declared. "It's a plumb coincy-dince, yer reasons fer comin' after this rascal. Ye'll see why when I tell ye . . . ye know what? Let's set down and gab this over some. It's too rich to rush through." He gestured to a nearby table with some chairs around it. Starting toward these, he turned his head and hollered across the room, "Hester! Get down here and fetch us some drinks, woman!" Before sitting down, Pap said to Archie, "Get back to yer lookout post, boy. Try not to let any more ornery cusses get by you . . . less'n you can guarantee they be as entertainin' as Mr. Independent here." Then he laughed some more.

Pap, Mase, Lucinda, and Lone took seats at a table off to one side of Jaime. He continued to hang, motionless and unconscious. Lucinda sat with her back to him so she didn't have to look at his torment.

When Hester arrived, Pap said, "A pitcher of cold beer would be just the thing for this hot day. That suit ye, Mr. Independent?"

"Sounds good."

Pap's eyes went to Lucinda. "Yer woman bein' Mezkin, I reckon she'd prolly favor some tequila instead?"

Lucinda's eyes flared, but to a controlled degree. "I am capable of speaking and answering questions for myself, Senor. If you have it, yes, I would appreciate a glass of tequila, *por favor*."

"You heard her," Pap said to Hester. She turned and waddled away. Pap's gaze rested on Lucinda for a moment, then cut to Lone. He chuckled. "I'm thinkin' ye got yerself a bit of a spitfire there, Mr. Independent. But then, that prolly suits you, eh?"

"We get along," Lone replied.

Pap continued to eye him. "Callin' ye Mr. Independent is gettin' kinda long-winded. What name ye go by?"

"I'm Trent. This is Lola."

"Trent and Lola. Ye make a handsome pair. Everybody calls me Pap, as I guess ye've heard."

"Pap it is."

"I gotta be honest, though . . . and meanin' no personal offense, Lola ma'am . . . but I don't generally cotton to Mezkins. Purty as ye are, ye surely rate an exception. But anyway, that's why I changed the name of this town," Pap boasted. "Useta be called Hernando Heights. Named by the Mezkins who founded it and started the old mission across the plaza. Where I live now. But when it became my town and my mountain, ye can bet I changed it. Binderville—now that's a red-blooded *American* name!"

Lone made a gesture to once again indicate Jaime and said dryly, "Is that what he's guilty of . . . bein' too Mexican for Binderville?"

Mase thrust forward in his chair. "What kind of smart-mouth remark is that? You might be amusin' to my pa, mister, but I ain't much liked yer tone from the first."

"Back off, son!" Pap said sharply. "I'm handlin' this."

Hester arrived just then with a tray containing a pitcher of beer, three mugs, and a glass of tequila. She placed the tray in the middle of the table then quickly departed.

When she was gone, Pap hitched forward as far as his gut would allow and began distributing the drinks. First he handed Lucinda her tequila. Then he slowly, methodically poured the beer, filling each mug and pushing one to Lone, one to his son.

After taking a long pull of his own drink and leaving a dripping smear of foam on his top lip,

Pap rested his gaze on Lone and said, "To answer yer question about the decoration we got hangin' yonder . . . yeah, in a manner of speakin', what put him thar has to do with him bein' Mezkin."

"Was up to me," Mase snarled, "he wouldn't be hangin' nowhere. The filthy bag of meat would be dead and buried!"

Ignoring this outburst and taking another swallow of his beer, Pap said, "The thing 'bout Mezkins that puts me on edge, see, is knowin' their blood ain't pure like white folks. Again meanin' no personal offense, Lola ma'am. I'm talkin' mainly 'bout the males. Mezkins, Injuns, niggers . . . they's all the same. The impure blood in the bucks has got too much animal rut in it. They can't help it, I reckon. But that don't change the fact they can't ever be trusted around decent, white womenfolk."

Pap paused to heave a great, weary sigh. "Still, I try to be tolerant. Like the Good Book says. After all, I tell myself, they's God's critters."

"Wolves and rattlesnakes and the like is God's critters too," Mase huffed. "But you don't invite 'em in friendly-like to take a chomp out'n ye."

"I draw the line sharp and hard on Injuns and niggers," Pap said flatly. "You won't ever see any of either in Binderville, by gar! But Mezkins, in spite of my rester . . . restiv . . ."

"Reservations, Pa," Mase said somewhat wearily.

"Right. In spite of my reservations," Pap continued, "I make certain allowances fer Mezkins. After all, like I said, they founded this place. They's still a few of the originals scattered around up in the hills. What am I gonna do—hunt 'em down and throw 'em off my mountain?"

The rhetorical question hung in the air for a moment and gave Lone the chance to slip in a question of his own, one that had been building in him increasingly stronger. "One of the reasons we came to Binderville lookin' for this particular skunk," he said, "is that he was overheard to claim he was on his way to join up with some friends who were already here—a gang from down along the border led by an hombre named Manolito. But since that bunch, and certainly Manolito himself, is mostly made up of Mexicans, then I guess his information about them bein' here was mistaken, eh?"

"Because, yer thinkin', thar's no way I'd allow a whole passel of Mezkins to settle here for a spell. That what yer askin'?" Pap prodded.

"I was just goin' by the things you've been sayin', that's all."

"Well, ye got it wrong! Only a foolish man'd let his personal feelin's about a thing get in the way of doin' smart bidness," Pap stated somewhat heatedly. The way he shot a sidelong glance over at Mase made Lone think the old he-bull had already had some kind of disagreement with his son over this very thing. Bringing his eyes back to Lone, Pap continued, "Matter of fact, Manolito and his bunch did show up here and I did decide to do bidness with 'em. Yeah, they was all Mezkins. But after I laid down the rules and laws of Binderville, me and Manolito looked eye to eye and I could see that he was enough like me—a man who ruled his bunch with an iron fist—so that when he gave his word his men would toe the mark I could trust, by gar, he'd make sure they did."

"So they're still here then?" Lone asked, surprised and a little perplexed.

Pap shook his head. "No, not right at present they ain't. They rode out the day before the one over thar showed up lookin' fer 'em. It was only 'cuz he said he was a friend of theirs, and I knew Manolito would be comin' back that I made the mistake of lettin' this lone buck stay."

"You say Manolito will be returning?" questioned Lucinda.

It was Mase who answered. "That's his plan. After him and his had been here a few days, some of 'em got to jawin' with a couple Coloradans who was on hand and was keen on a job up Pueblo way, but needed more men to get it done. Manolito decided he liked the sound of it, so he agreed to throw in with them Coloradans. They rode off together to take care of it. All goes well, they figure to come back and sit tight again fer a while."

Pap frowned. "Why are ye so interested in Manolito?"

"We're not, particularly," said Lone. He paused, flashed a rueful smile. "It's just that, all the way here, me and Lola been frettin' how willin' Manolito was likely to be when it came to lettin' us ride off with a member of his gang. Now, it turns out, he ain't even here."

Pap's frown deepened. "Maybe not. But I hope ye understand that, Manolito or no, it don't make the decoration pinned on that thar beam some kind of apple on a branch waitin' to be plucked off by just anybody. He's got hisself a, whatycall, prior ing . . . ing . . ."

"Engagement." This time it was Lone who supplied the word Pap was trying to come up with. This earned the former scout an even more unfavorable look from Mase than the ones he'd already been getting.

"Yeah, *engagement,*" Pap proclaimed. "That buck has got hisself an engagement come tomorrow mornin'—special doin's the whole town is het up to see. And no matter if the dirty deed he done Lola's sister happened first, what he done here is the one gonna get took care of. Plain and simple."

Lone ground his teeth. "Yeah, I had a hunch it was shapin' up that way. Reckon our questions about Manolito interrupted you tellin' what it was the varmint did here and what's in store for him as a result."

"What the foul villain did," Pap said after a big gulp of his beer, "goes to what I was sayin' before about the animal rut that drives his kind on account of ther tainted blood. The cur tried to force hisself on a Binder woman, an innocent young thing who was tricked by what was truly on his filthy mind!"

"*My* daughter," growled Mase. "I hadn't been held back, even after he was stopped short of ruinin' her, he'd be dog meat right now—not hangin' there with breath still in him!"

"Calm down, son," Pap said soothingly, placing a hand on Mase's shoulder. "Betty Belle is also my granddaughter, remember. But they's laws for this kind of thing, and we got to foller 'em same as everybody else. Proper justice will be served tomorrow. Believe that."

"This justice is the 'special doin's' you have spoken of?" Lucinda asked.

"That's right. I'm sorry to say it will rob yer sister of the husband and baby's father she's pinin' fer," Pap said, sounding genuinely sincere. "But surely you must know in yer heart that a no-good critter like what's over there wouldn't ever be true to her and would only torment her more. Let her be free of him . . . which she'll be when we's done with him here."

At that moment, Jaime stirred and groaned, showing signs of regaining consciousness for at least a moment. The balls of his feet pressed down on the floor and his trembling legs braced, momentarily relieving what had to be excruciating pain on his overstretched arms.

Something glinted in Lucinda's eyes. "Yes, I know you are right," she told Pap. "I promised my sister I would try to bring this cheat and liar back to her, but all the while I knew he would never be good *for* her or *to* her. I am *glad* it is working out this way—that we will not succeed in our attempt."

Pap smiled. "Ye are a wise woman. And a good sister, even if yer younger one never knows to fully appreciate it."

The glint in Lucinda's eyes flashed brighter. "Can I speak for a moment with the prisoner? I want this last chance to tell him what I truly think of him for what he has done to my sister, for the pain and shame he has visited on my whole family. I want him to meet his end knowing how much he is *loathed* so it is left to writhe in his mind for the eternity he will be spending in Hell!"

Pap's shaggy brows lifted high. "Whooee! Ye are one fired up gal, ain't ye?" He rolled his eyes over to Lone. "When I said ye had yerself a spitfire here, Trent, I wasn't wrong, by gar. Ye better watch yerself 'round this'n."

"Don't worry. I will," Lone assured him.

"My request, Senor. May I proceed?" Lucinda pressed.

Pap waved a hand. "Have at it. Long as ye ain't comfortin' him none."

Lucinda stood up, seizing her barely touched glass of tequila. "That is hardly my intent. I just want him alert enough to understand what I am saying to him."

She reached Jaime in three long strides and immediately flung the contents of the glass in his face. He gasped and sputtered and lifted his head. As soon as he did, Lucinda jammed her face close to his and cut loose in a loud, rapid-fire burst of Spanish that made the whole barroom ring. She stood with fists planted on hips, her lips curled back and her brows furled angrily as she continued to bombard him relentlessly with her words.

Pretty soon everybody in earshot was wearing sheepish grins and muttering under their breath, grateful it wasn't them on the receiving end of such a blistering dressing-down. None of them understood what was being said, they just knew they wouldn't have wanted any direct part of it.

Even stone-faced Mase managed a wry smile and remarked, "Man, is she tyin' into him. If'n words was knife blades, he'd be sliced to ribbons by now."

Only Lone realized what truly was going on. He

didn't understand hardly any of the words either, yet he nevertheless knew the message. Despite her gesturing and outward display of anger, the words Lucinda was pouring on her brother were actually ones of love and encouragement and promises of aid, pleading for him to just hold onto hope a little while longer.

Chapter Thirty-Two

The murkiness of dusk had the room shot full of long, sharp-edged shadows when Lone and Lucinda came through the door carrying their saddlebags and other gear. It was a second-floor space of the "Hotel" that they had secured for the night from Hermoine down in the general store. The structure's thick stone walls and sturdy flooring between its different levels kept the din from the ground floor saloon reasonably muted.

There was a wall-mounted coal oil lantern to one side of the doorway. Lone dumped his load on the room's only bed and then stepped back to snap a match to the lantern. When the wick was turned up it cast everything in an orangish-gold glow and chased away the pattern of shadows. Lucinda also deposited her gear on the bed before going to the window and adjusting the heavy canvas shade three-quarters of the way down. The room was relatively cool but not so much that it was desirable to shut out the evening breeze entirely.

Apart from the bed—a wide, lumpy-looking affair with a scarred wooden headboard and a matching night stand, equally scarred and additionally pocked with cigarette burns—there was a three-drawer dresser pressed flat against one wall and a washstand with a smeared, cracked mirror situated diagonally in one corner. A straight-backed wooden chair was hitched up to the washstand and a second chair, with a mashed-down horsehair seat, occupied the opposite corner.

Lucinda turned from the window and said, "Ordinarily I might make a less than flattering remark about such accommodations . . . but considering how my brother will be spending the night, I hardly have the right to complain."

Lone grimaced. "I know it's hard, but for right now, for tonight, try to blot out the image of how you saw him."

"You have no idea how impossible that is. What's worse, everything he *has* endured and *is* enduring is all based on a lie! Jaime was able to gasp to me—just as Brick Holland suggested—that it was the puta Betty Belle who slipped uninvited into his room and was making demands of the flesh when they got caught. All of which she then denied and turned into false accusation." Lucinda's voice trailed off in an anguished tone. Then: "Where is that bottle of tequila we purchased downstairs?"

Lone dug into his saddlebags and produced the requested item. He held it out to her. "Looks like the maid somewhere forgot to lay out the crystal drinking glasses. You want a tin cup from my mess kit?"

"Don't trouble yourself," Lucinda replied. She broke the seal on the bottle and hoisted it high for a long pull. Lowering it, she took a quick intake of breath, then said, "Not a very ladylike display, I know. But I am not feeling particularly ladylike at the moment."

"You got a right to feel however you want," Lone told her. "But it might be best to go a little easy on that stuff. You only pecked at your supper earlier. Liquor hits harder on an empty stomach and you don't want to be hungover for what we're gonna need to deal with tomorrow."

Lucinda made a frustrated gesture with one hand. "What *are* we going to have to deal with tomorrow? After all the talking and the veiled threats and the Mexican insults, we still have no clear idea what are these 'special doin's' in store for Jaime in the morning!"

Sad to say, she was right. Following her false tirade against her brother in the saloon—which, as Lone had recognized, was in truth a disguised way to let him know help was at hand and not to give up hope—Pap and Mase had soon parted company with them and went to attend other matters. Lone and Lucinda were cautioned to learn and adhere to all Binderville rules and warned specifically against plotting anything to achieve their own ends where the prisoner was concerned. Otherwise, they were ostensibly free to go about town as they wished. It didn't take long, however, before Lone spotted the fact they were being covertly shadowed wherever they went.

Pretending *not* to have noticed this, they proceeded to drift around idly and get somewhat acclimated to the layout. They talked a bit more with Brick Holland and a few others he introduced them to, and generally prepared for at least a night's stay. This included stabling their horses and arranging for the room they were now occupying. At Brick's recommendation, they took supper at a small, out-of-the-way diner on a short side street just off the plaza. The food was basic but not bad, even though Lucinda could not fake an appetite. Otherwise, all things considered, she was holding up remarkably well.

A back corner of the diner, where they requested to be seated, had provided their first chance to talk privately and freely practically since arriving in Binderville. Unfortunately, there hadn't been a lot to share. Lucinda did relate that, at a couple moments when she had her face jammed up near Jaime's during her false tirade, he'd been able to mumble recognition and an understanding she represented a ray of hope. Knowing she had gotten through to him at least that much had greatly buoyed her resolve to keep going. But still, seeing him like that and then having to leave him in such misery was extremely difficult. Adding to it was the frustration of not yet getting a straight answer to what was in store for him in the morning. It kept coming back around to mentions of something called the Choosing Ceremony and then mysterious indications that whatever came next would mark a grim finale.

Which was where they were right back to again now, with Lucinda expressing her anguish here in this drab stone hotel room.

Lone took the bottle of tequila from her and threw down a slug for himself. He'd never been a fan of tequila, and now he was reminded why. It tasted like shit and burned like hell. He said, "Look, I don't have any exact answers because I don't know all the goddamn questions yet. Like you, I don't know what the Choosing Ceremony is or what comes after. But I know this much . . . I kept my eyes open while we were strollin' around earlier and I saw a few things we can do that will amount to some rough preparations aimed to cover a range of what I think *might* happen."

Lucinda's eyes widened. "Truly? Or are you just trying to make me feel better?"

Lone grinned crookedly. "That, too. But there ain't no advantage for me to lay out false hope. I see givin' it to you straight and blunt as the best bet for all of us. You, your brother . . . and me, if you don't mind me givin' my own hide some consideration too."

"I could hardly hold that against you. So give it to me straight and blunt. Tell me some of these rough preparations you have in mind."

Lone handed her the bottle back and then reached down and gave the edge of her serape a little flip. "Well, for starters, I'm thinkin' this thing is prime for playin' an added part I never had in mind before. Yeah, it'll still hide some of your natural curves. But if I can get it rigged up proper, I got a hunch it could come handy for also hidin' some other curves. Specifically, the shape of a Greener shotgun . . ."

Chapter Thirty-Three

The next morning dawned bright and clear. No breeze, not the faintest wisp of a cloud in the sky. In a couple of hours, the plaza would be an oven. The "big doin's" were scheduled to start at nine. The expected crowd of onlookers for that would only make things hotter.

Lone woke early. Wrapped up his bedroll, and went to stand at the open window for a while. The morning air pushing against his face still had some crispness to it. Down on the edge of the plaza, he watched a handful of women and kids who were putting up stands and tables. With a sour twist to his mouth, Lone recognized the signs of what this was—making ready for serving food and drink to those who would be assembling before long. The fun, festive side to whatever lay in store for Jaime Rodero. Same as what took place when ghoulish, thrill-hungry throngs gathered to enjoy a good hanging.

Lone turned and regarded Lucinda sleeping in the bed. Sleeping finally. Not surprisingly, she had tossed and turned through much of the night before at last finding some rest. Lone had slept atop his bedroll spread on the floor. Lucinda had insisted they could share the wide bed—as long as it was only for sleeping. Lone politely but firmly declined. He didn't want to admit to her (nor to himself, when it came right down to it) that he didn't trust what might happen in the wee hours after lying for a time next to a woman of Lucinda's voluptuousness. After all, he wasn't made of stone.

While Lucinda continued to sleep, Lone stripped off his shirt and got cleaned up at the meager wash station. When he was done, he put his shirt and vest back on then pitched the basin of used water out the window. From one of the canteens they'd brought up to the room, he refilled the pitcher so Lucinda would have fresh water for her ablutions.

He completed getting dressed by stomping into his boots and buckling on his gun belt. Next he woke Lucinda and informed her he would leave her to get washed up in private while he went out for a little while to have another look at things in the daylight and would bring back some breakfast.

Downstairs, Lone found the saloon empty and quiet. Except for a couple of snoring drunks— one sprawled across a table, the other on the floor—sleeping off the effects of last night's drinking. What held Lone's interest far more than that was the absence of Jaime Rodero from the support beam where he'd been hanging. Lone wanted to believe he'd been taken somewhere less torturous. Perhaps some variation of the condemned man getting a last meal . . . not that that was an altogether comforting thought.

Outside, he took a slow walk around the perimeter of the plaza. More food and drink tables were being set up and a few additional people were beginning to straggle in, early arrivals for the upcoming entertainment. These all appeared to be Binder "clan" members. There was no sign of the outlaws or hard cases, men like Brick Holland, who were laying low here in Binderville and whiled away their time mostly in and around the saloon. The clan folk tended to be easy to spot, largely due to the preponderance of homespun clothing that didn't vary much in color or style and also the suspicious, humorless eyes that tracked openly and endlessly. It was hard to miss the signs of inbreeding, some of it disturbingly obvious and difficult to look at, most of it to lesser degrees.

One from the latter category, a pinch-faced little mutt with close-set eyes under a single ledge of furry black brow—the primary shadow Lone had spotted following him and Lucinda the previous evening—showed up again this morning about half way through Lone's meandering. The former scout had a notion to march back and give the mutt a chewing out not only for his sloppy work but for arriving on the job tardy. He talked himself out of it, though.

Lone took time for a stop at the livery stable

to check on Ironsides and Conquistador, making sure they were receiving good care. At the same time he also gave the other horses present a good looking over and decided on one who made the best prospect for a good third mount—Jaime's—if it worked out they had to beat a hasty withdrawal away from here. One of the "rough preparations" Lone planned on making, when the crowd was at its peak just before the actual event began, was to slip unseen back to the livery long enough to get three horses saddled and ready in case said withdrawal became suddenly necessary.

The final stop of Lone's morning tour was the little diner where he and Lucinda had eaten last evening. He bought four breakfast burritos wrapped in waxed paper and a clay pot filled with strong black coffee that he took back to the hotel room.

Lucinda washed up, dressed, and standing at the window when he came in. She looked fresh and radiant in the wash of sunlight pouring over her. Her hair was glossy from a vigorous brushing, her skin a rich cinnamon color. And the way she filled out her blouse, unbuttoned at the throat with the serape not yet donned, reminded Lone once again why it had been best for him to sleep on the floor.

They hitched chairs up to the side of the bed, spread the paper-wrapped burritos on the blanket, poured coffee into tin cups Lone produced from his gear.

"I am famished from not eating last night," Lucinda announced as she bit into one of the tacos. "Which is a good thing since these burritos are so far below the quality of the ones my Carlos serves." Despite this lament, she seemed in surprisingly high—though measured—spirits. "After the long hours of waiting and not knowing fully what to expect," she explained, "I just want the time to be at hand so we can decide what it will take to try and get Jaime out of the hands of these strange, menacing people."

Lone told her how he had found Jaime missing from the beam in the saloon. She wanted to find hope in that, hope he was experiencing conditions less cruel and painful. Lone joined her in that, but he had reservations about the lad's treatment being a whole lot better.

He also told Lucinda about his visit to the livery and locking on a third horse he planned to make ready, when the time was right, for Jaime's mount. "If it comes to tryin' for a flat bust-out," he explained once again, "it will be a big advantage for us to be on horseback while the plaza is clogged by a crowd of everybody else on foot."

Lucinda nodded. "And the arsenal of guns you have assembled for us is what we will use, if necessary, to gain the horses. I understand that much. But once we manage to break out of the plaza and ride away from town—what then?" Her expression grew concerned. "Judging by what we saw, Jaime will be in poor condition to hold up for a long, hard ride. What if a horde of those creepy clansman give chase? You really believe we can outdistance them?"

"Let me worry about that. I ain't out of ideas yet," Lone told her. What he had in mind was, if they successfully escaped as far as the wagon road leading back down the mountain, there were enough narrow spots in it where he could lag back and hold off any pursuit for hours. Hell, a day and maybe more if he had to. Long enough for Lucinda and Jaime to gain a safe distance. And when it came for him to finally pull out and kick up some dust of his own, he had no doubt that Ironsides could run any hayburner they sent after him plumb into the ground.

But Lone wasn't ready to go into those details with Lucinda just now. He didn't want to hear her protests or have her weighed down by extra worry for his safety.

"Speakin' of our arsenal," Lone said, lowering his cup after washing down a last bite of burrito. "It's time we start gettin' the pieces properly distributed. We're gonna want to get on down to the plaza pretty soon. Crowd's gatherin'. We'll need to claim a good spot."

The next handful of minutes were spent

checking weapons and then outfitting their persons. Lone would have the big Peacemaker on his hip, the Colt Lightning tucked at the small of his back, and would be carrying his Yellowboy. Lucinda would have both the Baby Russian and the Walker Colt tucked in a wide sash around her waist. Her serape would cover these. The heaviest firepower, the double-barreled Greener, would also be worn by her under the serape. It would hang down the middle of her back, suspended by a leather thong looped up over her left shoulder and knotted there. A single yank on the tail of the knot would loosen it and free the Greener to be pulled—by Lucinda or Lone, either one—out from under the serape and into action.

With the handguns in place and Lone's Yellowboy resting temporarily on the bed, they practiced "drawing" the Greener several times until Lone was satisfied they had it down pretty good.

"Okay," he said. "Reckon all that's left is to go down and finally find out what the 'big doin's' is. And then, once we do, let everybody else find out how we feel about it."

"How I feel right now, with all this iron on me," Lucinda replied, "is like a display in a hardware store."

Lone grinned. "Just remember. All that iron *on* you is a good counter against endin' up with lead *in* you."

Chapter Thirty-Four

A few minutes short of nine. The eastern side of the plaza was packed with scores of people arranged in a C-shaped pattern facing in toward the center. All of them, as far as Lone could tell, appeared to be clan folk. He further judged that some of them must have come from higher up in the hills since his earlier wandering about the town had given him no sense of this many citizens occupying the numerous rundown buildings. Wherever they came from, an excited, jovial mood ran through the lot of them. There was laughter and calling back and forth while clusters of little kids darted in and out between their legs. The vendors at the tables Lone had seen being set up earlier were busy dishing out sandwiches, donuts, hard-boiled eggs, chunks of boiled ham on sharpened twigs, coffee and wine, and sweetened water for the youngsters.

A dozen or so hard cases were lined up in front of the saloon, leaning casually back against the outer wall, smoking and passing around a couple bottles as they looked on with bemused interest.

Lone and Lucinda had pushed themselves into position on the edge of the plaza about half way between the saloon/hotel/store and the livery. Because they were recognized as clearly being outsiders, folks in their immediate vicinity held back from crowding too close and occasionally shot them disdainful looks. For the most part, though, they were ignored. This had given Lone the chance he needed to briefly slip away, unnoticed amid the festive atmosphere, for the purpose of transferring their gear and saddling the horses as planned.

At nine o'clock sharp, a small group of people was seen emerging from the old mission across the way, the building that housed Pap and his immediate family. A ripple of heightened excitement ran through the crowd as the group proceeded slowly, with something of a ceremonial air, toward the center of the plaza.

Pap strode in the lead, chin up, eyes locked straight ahead. He was dressed as before, except for the addition of a swallow tail coat, strained at the seams due to being at least one size too small. Behind him walked Mase and another middle-aged man of similar size and features—Pap's other son Romer, was Lone's guess. Like Mase, Romer had a gun belt and holstered six-gun strapped around his waist. In his roaming about, Lone had noticed—somewhat to his relief, considering how things might erupt—that only a handful of the townsmen went armed. The exception, of course, were the hard cases present as temporary residents.

Between Mase and Romer, largely supported

by the grips they had on his arms, staggered Jaime Rodero. He was still shirtless and barefoot, his wrists still bound in front of him. Clearly no attempt had been made to clean up his cuts and bruises. His battered face hung down and his knees buckled frequently as he tried to walk. However he'd spent the night, it appeared he hadn't been beaten additionally—but neither, by a damn sight, had he been given any succor. Seeing this, Lucinda gasped and went rigid beside Lone. But then she steeled herself and showed no further outward reaction.

Bringing up the end of the procession was a plump young woman of about seventeen wearing a prim homespun blue dress and a sad, somber expression. She had stringy, reddish blonde hair, one crossed eye, and her lips were pooched outward in what looked like a well-practiced pout. This, Lone guessed, was Betty Belle, Mase's daughter, the alleged "innocent, vulnerable victim" of Jaime's improper advances. Walking beside her was a misshapen young man, maybe a couple years older. He had a shriveled right arm and a severely bowed left leg that made him walk with a pronounced limp. His face carried the perpetual scowl of someone always in physical discomfort and mentally harboring resentment for what the fates had done to him. Where he fit into all of this, Lone wasn't quite sure.

The group of seven reached the middle of the plaza and shuffled to a halt. Pap turned to the C-shaped gathering that had gone mostly quiet now, looking in at him and waiting to hear him speak.

"Citizens . . . Clan family," he began in a booming voice. "Ye know our purpose here today. Ye all have heard by now the charges declared against this bound man, this tainted villain. He's been found guilty—by me, makin' judgment after hearin' all the facts—of tryin' to force his unclean self on one of our own. A poor, innocent child who ye also see before ye—my own granddaughter. By the grace of Providence, she was barely saved from ruination. The animal responsible must and will be punished!"

A cheer went up from the crowd.

"As is our custom, and keepin' to our laws and rules," Pap continued when he was able to speak again, "we don't have a set punishment fer crimes. We put such to the party been wronged, along with his or her family." Another pause for more cheers. Then: "As ye know they get allowed to put forth three acceptable punishments. And that brings to today's doin's. The Choosin' Ceremony where ye, the whole clan, get to decide which of the punishments they named ye want to see carried out—then we go ahead and proceed with doin' it!"

This brought forth the loudest and longest

cheering of all. In the midst of it, Lucinda looked up at Lone with a deeply plaintive expression.

Pap finally had to raise his arms to get things settled down to a level where he could carry on. "All right. Now . . . here's where the noise ye make counts . . . the first punishment you got a chance to choose is: Hangin' by the neck 'til dead!"

This received a moderately strong response.

"Okay. The second one ye can choose is . . . now ye gals gotta excuse if this is kinda crude and maybe ye want to cover the ears of yer kids . . . but ye can go fer havin' this critter nutted, to take away the animal drive caused by his impure blood, and then be banished off our mountain with no equipment left to threaten nobody no more!"

This earned a smattering of cheers but more titters of laughter than anything else.

"And finally . . . a strap and knife fight to the death that would snuff out the condemned man's candle permanent-like or, if'n he was to win, give him a chance to live and be initiated into our clan!"

That settled it. The roar of approval that erupted from the crowd made it clear beyond any doubt that this was what they wanted to see. It was clear this was a popular outcome and Lone had a strong hunch that such votes in the past had almost exclusively gone this way. What was more, if the guilty parties had all been mistreated beforehand to the degree Jaime was, then it wasn't likely any of them had ever reached the subsequent initiation stage.

The former scout looked around, getting poised for the right opening. Because it was looking almost certain that some gunfire and hard riding was going to be necessary to get Jaime out of this.

Pap was addressing the crowd again. "Now ye also know how the rules say the wronged party has to hold up his end of the fight. In this case, though, that clearly can't be Betty Belle. In place of her it should then fall to Adolphous"—here he gestured to the lad with the shriveled arm and bad leg—"her betrothed for marriage. But the rules also say that the fight has to start reasonably even, so's somebody with a . . . a fisky . . . er, fal . . ."

"Physical impairment, Pa," said Mase and Romer in unison.

Pap scowled. "Yeah, one of them. In other words, it wouldn't be right for Adolphous, crippled like he be, to try and fight this fight. So the rules got an allowance for that. They say that somebody in that kind of fix can pick hisself a champion to stand in for him." A low, anxious buzz grew in the crowd, like they knew what was coming next. "And in this case, Adolphous has picked, for his champion . . . his cousin Orville!"

This brought forth another long, loud cheer and from out of the heart of it stepped a towering, musclebound giant who proceeded to lumber toward the group in the middle of the plaza. He easily stood six-six, had a sagging gut but massive shoulders and arms to offset it. His face had a pounded-on look, bracketed by two cauliflowered ears, and topped by bristles of rust-colored hair.

"Orville! Orville!" the crowd chanted.

Under his breath, Lone muttered, "Jesus Christ."

As Orville came to a stop next to Adolphous and Betty Belle, two young boys, barely into their teens, came trotting out of the crowd. One carried a flat leather strap, about eight feet long, with adjustable loops on each end. The other carried a matched pair of Bowie knives with bone handles and ten-inch blades.

Gesturing to Jaime, Pap said, "Somebody cut his bonds. Get him ready. Orville, step up here. Take yer knife, get yer end of the strap slipped—"

"Wait a minute," rang a loud, clear voice from out of the crowd.

Everything went dead quiet. Necks craned and scores of eyes swung around to try and find the speaker. It was Lone.

Pap bared his teeth. "Mr. Independent. Trent. What's the big idea of interruptin' these doin's?"

"I just have a question," Lone said, raising his

voice to be heard above the grumble of protests arising from all sides.

"Yer an outsider! Ye got no say in this!" Mase hissed.

Pap raised a hand. "Give it a minute. Let him speak." Then to Lone: "Go ahead. Make it quick."

"I was just wonderin' about these here rules of yours," Lone drawled. "I understand how it's reasonable for the fella there with the physical problems to have the right to a champion representin' him . . . but what about the other fella?"

Pap's eyes were blazing slits. "What about him? What are ye drivin' at?"

"Well, anybody can see he ain't a hundred percent neither," Lone pointed out. "Look at him, how he's been worked over. The way he's hunched to one side, I'm bettin' he's got some busted ribs there. His one eye is swole shut. And from the way I saw him hangin' on that saloon beam yesterday, his shoulders are almost certain to be wrenched half outta their sockets."

"I still don't get yer point," Pap rasped.

Lone replied, "My point is . . . in that condition, don't *he* have the right to a champion? You spoke of the fight startin' out reasonably even. How is it even for that big lug"—Lone jabbed a finger at Orville—"to square off against a fella so beat-up to begin with?"

The tone of the crowd's murmuring shifted

slightly, as if some might be—cautiously—finding validity in Lone's questions.

Romer leaned over and whispered something in his father's ear.

Very slowly, Pap's mouth spread into a wide, sly smile. "Okay, Mr. Independent . . . ye pose questions that rate thinkin' 'bout. Maybe even takin' action on . . . but the thing is, no one, just on account they be asked, *has* to agree to be a champion. They gotta be *willin'* to step into the fight. If none are, then the fight's gotta go on as demanded by the Choosin' Ceremony." He paused and his sly smile stretched wider still. "So . . . my people, my clan . . . who among ye be willin' to go against Orville and fight as the champion for this judged guilty cur standin' here?"

Dead quiet again. For several beats.

Until a by now familiar voice—Lone's—rang out once more. "I will."

Chapter Thirty-Five

Pap's attempt at craftiness had backfired on him and the look on his face showed he didn't like it worth a damn. By the way Mase was grimacing and balling and unballing his fists, he liked it even less. But the growing calls of encouragement coming out of the crowd was pressuring them to go ahead and play the hand Lone had dealt. Even big Orville seemed to want it, glaring and sneering at Lone and making "come ahead" gestures with his hands.

"Awright, by gar!" declared Pap. "If ye want to strap up and lock knives with Orville, ye be a bigger fool than I took ye fer. Shuck yer iron and step on out here then—Let's get to it!"

As Lone began unbuckling his gun belt, Lucinda stepped close and whispered urgently, "I hope you know what you are doing!"

"So do I," Lone told her with a wry grin. "But keep that shotgun handy. If things go south on me, the only chance for you and your brother will be to blast your way to the horses and kick dust outta here. Ironsides and Conquistador are sure to smoke anything they send after you."

Lucinda looked like she was going to say something more but instead held it in check.

Lone laid his gun belt, the Colt Lightning, his

Stetson and his Yellowboy at her feet. Then he straightened up and began peeling out of his buckskin vest and shirt. Once he was stripped to the waist, the sight of his muscle-corded frame and the numerous scars adorning it generated an audible gasp from several onlookers. Here, clearly, was a veteran fighting man—and a survivor, as the marks left by his battles mutely testified. Even Orville abandoned his taunting "come ahead" motions.

Lone moved toward the center of the plaza. The sun was hot on his bare back. He opened and closed his hands as he walked, lifted on the balls of his feet to flex and loosen his leg muscles. Tiny muscles and nerves fluttered under his skin.

Betty Belle and Adolphous left the plaza and merged into the crowd. Romer led Jaime away. Pap and Mase remained, the latter holding the strap and the two knives delivered by the two boys. Lone and Orville moved up on either side of the Binders and stood silently glaring at each other.

"The rules is simple," Pap intoned. "Once the strap goes on yer wrist, it don't come off 'til the fight is over. Either of ye turn yella and try to pull loose of the loop or purposely cut the strap to try and break free, one of my boys will shoot ye dead. It don't end 'til one of ye is ended . . . other than that, anything goes. Ye can cut, slice, kick, gouge, spit, call each other nasty names, whatever it takes . . . that clear enough?"

"Is for me, Pap," Orville grunted. "I've heard it all before . . . and when this is done, I'll be around fer hearin' it again."

"All I want to know is when do we quit talkin' and commence cuttin'," said Lone.

Half a minute later he and Orville were strapped up and each was gripping a knife in his free hand. They only awaited the start signal from Pap as he and Mase backed off toward the crowd. When the old man was far enough, he bellowed, "Get to it!"

The crowd let out an encouraging roar and it was underway.

Big Link had surprised Lone a few nights ago back in Rio Fuego by *not* coming in a bull rush. This morning, Orville followed the more common practice of larger combatants—instantly hurling himself forward in a charge. Anticipating this, for just a fraction of a second, Lone was tempted to meet him in kind. At six-three and weighing two hundred and thirty pounds, Lone was a big, powerful man who could have braced himself and not been easily bowled over. But Orville still had three or four inches and a good fifty pounds on him. Butting heads with an onrushing force that big just wasn't smart.

So instead of doing it head-on, Lone met the charge in a different way. He dropped low and threw a cross-body block at Orville's knees. Orville could neither halt nor adjust his forward momentum. All he could do, finding himself upended and pitching forward, was tuck a massive shoulder and tumble into an awkward somersault as he crashed to the ground.

But in the midst of this, the leather strap, with Lone on the opposite end, suddenly played a role. Nimbly springing to his feet as soon as the big man passed over top of him, Lone grasped the strap and immediately hauled back on it with all his strength. This resulted in Orville's strap arm, while he was only partly turned over in his somersault, being yanked hard in reverse. It ended up getting levered briefly though punishingly square into his crotch. The big man howled in pain as he finished flopping the rest of the way over. Once he slapped onto his back and could kick his legs out and away, the grinding pressure to his groin was released.

The crowd clamored through all of this, several of the men groaning in sympathy.

Lone let some slack form in the strap and adjusted his balance, getting set and waiting for Orville to struggle back to his feet. Orville rolled onto one hip, twisting around to face Lone, cussing him furiously as he started to push up. Lone timed it perfectly—surging forward in two long, smooth strides. On the second one, he extended his leg out full and swung it upward, driving the toe of his boot as hard as he could under the point of Orville's chin. On impact

Orville's teeth were driven together with a loud *crack!*, like the sound of two wooden blocks being clapped against each other. The big man was knocked down again, falling heavily once more onto his back.

The rumbling from the crowd now began to include some wails of despair and concern.

Lone closed on his opponent. But he hurried it, mistakenly thinking Orville was more stunned than he turned out to be. As soon as Lone was within reach, Orville snapped to a sitting position and his knife hand flashed in a sweeping, slashing flat arc. Lone twisted and hopped sideways, barely avoiding getting the side of his right calf laid wide open.

Lone got fully re-balanced and started to circle. Orville's eyes followed him; glaring, hating. Blood was running freely from both corners of his mouth.

Lone readied himself, expecting his opponent to try scrambling to his feet. But once again, he misjudged. This time it was Orville who took the slack out of the strap and used it to his advantage. Making a quick wrap of it around his forearm, shortening the overall length by nearly two feet, Orville then gripped the leather in a meaty fist and yanked, jerking Lone down toward him. At the same time, he swung a tree trunk leg in a side sweep and knocked Lone's feet out from under him.

The big lunk was fast. Damned fast. Lone couldn't do anything to keep from falling, but at least he could control the drop somewhat. Knowing Orville would be aiming to meet his descent with a knife blade, Lone rotated his body in midair and pitched to one side. He was right about the knife attempt. It streaked up in a stabbing motion. His twisting, turning maneuver spared him from having it plunged into his chest. As it was, the blade merely sliced a short, shallow track on the outside of his right shoulder.

Lone hit the ground on his stomach right alongside Orville. The big man's knife arm remained extended straight out from its thrusting motion. Having Lone now jammed against him prevented him from being able to draw it back in a way that presented any kind of angle from which he could make another quick try. In the meantime, Lone's knife arm was also shoved out as part of breaking his fall and likewise blocked him from twisting his hand around to make use of the blade. What he could do, though, was bend the arm inward and then drive the elbow back sharply against the side of Orville's head—which he proceeded to repeatedly do. One, two, three, four times in rapid succession, the elbow crashed into ear and cheekbone. Each time Orville roared and spat blood.

The two men finally rolled away from each other and clambered to their feet. They separated as far as the length of the strap would allow and began circling warily. Both were smeared with dust-caked sweat. Lone's cut shoulder burned, but not that bad. Orville was puffing hard and blowing spittles of blood with each exhalation. His sagging gut swelled and deflated visibly.

It was that gut, Lone told himself, that presented him his best opportunity to come out on top of this. If he could prolong the fight long enough, keep Orville on the move, keep pressing him hard, then his endurance would falter under the weight of all that blubber. His speed and strength and reflexes would soon follow. Although it sounded like Orville had been the victor in more than a few past fights such as this, Lone was willing to bet they were of relatively short duration. One that ground on long and grueling could tell a different story.

But that story wasn't written yet. Orville was laboring, but he was unfortunately still far from done.

He proved that by suddenly launching another attack. First he gave the strap a hard tug, catching Lone momentarily off guard and yanking him two or three steps closer. Lone quickly braced himself and dug in his heels to get stopped. But by then there was enough sag in the strap for Orville to grab it, pinch it off, and create a short dangling loop. Then, continuing forward in a rush, he swung this like a whip at Lone's face and eyes. Lone turned his head to keep the biting leather away from his eyes, but the impact of it on his jaw and the side of his neck cracked loud and stung like hell.

Lone staggered momentarily, swinging blindly with his knife, back-and-forth slashes that cut nothing but air. Orville dodged these easily then swung the whipping loop again, backhand this time, and cracked it across the opposite side of Lone's face. The former scout staggered again, cursing as he pivoted away. Orville bulled forward, now swinging his knife in a chopping downward motion aimed at Lone's neck. But Lone's pivot carried him farther than Orville anticipated so the point of the blade instead only raked a long, deep track down across Lone's left shoulder blade.

Lone ground his teeth in pain and his knees buckled, dropping him low. But this was only partly in response to the knife strike driving him down. There was also a calculation to it. He sensed Orville hovering over him now—right arm extended out ready to hack down with the knife blade again; left arm extended ready to hit with the whipping loop again. Lone suddenly whirled back in reverse of his earlier pivot and straightened his legs, propelling himself upward and forward, ramming the top of his head deep into Orville's swollen gut.

A wail of surprise and pain and a great gush

of air was driven out of the big man as he was driven back and knocked off balance. He fell hard, once again flat on his back. Lone landed full on top of him and immediately began pistoning his knees—first right, then left—repeatedly into Orville's ribs. Aiming to hammer every last morsel of breath out of him. In this frenzy, Lone seemed to forget all about using his knife.

But Orville didn't. Amazingly, despite a relentless pummeling and with all the air pounded from his massive lungs, the big man dug down and found more fight somewhere deep inside himself. Demonstrating this, his knife arm, outflung and limp-seeming though still gripping the knife in its fist, started to lift off the ground. It gained speed as it rose higher and it became clear that the point of the blade was aimed straight for Lone's throat.

Only the weakened sluggishness of the rising arm and Lone's keen peripheral vision saved him. At the last instant, still astride Orville, Lone twisted at the waist and swung across and down with his Bowie, blocking the upward motion of Orville's. The blades locked, hilt to hilt, and held quivering at a midpoint. Lone started to push Orville's arm steadily back down . . .

And then, with a ringing metallic twang, Lone's blade snapped clean off!

Lone was pitched momentarily off balance. And Orville's fist and blade, suddenly without resistance, shot harmlessly upward.

Lone recovered quickly. Hooking the outstretched arm, he flung himself back and pulled on it as he rolled off Orville's body and used the arm like a pry bar to turn the big man over onto his stomach. Then, spinning and squirming into the position he wanted, Lone planted his right knee between Orville's shoulder blades. Leaning forward, gripping a length of the strap between his two fists, he slipped it roughly down over Orville's face and chin, then yanked it back hard and deep into the rolls of fat covering his throat. Throwing his head and shoulders back, Lone strained in the strap for several beats. Orville gagged and gasped and his hands and legs flailed frantically at first but quickly weakening. When there was barely any movement left, Lone quit pulling on the strap.

He was breathing hard, his own chest rising and falling rapidly.

His gaze fell on Orville's knife, lying on the ground mere inches from the man's limp, outstretched fingers. Lone reached down and picked it up. He held the blade extended upward and his eyes traveled from it to the back of Orville's thick neck.

He became aware once more of the crowd noise. It had been there all along, he supposed, but for the past several minutes he'd quit hearing it. It was hard to keep doing so now. They were chanting loudly, demandingly.

"Kill him! Kill him! . . . Finish it! . . . Kill Orville!"

Lone's stomach turned. In the beginning, they'd been cheering their champion's name. Now they were cheering for his death.

Lone raised the knife high.

The voices clamored with approval . . . until Lone thrust the blade downward and sank it into the ground a half inch off to one side of Orville's head.

The voices went silent. Lone stood up and looked straight at Pap.

"Ye must finish it. Ye must kill him," the old man declared. "That be the rule!"

"Then your rules stink! It's time to change 'em," Lone fired back. Pointing down at Orville, he continued, "This man fought hard and brave—for something he didn't even have a direct stake in. Because he lost the fight he deserves to die?"

"That be the rule," Pap stubbornly said again. "A death for a life!"

"Why not a life for a life?" Lone insisted. "Do you really want him to die and be replaced by initiatin' me—or the Mexican kid with his impure blood, since I'm only actin' as *his* champion—into your clan as a replacement? Does that make a lick of sense? Men have suffered and bled to defend your granddaughter's honor. Let that be enough. Let her and Adolphous marry and live their lives without shame, not have the shadow of *their* dead champion hangin' over 'em."

The murmuring of the crowd suddenly sounded a lot less bloodthirsty.

Mase stepped up beside his father. His face was clouded with anger and his hand was resting threateningly on his holstered Colt. "Ye have cut this stranger too much slack right from the first, Pa! Listen to him—he's not only disrespectin' ye right to yer face, but he's runnin' down the rules and laws we live by in front of our whole clan. That can't be let go! If he tries slippin' out'n that strap 'thout killin' Orville, then it's my job to shoot him dead and, by gar, that's what I fully intend to do."

Before Pap could respond, there was a hellacious roar directly behind the two men. Flame and smoke belched high from one of the Greener's skyward-aimed barrels, the ground shook, and people anywhere within a dozen yards ducked and spun sharply away. Lucinda stepped through the blue powder smoke haze and rested the Greener's twin muzzles—a twist of smoke curling lazily out of the spent barrel—on Pap's right shoulder. "I would advise you to hold very still, Papa," she said calmly. "And tell your *bravado* son to do likewise. I only have one barrel not yet discharged but I have it on good authority that at this range it would be enough to turn the two of you into extra chunky salsa. In case you do not know, that is a dish served by us Mexican subhumans of impure blood."

From elsewhere in the crowd, Pap's other son Romer called out. He was standing with his Colt drawn, Jaime collapsed at his feet, and was aiming rather shakily at Lucinda. "I got her in my sights from here, Pa," he said in a strained voice. "Say the word, I'll burn her down."

"No, ye fool!" protested Mase. "Her finger jerk could still blow us to smithereens!"

It became a moot point a moment later when another shot flatted in the shimmering air. It was a pistol shot, but not from Romer. In fact, the bullet thus released took Romer's Colt and one of his fingers and sent them flying out into the dusty plaza. Romer sank to his knees, keening in shock and pain, and scores of eyes swung looking for the source of the shot.

What they came to rest on was Brick Holland, having stepped out away from the saloon wall. He was braced with feet planted wide, his black-handled hogleg extended at waist level, a wisp of smoke rising out of its muzzle. Several of the other hard cases who'd been leaning casually back against the saloon were also standing up straight now, slitted eyes raking over the crowd, hands hovering close to their guns.

"Okay, everybody, listen up," Brick said. "It's like the shotgun lady said a minute ago—just stay still and take it easy. Me and my pals had no intention of getting involved in any of this today.

We appreciate your hospitality for letting us stay among you for as long as you have, and most of us hope to stay a while longer.

"But the turn all of this has taken . . . it flat got out of hand. Like was said by Trent out there—or whatever his name is—two brave, tough hombres just put on a hell of a show. Enough's enough. Ain't no sensible reason for one of 'em to have to die to finish it up. It's plenty good enough just the way it is."

Brick paused, sweeping his gaze over the faces looking back at him. They were quiet, seemed to be listening with interest and at least a touch of deeper consideration. Pap and Mase stood with their heads hung, expressions as blank as the muzzles of Lucinda's shotgun still resting on Pap's shoulder.

"What I say," Brick continued, "is this: Today's 'special doin's' are over. It's time for everybody to go on back to the normal swing of things. Orville's people need to go out and get him and take him to be cleaned up and cared for. Same for Romer, though leave his gun where it is for now. Trent, Miss Lola, and the Mexican kid—whatever the hell he truly is to them—need to be allowed to leave with no more bother, soon as they're ready. Anybody got a problem with that, me and my pals . . ."

He stopped and scowled at Lone. "Goddamn it, Trent, I've talked enough. Worked myself up a thirst. Take that stupid strap off your wrist, come over and reclaim your shootin' irons. Finish cleanin' up your own mess. It's too hot out here, me and the boys are going inside for some cold beers." He started to turn away, then stopped and looked back over his shoulder. "Helluva show, hombre . . . helluva show."

Lone let the strap drop off his wrist, grinned crookedly. "I'll be in to buy a round before we pull out."

Chapter Thirty-Six

"Harriet . . . don't cry out, it's me."

The deep, reassuring voice . . . the gentle nudge to her shoulder . . . Harriet Munro came quickly awake, feeling no sense of alarm. Her eyes swept the darkened room, the guest room of the Thorndike house to which she had become quite accustomed after having spent so many recent nights here. In the faint wash of silver-blue moonlight slanting in from the open window she could make out the shape of a man standing by her bed. Somehow the murky shape—just as the voice murmuring the few words that interrupted her slumber had been—was immediately familiar to her.

"Lone," she whispered, raising on one elbow.

She sensed rather than saw his equally familiar lopsided grin. "Sorry for the late-hour visit. Just reportin' in on our little trail ride."

"God, it's good to have you back! I've been so worried. Partly out of guilt, I suppose, for my role in sending you in the first place . . . did everything go okay?"

"We fetched Jaime back with us, if that's what you mean. Can't say there wasn't a few rough spots gettin' it done, though," said Lone. "But, from what we've heard since returnin', sounds like things ain't been goin' overly smooth around here neither. That's why we held off bringin' the kid all the way in right away and why I'm showin' up now, so late and kinda roundabout—to get the straight of the situation from you."

Harriet heaved an exasperated sigh. "Boy, you're so right about things going less than smoothly around here. You would have thought that the two killings—first the judge and then the marshal—were bad enough. But the aftermath is only adding to the strain on this town. The overall mood is uglier than ever, and still building. And some of what's driving it is nothing short of shocking."

"How are the two lawmen—Zack and Steve—holdin' up?" Lone asked.

"Those poor devils. They're getting whipsawed from every direction." Harriet sat up the rest of the way. "Let me slip on a robe and light a lantern. No need for us to sit talking in the dark like we're plotting some under-handed deed. After all, we're the ones on the right side of things in all of this."

Lone said, "I'd just as soon keep it to the two of us for right now. No need to wake up Mrs. Thorndike."

"Don't worry about that. Dr. Praeger still has her on sedatives," Harriet explained. "It would take a cannon blast to roust her at this hour. The only other one in the house is Mrs. Gladstone. Her bedroom is off in a corner of the downstairs and she's a heavy sleeper."

In less than a minute, the room was bathed in pale gold light from a table lantern and the two old friends were seated facing each other. Harriet had donned slippers and a patterned dressing gown with a silk collar. She sat on the edge of the bed, Lone had hitched up a high-backed reading chair.

"So when did you actually get in?" Harriet wanted to know.

"A little before dusk. Figurin' word had probably spread about me and Lucinda goin' after her brother and rememberin' all too well how unpopular he was when he lit out," Lone told her, "we reckoned it'd be best to sidle back kinda careful-like. There was even some talk, you'll recall, of me deliverin' Jaime to Ford City instead of directly here. His sister balked hard against that, though, at least until we got a feel of how things might've changed while we was gone. So we held back at a little ranchero south of town, some friends of the Acunas, and sent word for Carlos to come meet us there. He did, and that's when we heard about some of the rest of what's takin' place hereabouts."

"God knows there are plenty of fingers in the pie," Harriet said bitterly. "But the ones jammed in the deepest and coming out the dirtiest belong to none other than that conniving snake Hank Birchfield!"

"That's the fella been ramroddin' the JT Connected all these years, right?"

"The same." Harriet nodded. "He was in on it with Reginald Thorndike from the get-go. He did all the hands-on work, took the ranch from a dream and a handful of cattle and built it into one of the biggest spreads around. When it came to the ranch, he was the judge's right *and* left hand, and the judge counted on him and treated him practically like a brother."

"I remember hearin' that. I remember Zack and Steve sayin' how tore up Birchfield was when the judge got killed."

"That's the way it appeared," Harriet conceded. "If it was an act, it was an awfully convincing one. Right up to the blubbering he did standing beside the coffin on the day of the funeral . . . but then, just days later, right after Marshal Bartlett was laid to rest, a different Hank Birchfield—maybe the *real* one, waiting all these years to shed his skin and show his true self—emerged."

"Carlos was kinda sketchy on understandin' all of it. But it's something about the judge's will. That it?"

"It's *everything* about the judge's will!" Harriet said fiercely. She stood up. "Every time I think about it or try to talk about it, I get more worked up. Not very professional, I know, but I can't help it. The lies and deceit are so damnedably obvious—but there's no way to prove it!"

"Sorry. I didn't come here aimin' to upset you."

Harriet shook her head. "Don't be silly. You're the least of what's upsetting me. In fact, whenever you're around, I always find myself feeling more hopeful. That somehow, some way you'll manage to straighten things out."

"I'm honored at bein' well thought of," Lone said. "But don't sell yourself short in any way. You're a mighty tough, resourceful gal and you know it. You climbed your way up the big city legal ladder all on your own, didn't you? How much good would I do you in a courtroom flingin' points of order and habeus corpuses back and forth? The only kind of corpuses I know about are the kind you leave in the street or trail behind you and ride off from."

Harriet arched a brow. "You never get tired of downplaying yourself, do you?"

"I'll tell you what I am gettin' tired of," Lone replied, his tone changing. "I'm gettin' damned tired of runnin' into one lowdown skunk after another bent on makin' life miserable for decent folks who otherwise could have something good and nice here in Rio Fuego. It's them decent folks who'd better learn how to start pullin' together and get things righted again.

"Yeah, they lost a couple important leaders in the judge and the marshal. But there are others—

Doc Praeger, Zack and Steve, a brave little man named Carlos Acuna, if they'd open their eyes—right in their midst who they could get behind. Me, I figure I've done my share of lendin' a hand. After we get Jaime safely turned over for a fair trial, all I want is to finish makin' a deal on the horses I came to buy and be on my way."

"Then in accordance with how things currently stand," Harriet informed him somewhat stiffly, "the horses you're interested in buying have become the sole property of a freshly revealed skunk by the name of Hank Birchfield."

Six years earlier, when the JT Connected, under the hands-on, hard-working guidance of Hank Birchfield, first began to show signs of growing into something more substantial than Judge Thorndike ever dared hope, the judge had drawn up a will. Simple yet sufficient. With no children or other close relatives involved, the will stated that, in the event of his death, the town house and sixty percent of the ranch holdings would go to his then wife Katherine. The remaining forty percent of the ranch holdings would be left to Hank Birchfield. An addendum stated that should Katherine expire before making changes or provisions otherwise, her portion of the ranch holdings would automatically transfer to Birchfield; and the town house would be gifted to the town of Rio Fuego to use however deemed fitting.

All of this was related to Lone by Harriet as they continued to talk into the night. "For whatever reason," she went on, "the judge never revised that will after Katherine died. He was busy with other matters, he was just a procrastinator about such things . . . nobody can say for sure. Not even after he married Amanda did he set out to officially change anything. At least not right away."

"So with the will existin' for all that time the way it was written," said Lone, "it basically made Birchfield his sole heir."

"Exactly," Harriet agreed. "But even if the judge ever stopped to consider it that way, I doubt it would have mattered to him. He and Birchfield were that close."

"Yeah. Close enough that, was I the judge, the hairs on the back of my neck would have prickled every time Birchfield moved up behind me," Lone said wryly.

"Too bad the judge didn't have your instincts. But still, finally, after he was diagnosed with cancer and knew he had limited time to live, he began to start making some changes. In addition to setting in motion the selling off various holdings for the sake of building up a money fund to care for Amanda when he was gone—which included, as you know, shedding JT Connected livestock and property since he knew she had no interest in the ranch without him—he was re-writing a will to address how all of this was to be disbursed."

Lone cocked a brow. "Soundin' like, somewhere along the way, it might have started brewin' a serious case of chapped-assedness in one Hank Birchfield."

Harriet smiled. "I definitely must find a way to work that—'chapped-assedness'—into a legal brief someday. But for this current discussion, there was never any sign of Birchfield having concerns about how the judge was proceeding. It was generally expected, by everyone else and apparently by Birchfield as well, that due to their close and long-standing relationship, the judge would be very fair and accommodating."

"So let's cut to it. What happened then—what's got everybody in this current tizzy?" Lone wanted to know.

Harriet sighed. "Long story short, the new will the judge was allegedly writing—something numerous people saw him working on when they went to visit him as his illness worsened—never got officially filed. What's more, any sign of it, any of the pages he was seen to have about him in what turned out to be his final days, have all disappeared. No trace, in spite of much searching."

"So the only will to be had is the old one—the one givin' the complete ranch holdin's to Birchfield."

"And Amanda, since she was never part of the picture at the time of that will," added Harriet, "is left out totally. She doesn't even technically have a place to live. This house, with both the judge and his first wife, Katherine, gone, now belongs to the town."

Lone let out a low whistle. "One tough break after another for that gal."

"You can see why Dr. Praeger still has her on sedatives."

"Wait a minute," said Lone, scowling. "Don't I remember hearin' that one of the first ones on the judge's murder scene, right after the nurse who found him, was Birchfield arrivin' for a visit?"

"You remember exactly right."

Lone's scowl deepened. "Don't it seem mighty damn fishy to anybody but me that those papers for a new will—known to be right there close about the judge and no doubt containin' changes bound to affect Birchfield different than before—all of a sudden went missin' and left the ramrodder the whole ball of wax?"

Harriet spread her hands. "See why I said the lies and deceit are so damnedably obvious? And it gets worse. The nurse—the other person who was on the scene first? It turns out she's Birchfield's sweetheart. He's moved her out to the ranch now, living with him in his foreman's cabin. Until, one can assume, he finishes the grand new house—the one the judge had begun having built for Amanda—so they can move into that together."

"Jesus," Lone growled. "Can't nobody do nothing?"

"Nothing legal. Not that anyone's been able to come up with so far." Harriet shook her head in frustration. "It all happened so fast, needless to say so unexpectedly. And the change in Birchfield, his whole demeanor, his lack of remorse or any hint of compassion for Amanda. A handful of JTC riders quit over the change in him, the suspicion. It appeared he already had some other men lined up to replace them—men more of the hard case mold than just wranglers. It didn't take long for a couple saloon fights to break out, even a shooting. Nobody was seriously hurt, at least not yet. But everybody can sense more trouble brewing. That's what's been keeping Zack and Steve so busy."

"You mentioned suspicion of Birchfield by some of the JTC riders," Lone said. "You mean suspicion he might've been the one who actually killed the judge?"

"Lord. I don't know." Harriet shook her head again. "I haven't heard anybody suggest that out loud before. Though I can't imagine it hasn't crossed a few minds. Mostly, though, I think people are just stunned and suspicious of the cold-blooded way Birchfield is taking advantage of the judge's death. Remember, too, in the minds of many, Jaime Rodero is still the prime suspect for the murder."

"Yeah, well we now have things lined up to fix that. Unless," Lone questioned, "all of this other crap has changed Amanda's mind about speaking up for the kid?"

"No, she's still steadfast on that. How is Jaime, by the way? Did you have much trouble getting him away from that outlaw gang? My goodness, we got off on this other business and never even discussed that."

Lone grinned. "Actually, the outlaw gang never really entered into it. Leastways not the bunch we figured we were gonna run into. But that whole tale can wait for another time. Main thing for right now, now that we got him here, is to set up Amanda givin' her alibi so we can get that much over with."

"Does he know she's willing to do that?"

"He does now. It came up durin' our trip back. He was pleased to hear it. So was his sister"—here Lone made a rueful face—"*after* she got done chewin' the both of us out for neither of us lettin' her know sooner about what had been goin' on between Jaime and Amanda."

Harriet lifted her eyebrows. "You make that sound like it might have been the worst part of the experience."

"You ain't seen Lucinda riled up," Lone told her. "But thankfully, she let us survive. So it sounds like the thing for me to do now is to let Zack and Steve know I'm back and make plans for the smoothest way to conduct gettin' Jaime's name cleared." He stood up. "I'll leave you to catch some more sleep while I get that set in motion."

Harriet stood also and placed a hand on his arm. "I'm glad you're back safely, Lone . . . despite what you said a little while ago, I hope you're not in too big a hurry to be on your way again."

Chapter Thirty-Seven

Harriet had told Lone that Zack and Steve had taken to sleeping at the jail of late, due to having prisoners in custody and just in general because of the tensions gripping the town. It was past midnight when he went calling on them there, but despite the hour, they were glad to see him.

"Might've known you wouldn't show up at no civilized time," groused Steve. "But then, you wouldn't be you if you did something like that."

They put on a fresh pot of coffee to brew and sat down to talk.

Before they got into the events that had transpired in Rio Fuego while he was away, Lone told them a condensed version of how he'd succeeded in bringing back Jaime Rodero. He then gave them the rest, the part he hadn't been totally open about before—how Amanda Thorndike was willing to provide an alibi to clear Jaime of having been the one who'd knifed her husband.

"Ho-lee balls," Zack expelled in an exasperated breath. "That's just what our town needs right now. One more bombshell dropped in the middle of everything else that's got nerves already stretched tight as barbed wire."

"Sorry for the inconvenience," Lone said. "But ain't the truth always best in the long run?

Ain't it better than havin' Rodero on the run and maybe gettin' deeper into trouble, screwin' up the rest of his life, over something he's innocent of? And you can understand, can't you, how Mrs. Thorndike didn't want to come forward unless the kid was on hand to get the benefit out of it?"

"Yeah, yeah, I get all of that," allowed Zack. "But even though Rodero was on the run, folks at least thought they *knew* who the judge's killer was. So if we clear him—and I ain't saying we shouldn't, mind you—then we put the wonder and the worry in everybody's head: Who *is* the killer? And what are them lazy damn law dogs doing about catching him before he kills again?"

"We already got two potential killers back in the holding cell," Steve said, "that some folks think we're not dealing with fast enough. They'd be Reece Dooley and Gus O'Toole, two of the names you gave us from what you overheard that night at Coyote Pass. We arrested 'em right after Marshal Tom's funeral. There was a third—Merl Brown. But he didn't take to being arrested so easy. He tried to shoot it out. They buried him yesterday."

"So as far as the two you've got—what are they sayin'?" Lone wanted to know.

"Oh, they're admitting to being there that night," Zack said, taking the bubbling pot off the stove as Steve snagged three cups and set them out to be filled. "They own up to being part of the went on. "And while I walked, I rolled a lot of things around in my head until some of 'em started fallin' into place in ways that only fitted a certain pattern. Two of those pieces were named Trent and Bone Harper. I know you've heard of Trent, I'm bettin' you recognize Harper too. Been ridin' a long time for the JT Connected, right? Loyal to the brand and to Hank Birchfield. And now you tell me Trent also worked for the JTC, but supposedly got fired. Yet Harper was *aidin'* Trent in trackin' me into New Mexico for the sole purpose of killin' me. As you can see, they didn't quite get the job done. They're the ones rottin' away and servin' up worm food in the New Mexican dirt.

"So what's the link between Trent first headin' up a necktie party to make sure Jaime Rodero swung real pronto-like before makin' trial, and then goin' to a lot of trouble all over again to track me down and try to kill me in order to make sure I don't bring the kid back for another crack at that trial? One answer that comes to mind is what you said a little bit ago about how, as long as Rodero was in the wind—or dead, if he'd've swung from that cottonwood tree out by Coyote Pass—folks would believe they *knew* who the judge's killer was and wouldn't worry much about lookin' any farther. So the next question is, who benefits more than the real killer if everybody stops lookin' for 'em?"

to some people," said Zack. "And when a quirk of luck walloped Hank with a big dose of both, it went straight to his head."

Lone drank some coffee. "What if," he said when he lowered his cup, "it wasn't just luck that served up that dose of power and money to Birchfield?"

"Oh, no. Not you too, McGantry," groaned Zack. "Don't tell me you been back in town a half hour and you're ready to buy in that Birchfield and his girlfriend hid the judge's new will so Hank could gain the full benefit of the old one."

"Okay. I won't tell you that."

"It sure sounded like that's where you were headed," Zack insisted. "In the first place, even if Thorndike had a dozen pages of a new will written right there for everybody to see, it was never filed. So it wouldn't have meant crap!"

"But Hank might not necessarily know that. Or, in a moment of panic, he might not have thought it through," pointed out Steve.

Zack pointed a finger. "Now don't *you* start in with this nonsense!"

"Can you calm down and just listen a minute, Zack? Not that hearin' this is gonna help you do that," said Lone, "but we might even be lookin' at something more than just throwin' away a few papers."

"Oh, Jesus," Zack muttered.

"I took a long, slow walk over here," Lone

before and Dooley thought he heard he worked for the JT Connected. When we asked Hank Birchfield about that, he told us yeah, he'd hired the hombre for a couple weeks but then canned him for being lazy and a troublemaker. He didn't know anything about him beyond that."

"Wasn't there a US Marshal due in with those dignitaries who came for Judge Thorndike's funeral?" Lone asked. "He should have been a source for possibly gettin' a handle on Trent. Didn't he do you any good?"

Zack grunted. "Not so's you could notice it. He came and went with the dignitaries and that was that. And the local added deputies we took on just as you were leaving? They lasted long enough for some of those new hard cases Hank Birchfield has been hiring to start showing up and all of a sudden they had better things to do than pack around a star."

Lone blew a cooling breath across his coffee before saying, "This big change in Birchfield . . . from what I heard about him before to what I'm hearin' since I got back—none of that can be helpin' the tensions around town, is it?"

"Ha! Not by a long shot," declared Steve. "And you're sure right about a big change. Never saw anything quite like it in a person. Hank always seemed like a pretty decent fella before. Now he's turned into a total jackass!"

"A sudden taste of power or money can do that

lynch mob and even doing some of the shooting that broke out. But what neither of 'em will admit to is that they fired any shots anywhere in the direction of Marshal Tom. So we got a whole fistful of charges we're holding them on, but none that hold up as a clear-cut case of murder."

Steve handed Lone a cup of coffee. "There's a circuit judge due around in a week or ten days. He's supposed to help us sort some things out and set the basis and dates for their trials. In the meantime, they remain our guests and most every night we get a handful of belligerent drunks who come around offering to take 'em off our hands an hang 'em for us. Nothing very serious, but it gets damned tiresome yet can't be merely ignored."

Lone asked, "What about our mystery man— Trent? Ever come up with anything on him? O'Toole and Dooley must have been able to provide something, didn't they? Trent was obviously runnin' the show on that lynch mob ambush. How'd they fall in with him?"

"Yeah, he was running the show. That's something else they admitted. But it just grew out of drunk saloon talk, they claimed. Trent somehow knew about the plan to transfer the prisoner and he had a persuasive notion on how to intercept it and string up the Mexican kid the way everybody knew he deserved. As far as who Trent was, they'd only seen him around town a couple times

Zack wore a pained expression. "Oh, come on. You're not working up to saying you think Hank Birchfield actually *killed* the judge, are you?"

"Why not?" Lone demanded irritably. "Because it seems *too pat?* More often than not, something looks like what it turns out to be. If the critter sittin' on your backyard fence looks like a skunk and smells like a skunk and ain't yowlin' in heat—then it's probably a goddamn skunk and not your neighbor's cat! I'm sayin' there are some pretty strong signs pointin' to Birchfield bein' a skunk."

"If so, what about 'em makes anything legal action could be taken against?" Zack said, finally showing a chink in his resistance. "Yeah, there are things about that morning—Birchfield and his girlfriend being the first ones on the scene, the new will papers suddenly disappearing, Hank benefiting so much—I don't like the smell of either. But why *that* morning? What changed, after the old will had been in place so long, to suddenly make it worth killing over?"

Lone shook his head. "That I can't say. Maybe the nurse or Birchfield saw some objectionable wording in the new will. Maybe a wrong word got said . . . a few nights ago we were in this room when Steve told Harriet Munro about the old gal who stove in her husband's head with a fryin' pan because he made her mad. Bad things happen when people get mad."

"Boy, ain't that the truth."

Lone drank some of his coffee. "Listen. I got an idea how maybe to get Birchfield to show his hand. If it works . . . well, it'll work. If it falls flat, I'll be left lookin' a little silly. But it wouldn't reflect bad on you fellas even if I did. I'll need your cooperation, though, to give it a try."

The marshal and deputy exchanged looks.

Finally, Zack heaved a resigned sigh. "No denying you've steered us pretty good on a number of things, Lone. And, like I said, I haven't liked the smell of certain things about the judge's murder either. So okay, let's hear what you got in mind . . ."

Chapter Thirty-Eight

Coyote Pass. Dusk.

Right back to where, as far as Lone was concerned, it had all started. Making it seem a good place to bring it to an end.

An afternoon wind, though died down now, had kicked up a lot of dust that left a haze in the air through which the sinking sun now filtered and cast the countryside in a rosy hue. A bloody red foreboding? Lone hoped not. But if more blood had to be spilled—as long as it was guilty blood—then so be it.

Lone had been awake all night, first fine tuning his plan with Zack and Steve and then explaining it to Jaime and Lucinda. The hardest part was convincing the last two to remain at the outlying ranchero for another day, staying unseen in order to allow Lone's ideas to take shape and play out. They had complied in the end, putting their trust in him. Lone had also gotten word to Harriet, via Steve, for her and Amanda to keep absolutely mum—for the time being, until they were informed otherwise—about him and the others being back.

In the middle of the day, Lone had finally caught a few hours' sleep at the ranchero. Then it was time for him to be on the move. To get here and get ready. To find out if his bait would be taken or ignored.

When the two hard cases showed up—well ahead of when anyone should have, and clearly ahead of when they expected his presence—Lone knew the bait was working. Then it became a question of whether the real prey would show up to take a bite, or if he'd rely on this pair to empty the trap and eliminate the trapper as well?

Operating covertly in a rugged outdoor setting, especially going against someone with Lone's skills, was not a smart assignment for the two hard cases. They might have amounted to something in a shootout or a rawhiding where they had the numbers advantage, but for whatever they were sent to accomplish at Coyote Pass, they fell damned short.

Within minutes of them taking up positions in the rocks on either side of the pass, Lone easily and silently eliminated each one. At a different time, under different circumstances, he likely would have gone ahead and killed them. But given the legal angle to this particular matter, he settled for leaving them hogtied and gagged until somebody cared enough to do something otherwise.

Then Lone waited.

He pushed the limits of dusk before he finally showed. A husky, ruddy-faced man astride a steeldust stallion. He wore a flat-crowned, cream-colored Stetson and a loose-fitting corduroy jacket. A tooled leather gun belt with a big JTC buckle was around his waist. For as much time as he'd spent in and around Rio Fuego and as much talk as he'd heard about this man, it brought a wry smile to Lone's lips to think that he was laying eyes on Hank Birchfield for the first time.

Sitting Ironsides about a yard out from the center of the pass's mouth, Lone studied him now as he approached and drew rein ten feet away.

They eyed each other for a long count.

Then Birchfield said, "So it is you. I thought maybe there might be another player in the game."

Lone's head gave a faint wag. "No. There's just me. And I don't play games."

"So everything in the note is true? Trent and Harper are both dead?"

"Just as dead as I could make 'em."

The note Birchfield referred to was one Lone had arranged to be delivered to him out at the ranch he now claimed as exclusively his. It was contained in a wax-sealed envelope and said simply:

> *Trent and Harper are dead. Before they died, they talked. I know ways to make men do that. Now it's time for me and you to talk. To deal. Coyote Pass. Dusk. Come alone.*

No signature had been included. Lone reckoned if Birchfield couldn't figure out that part, then he was either innocent of everything Lone suspected or hopelessly stupid. Looking into his eyes now, Lone could see he wasn't stupid, and the fact he was here at all and had sent two henchmen on ahead pretty much proved he wasn't innocent.

"So what's this business about some kind of deal you're lookin' to make?" Birchfield said. "And what makes you think you have anything to bargain with?"

"Like I said in the note, Trent and Harper both talked. Plenty."

"So what?" Birchfield sneered. "Who gives a shit what they blabbered about? They're just a couple of quarrelsome cowpokes I fired for not carryin' their load. Naturally they'd have nothing good to say about me. So who's gonna take their word over mine?"

"If you're so unconcerned," Lone drawled, "then why are you even here?"

That caused the muscles in Birchfield's face to involuntarily pull tighter. His eyes flicked past Lone, making a quick scan of the higher rocks on either side of the pass.

Lone smiled a wolf's smile. "If you're lookin' for those two rannies you sent ahead to put the squeeze on me, they're too tied up to join us right now. I only had time for a short visit with each of 'em, but they told me some interestin' things you had to say about me and what you was wantin' them to do to me . . . or are they just a couple more disgruntled former employees you had to fire?"

"Now just a goddamn minute!" Birchfield licked his lips. "Who the hell do you think you are, runnin' roughshod over everybody and thinkin' you can get away with it?"

"Don't get high and mighty with me, you back-stabbin' bag of wind," Lone snarled in return. "Not after what you're tryin' to get away with—you and that connivin' hussy you got for a partner."

"You leave Rose out of this, damn you!"

Lone barked out a quick, harsh laugh. "I'm glad we both know who and what a hussy is."

"If it wasn't for Rose takin' care of that sick, droolin' old bastard for all the while she did—doin' things his prim and proper little wife was too delicate for," Birchfield said, his lips peeling back and his face purpling, "he would have been in more misery and died even sooner! And what thanks did she get when it was over? Shown the door and a boot in the ass on the way out, that's what!"

"So why did she bother if you two were gonna hurry the old boy on his way anyhow?" prodded Lone, seeing he'd hit a raw nerve.

"It was never meant to be that way!" Birchfield roared in protest. "I loved that old sonofabitch like a father! I worked my fingers to the bone to make the ranch prosper. After Katherine died, it was gonna be me and him makin' it bigger than ever—more cattle and a strain of fine horseflesh. But then he met that bitch Amanda!"

Birchfield's glaring eyes were catching some of the dusk's reddish glow, making them blaze like points of fire.

"It killed me when he started sellin' off pieces of the JT Connected. But I knew he was sufferin', I tried to understand. And I counted that he'd still do right by me." His mouth twisted into a fresh sneer. "But then Rose saw what he was puttin' in the new will . . . twenty-five thousand dollars! That's what he was gonna leave me. After near ten years of blood, sweat, and toil. My prime years . . . and when I 'fronted him about it that morning, you know what he said? He said he had to make sure *he left Amanda well enough off!*"

He was wailing now, his voice trembling with anger and also, Lone sensed, a deep torment over what he'd been driven to do. "I had my hunting knife right there on my belt," he went on. "I'd killed and skinned a jackrabbit on the way in. His appetite had been off, and I knew how much he liked rabbit stew, so I was gonna . . . but when he told me that—how Amanda was what he had to take care of above all else . . ." His voice trailed off and he was quiet for a beat. Then those blazing eyes flared bright again, and he aimed their fire straight at Lone, saying, "And after doin' what I did to get what's comin' to me, if you think some meddlin' saddle tramp bastard like you is gonna show up and try—"

"That's enough, Hank," a sharp voice cut him off. "After what you just admitted, you're damn sure gonna get what's coming to you."

These were the words of Marshal Zack Mercer, spoken as he and Deputy Steve Leonard reverse melted out of the thick, shadowy underbrush bracketing the mouth of Coyote Pass just behind Lone. Both had Winchesters aimed steadily at the confessed killer.

Birchfield went rigid in his saddle and for a tense moment, it looked like he was going to go for the gun on his hip in spite of the odds against him.

"Don't try it, Hank," Zack warned.

Birchfield held rigid for another beat, then all the fire in his eyes suddenly died and his shoulders slumped.

Sounding weary and somewhat sad, Zack said, "Go take his gun and cuff him, Steve."

Epilogue

Three days later, Lone rode away from Rio Fuego.

Minus any horses.

With the JT Connected ranch and all other Thorndike holdings now considered intestate due to the only existing will being contested over Birchfield's murder charge, all business transactions were frozen. In a cockeyed kind of way, Lone was relieved. Even after a respite, he was still feeling too damned worn down for the prospect of pushing a couple dozen hammerheads near four hundred miles north to his Busted Spur spread in Nebraska to sound very appealing, not anytime soon. There'd be other horses for another day.

As far as how things stood in Rio Fuego, for the first time in weeks, there was a sense that the town could finally take a breath and relax a little bit. The murder of Judge Thorndike was solved. The real killer and his accomplice were behind bars in Ford City, awaiting trial. All charges against Jaime Rodero had been dropped, saving Amanda Thorndike the personal embarrassment as well as any peripheral tarnishing of her husband's name by not needing to come forth with the alibi she'd been prepared to give; the few who knew the full story kept it tightly contained. Dooley and O'Toole, the only survivors of the lynch mob ambush that resulted in the death of Marshal Bartlett, eventually served time for involuntary manslaughter and a handful of related charges.

On the morning he rode out, Lone was sent on his way by a gathering of well-wishers at Carlos's *restaurante*. Jaime and Lucinda were naturally on hand, along with numerous relatives Lone had never met before and could understand only to the extent they were grateful for what he'd done to help Jaime. Zack and Steve were there too, and by Lone's count, Steve fell in love with at least three different pretty senoritas in less than half an hour. Harriet and Amanda Thorndike were present as well. Amanda, who by a special meeting of the town council had been granted the right to remain in the Thorndike town house pending litigation, was profoundly apologetic for being unable to pay Lone anything, due to her assets being frozen, either in horses or money for his perilous journey at her behest to retrieve Jaime. He tried telling her not to worry about it but she insisted he would be hearing from her as soon as things were settled.

When Lone was finally able to slip away from the rest of the throng, Harriet followed him out to where Ironsides was saddled and literally champing at the bit.

"He's restless to get back on the trail, just like his master," she noted.

"Shhh. Careful what you say," Lone told her. "He thinks he's the master."

Harriet gave a little laugh. "I'll be sure to remember that. But, tell me, whichever one of you is calling the shots . . . you think there's any chance you might end up over Denver way before another four years go by? It's not that terribly far, you know. I'd think a veteran scout like you ought to be able to find your way if you set your mind to it."

"Yeah," Lone allowed. "I expect so."

She placed a hand on his arm. "I really wish you would. I'll even promise to try and not involve you in another dangerous undertaking."

Lone was very aware of the heat of her hand on his arm and a part of him wanted badly to take her in his arms. He sensed she wanted it too. But another feeling in him, the ache that throbbed like a still raw wound from the loss of his Velda, wouldn't allow it. Not yet. Maybe not ever.

He pushed the moment aside with a lopsided grin. "Tell you what. When you find a way to work 'chapped-assedness' into one of your legal briefs, let me know. I'll come to Denver, and we'll celebrate."

Harriet managed a grin too. "You just made a date, mister. I'll get to work on it as soon as I get back. You make sure you're ready!"

About the Author

Wayne D. Dundee is an American author of popular genre fiction. His writing has primarily been detective mysteries (the Joe Hannibal PI series) and Western adventures. To date, he has written four dozen novels and forty-plus short stories, also ranging into horror, fantasy, erotica, and several "house name" books under bylines other than his own.

Dundee was born March 24, 1948, in Freeport, Illinois. He graduated from high school in Clinton, Wisconsin, 1966. Later that same year he married Pamela Daum and they had one daughter, Michelle. For the first fifty years of his life, Dundee lived and worked in the state line area of northern Illinois and southern Wisconsin. During most of that time he was employed by Arnold Engineering/Group Arnold out of Marengo, Illinois, where he worked his way up from factory laborer through several managerial positions. In his spare time, starting in high school, he was always writing. He sold his first short story in 1982.

In 1998, Dundee relocated to Ogallala, Nebraska, where he assumed the general manager position for a small Arnold facility there. The setting and rich history of the area inspired him to turn his efforts more toward the Western genre. In 2009, following the passing of his wife a year earlier, Dundee retired from Arnold and began to concentrate full time on his writing.

Dundee was the founder and original editor of Hardboiled Magazine.

His work in the mystery field has been nominated for an Edgar, an Anthony, and six Shamus Awards from the Private Eye Writers of America.

Center Point Large Print
600 Brooks Road / PO Box 1
Thorndike, ME 04986-0001 USA

(207) 568-3717

US & Canada:
1 800 929-9108
www.centerpointlargeprint.com